THE DELAY

THE SEQUEL TO THE HAZE

JACK HUNT

ISBN: 9798395698711

ALSO BY JACK HUNT

If you haven't joined *Jack Hunt's Private Facebook Group* just do a search on facebook to find it. This gives readers a way to chat with Jack, see cover reveals, enter contests and receive giveaways, and stay updated on upcoming releases. There is also his main facebook page below if you want to browse. facebook.com/jackhuntauthor

Go to the link below to receive special offers, bonus content, and news about new Jack Hunt's books. Sign up for the newsletter. http://www.jackhuntbooks.com/signup

A High Peaks Mystery series

In Cold Blood

Vanish From Sight

Her Final Hours

After it Turns Dark series

When the World Turns Dark

When Humanity Ends

When Hope is Lost

When Blood Lies

When Survivors Rise

The Great Dying series

Extinct

Primal

Species

A Powerless World series

Escape the Breakdown

Survive the Lawless

Defend the Homestead

Outlive the Darkness

Evade the Ruthless

Outlaws of the Midwest series

Chaos Erupts

Panic Ensues

Havoc Endures

The Cyber Apocalypse series

As Our World Ends

As Our World Falls

As Our World Burns

The Agora Virus series

Phobia

Anxiety

Strain

The War Buds series

War Buds 1

War Buds 2

War Buds 3

Camp Zero series

State of Panic

State of Shock

State of Decay

Renegades series

The Renegades

The Renegades Book 2: Aftermath

The Renegades Book 3: Fortress

The Renegades Book 4: Colony

The Renegades Book 5: United

The Wild Ones Duology

The Wild Ones Book 1

The Wild Ones Book 2

The EMP Survival series

Days of Panic

Days of Chaos

Days of Danger

Days of Terror

Against All Odds Duology

As We Fall

As We Break

The Amygdala Syndrome Duology

Unstable

Unhinged

Survival Rules series

Rules of Survival

Rules of Conflict

Rules of Darkness

Rules of Engagement

Lone Survivor series

All That Remains

All That Survives

All That Escapes

All That Rises

Single Novels

The Haze

The Delay

15 Floors

Blackout

Defiant

Darkest Hour

Final Impact

The Year Without Summer

The Last Storm

The Last Magician

The Lookout

Class of 1989

Out of the Wild

The Aging

Mavericks: Hunters Moon

Killing Time

For my Family

PROLOGUE

Lower Manhattan, New York
Two years and four months since event

Immunity was a double-edged sword.

Although she could survive the Haze virus — making her humanity's best chance of continued survival — it also made her a target.

Nothing made that clearer than a trip beyond the island after her arrival on the East Coast. It had been a trip for medical equipment, supplies, and a doctor who was supposed to have expertise in blood. A trip they'd done numerous times before without issue.

She would have liked to say that she was unwilling to be confined to Governors Island and drained like a cow only for the benefit of society, but she'd convinced those in charge that her training as a former U.S. Marshal could be an asset.

It was a mistake.

"Get her up to the helipad, we'll hold the doors!"

Alice Walker fired a single round at the charging savages before dashing across the ground floor of the skyscraper with three of the twelve remaining soldiers. Five others were already dead. Two never stood a chance. The others fell as they retreated to the extraction point.

It was a coordinated attack.

A clear ambush.

As she raced through the lobby of one of the tallest residential buildings in Lower Manhattan, flashbacks of her escape four months earlier from 19 Wing CFB Comox, a Canadian Air Force base on Vancouver Island, came rushing back.

The panic in the chest.

The urgency to leave.

The assistance of resistance soldiers.

The grisly sight of her sister being shot.

It bombarded her mind, trying to paralyze her from taking another step.

"This is why I was against bringing her along," Sophia 'Viper' Alvarez barked, unloading her M4 before directing them into the stairwell. Glass shattered around them. A slew of gunfire obliterated what few windows remained on the ground floor.

"The admiral cleared it," Captain James 'Hawk' Monroe replied.

"Yeah, we all know why."

Her immunity had placed her in a unique position. While the inherent risk should have caused them to restrict her, the admiral had no intention of making her a prisoner on the island.

"What is done is done," he replied, his hand forcefully pushing Alice forward. "Now keep moving!"

"Keep moving? Our men are dead," Alvarez shot back.

"And we will join them if you don't keep moving."

"It won't happen again," Alice promised.

"You're damn right about that. Once the admiral gets wind I will—"

"He won't," Monroe replied, cutting Alvarez off. "You keep your mouth shut, corporal."

Alice looked back at Monroe for but a second before they were in the chamber of the stairwell. "Wolf. Hold the door for the others," he cried.

"You got it, Cap."

Michael 'Wolf" Johnson hung back, weapon at the ready. A chorus of gunfire continued as they made the steep climb. Their feet echoed as they hauled ass up flights of steps. The high-rise was at one time a luxury condominium complex. In almost two and a half years it had fallen apart and given way to the weight of the disaster. No one wanted to be trapped inside a building, let alone found in the city.

No, New York had become one of the most dangerous cities in the United States, a mishmash of marauders, trappers, scalpers, beaters, and every other lowlife.

"Only ninety-one floors remaining," Alvarez grumbled, shaking her head. "If ever there was a time I wished the power was on, it's now."

All the soldiers on the island had worked at one time for Global Emergency Response Management — GERM — an extended arm of the government. A unit formed to handle disasters that no one knew existed until the Haze swept across the nation. But as the years passed, many turned coat, refusing to prey upon the innocent.

Moving with purpose and speed, they had ascended to floor twenty-one. They were about to go up the next steps when... "What the hell?" Alvarez said, taking a step back.

The way ahead was blocked by an insane amount of furniture: tables, chairs, beds, and even kitchen appliances. They couldn't have climbed over it even if they tried. And there was too much of it to attempt to move it. "There's a staircase on the south side of the building," Monroe said, opening the door to the floor.

Alvarez darted in, only to take a bullet to the temple.

She was dead before she hit the floor.

Another round unloaded, striking Monroe in the leg.

He fell, pulling back, grasping his thigh.

Alice exchanged fire with multiple assailants who

were lying in wait, taking out several, before grabbing Monroe by the collar. "Let's go."

Monroe hobbled toward the stairs. Alice shouted over the banister, "Johnson!"

His face appeared far below. "Pull back!" she yelled.

"The others are still under fire."

"Alvarez is down. Monroe is injured," she said.

"On my way."

Alice reached for a smoke grenade from Monroe's ballistic vest.

"Move it. I'll follow," she said.

She pulled the ring and tossed the smoke grenade into the corridor before closing the door. Next, she dragged some of the furniture toward the doorway to block the entrance.

Alice hustled down the staircase to find Monroe applying a combat tourniquet to his leg.

Blood covered the floor. It was a mess.

Without saying a word, Alice reached down and slung her arm around his waist, and hauled him to his feet. Monroe grimaced with each step. It was slow. Too slow. It was clear whoever had targeted them had every intention of cutting off their passage to the roof. "Did you call in the helo?" Alice asked.

"It's on its way," Monroe replied, grasping her tightly as they worked their way down steps only to be met by Johnson.

"Where are the others?" Alice asked.

Johnson shook his head.

That was all that was needed. Without wasting any time, Johnson helped carry some of Monroe's weight as they prepared to enter a new floor. This time, Alice made sure to check it by slicing the corner. "It's clear." They hurried in, following the corridor around and hoping that the second stairwell would be clear, but knowing that if any of the assailants on the floors above had survived, they'd no doubt be using it also.

They were within ten feet of the door when she heard voices coming from the stairwell.

"In here," she said, moving into one of the many condos. Inside it was a disaster, furniture overturned, blood on the walls. She could only imagine the horrors that had befallen the occupants. It was a snapshot — a moment in time — a reminder that the world had become unsafe as many sought out unwilling donors to be used for blood and plasma transfusions. It was a temporary treatment for a variant of bradyphrenia and encephalitis lethargica — a man-made virus believed to have no cure — whipped up in some lab by Weston Sciences owner Robert Weston.

In the silence they waited, hearing a slew of footsteps pass by.

"Wait here," Alice said, stepping out from behind an overturned sofa. She ventured out into the corridor, crossed to the stairwell, and lingered in the doorway, listening for movement.

Nothing.

Hurrying back, she beckoned them out.

She watched their backs as they made their way up the next flight of steps only to find another floor blocked.

"Shit. They must have seen us land," Johnson said.

Monroe replied, "You think? We'll revert to extraction point B."

"We won't make it."

"We don't have any other option," Monroe barked.

Alice understood Johnson's hesitation. Plan B was a fail-safe. The last option if the immediate extraction point became compromised. A lot of time had been spent on selecting a building the helicopter could land on. With only a few helos flying overhead, like her, they were a target, if only to bring down the bird and see what could be salvaged. Madness drove people to do all manner of things to stay alive, and the resistance wasn't any different. The Lower Manhattan financial district was close to Governors Island, and less inhabited, at least if their early assessment was anything to go on.

But they couldn't see those that were hidden.

Rumors of residents living in the sewers abounded. It seemed that dwelling with rats was considered safer than being above ground.

"We're on floor 19. The exit is on the thirteenth," Johnson said, turning and heading back down. "There's no telling how many are on their way up."

"Then we better reach it first," Alice said. On the way down, Johnson got back on the radio to give the pilot a heads-up on the change of plans. His stress was evident in the tone of his voice. Frantically they moved as fast as they could. Aware that at any second they could come face-to-face with those who had breached the building and were making their way up the north and south stairwells.

Extraction Plan B required reaching a window on the north side and crossing to another building via makeshift bridges. There was an endless array of rope, wooden planks, and steel interlinking buildings throughout the city. Alice had seen it back in Seattle in the quarantine zones.

Where buildings weren't joined, people had any number of creative ways to reach the next one without having to go to the ground. Some said it was designed after the Haze as a means of escape, another form of navigation. Either way, it was a precarious way to go between buildings as the planks weren't designed to hold a lot of weight or many people crossing them at once.

Whether by fate or a miscommunication between those chasing after them, they arrived on the thirteenth floor in one piece. "C'mon," Johnson said.

"I'm moving as fast as I can," Monroe shot back.

Hope ignited for but a moment only to be dashed by the sight of a sheer drop and no bridge. A strong breeze whipped at their clothes. Johnson released Monroe and stared out, shock getting the best of him. "The walkway was here. It was right here."

Monroe groaned. "As was the staircase to the roof. They've already taken it out."

Johnson tried to look down but it was too high. The ground was littered with debris.

"What now?" he asked.

"Those were our only options," Monroe said, resigning to the thought that this would be where they would die.

Alice got close to the huge, gaping office-style window. "Tell the pilot to come down to the north side."

"Um. Have you seen the gap? The rotor blades can't get close to the building," Monroe said.

"It can get close enough. Tell him."

She turned, charging back toward the corridor.

"Walker, where are you going?"

She didn't answer. Alice returned several minutes later, dragging a large hose that every floor had for the fire department to use if necessary.

Johnson shook his head. "No. No way."

"You want to get out of here alive?"

"Yeah, but what you are suggesting is pure madness."

"As is going back down that staircase and running into those coming up. This is it. Have you told the pilot?"

"You can tell him." Johnson tossed the radio to her. She scowled and got on the line. There was a moment of back and forth, reluctance on the pilot's part before she reminded him that if she was captured, he could all but forget about seeing his wife's health restored. It was a promise of life. Alice saw it as a fair exchange. Him risking his life for the sake of his wife. It wasn't like everyone on the island was entitled to her blood. The tests they were running were noninvasive. She'd only been able to give blood every eight weeks, otherwise, she ran the risk of developing anemia or worse — dying. So, the admiral made arrangements for only the young or valuable to be first in line.

Proof that it worked was Jade and Jonah.

Since receiving transfusions from her, they had yet to require another one. Jade had been brought out of a coma, a feat that no one had seen with regular transfusions. Alice's blood was rare. RH-null, otherwise referred to as Golden Blood. To date there were only forty-three people in the world known to have it, and with no way of knowing if those people were alive or where they were, that made her even more valuable.

The thump of rotor blades and the wash of air grew heavy and loud as the helicopter came into view, drawing close. The side door opened on the helo and two soldiers prepared to catch one end of the hose.

"I don't like this," Johnson said.

"Nor do I but it's the only way. Take this. Don't drop it," she said to Johnson while she tied off the other end of the hose around a pillar. The helicopter would have to hover in place while they worked their way out.

While Johnson was handling that, Alice crossed to the doorway, expecting war.

"Okay, okay, we've got this!" Johnson repeated to himself to boost his confidence. "Monroe, you're up!"

Although he'd lost blood from his leg, he felt strong enough to work his way out. It was a shot in the dark. There was no guarantee any of them would make it out and that included the pilot, but desperate situations called for desperate measures.

And the situation was about to get worse.

Bursting out of the stairwell into the corridor, multiple armed men appeared. Alice eyed them through her sight. She let out a three-round burst from the M4 catching them off guard and taking them down. Another three pulled back.

"How's he doing?" Alice shouted over her shoulder.

"He's on. You're next," Johnson said.

"No. You go!"

"We didn't go to all this trouble to lose you."

His words were lost in the bark of the M4. Alice unloaded more rounds as two of the hostiles darted across the corridor into a room. Now with men on both sides, they stood a chance. What came next only amplified that chance, as two smoke grenades were hurled down the corridor, filling it almost immediately with thick smoke.

Alice squeezed off multiple rounds into the smoke, expecting them to push forward using the smoke to get closer. She heard the cries of the fallen, caught in the hail of bullets.

Alice glanced back to see Johnson almost at the helicopter.

She removed a grenade, hooked the pin, and tossed it down the corridor to take out the brave or foolish as she turned and raced toward the opening.

She heard the familiar pop.

Extracting her knife, Alice cut through the hose around the column, tied it off around her waist, and without thought for her life, launched herself out the window, swinging below the helicopter as it banked away from the building.

Like falling with a bungee cord wrapped around her, she felt the snap of the hose as it went taut.

Adrenaline and pain coursed through her system as the helicopter surged out of the city, lifting her away from the concrete jungle back to the island.

1

New York
Three months later

It was forbidden but that's what made it all the more enticing.

Although she didn't believe it was her mother's fault — as there were many involved in the decisions that fateful day — Jade Walker would have been lying to say that the last venture into the city wasn't to blame. As it was only days after her return that the new rule came into effect.

NO ONE IS ALLOWED TO LEAVE THE ISLAND UNLESS AUTHORIZED AND IN THE COMPANY OF ARMED SOLDIERS.

It was posted everywhere.

Maybe that worked for them but for an eighteen-year-old, it might as well have been a prison sentence. It was for this reason and more that she justified her actions that evening. And yet she would come to regret it far more than she could ever know at that moment.

Jade slipped out of her window just after the sun had gone down.

Darkness was critical to eluding security, Caleb Easton had said.

She was trusting that he knew what he was doing.

As a relative newcomer to the island, at least in terms of months, she'd bonded with him as they'd both lost a parent and were tired of being confined to 172 acres. Governors Island wasn't bad, it was safer than anything that existed on the mainland, but there was only so much to see before they started to lose their mind.

Isolated just off the southern tip of the city, it was sandwiched 800 yards south of Lower Manhattan and separated by roughly 400 yards from Brooklyn by the Buttermilk Channel. A historic site that had been used as a military base during the Revolutionary War and as a Coast Guard station during World War II, it had since become home to a large and growing community of people from the city who would ferry over each day to use the recreational facilities. That was before the event — the Haze — the disaster that had befallen the country and spread across the world.

Besides seasonal accommodations, no one had lived on the island until now.

Peering out into the night, Jade saw movement.

The perimeter was guarded 24-7 by armed personnel.

It wasn't fair.

The only ones that left the island were the highly trained. Those willing to risk their lives to bring back urgent supplies. What they returned with was as much a mystery as the resistance who ran the place. Food was as abundant as the fish in the harbor. Crops were grown on the island and they even had livestock, farm animals, and poultry.

To most, it was the perfect safe zone.

It couldn't be further from the truth.

A radio stolen from security crackled on her hip. She adjusted the volume, turning it down a couple of notches.

"Are you there?" Caleb asked, his voice barely a whisper.

"Sorry. My mother was giving me the usual spiel. I'm on my way."

"You know we're running on a tight schedule here. If you're late, this doesn't work."

"Not much I could do."

"Be sure to follow the route I gave you. Deviate from that and you'll be seen."

"Got it."

She was to meet him at the Hugh L. Carey Tunnel

Ventilation Building. It jutted out from the east side. It was a mammoth high-rise building that was part of the tunnel that passed under the East River and connected the southern tip of Manhattan to the neighborhood of Red Hook in Brooklyn.

Thousands of cars had used it to drive back and forth daily before the Haze. A ventilation system had been built along with the tunnel to feed fresh air into it. There were four buildings, two in Manhattan, one in Brooklyn, and the other on Governors Island.

No one was allowed over there. Two guards were posted at the concrete dock that extended out to it. Caleb said he'd timed the changeover of shifts and had noticed a two-minute gap. A window of opportunity that would allow them to reach it.

Jade whipped around as a rustle caught her attention.

She squinted into the darkness. Had someone heard the radio? Was someone following? Frozen in place, she waited another minute or two before darting around the perimeter of the Parade Ground, one of the largest fields that surrounded Fort Jay and divided Colonels' Row from Nolan Park. Caleb had told her to stick to the tree line. He didn't need to give her a map as after seven months of living on the island, she knew it like the back of her hand.

Hurrying in the direction of the Castle Williams fortification, she cut through the dense tree line until she made it to Andes Road. From there she still didn't feel safe. She wouldn't feel safe until she was with Caleb.

She'd already gotten in trouble once for attempting to leave the island by boat; a second infraction would cost her dearly. What that punishment might be was anyone's guess. Few stepped out of line on the island. Most abided by the rules because of the benefits. It was contained, protected, and in many ways a sliver of the life they once knew. They didn't have to worry about losing sleep at night as soldiers worked around the clock standing guard. Entertainment amounted to live theater, an almost forgotten art for her generation who were used to gazing mindlessly into tech devices.

That was a thing of the past.

Jade squinted toward the horizon.

At one time the skyline of Manhattan would have been aglow with lights and abuzz with the hum of the city. Now it was masked in darkness and silence. All she could see was the silhouette of towering skyscrapers looming in the distance.

Seagulls squawked overhead and the smell of salt water filled the air, giving the place a peaceful and serene atmosphere, although the world beyond the island was far from it.

Jade glanced at her watch. "Damn it."

Caleb would be pissed. What should have taken her only a few minutes to reach him ended up being extended by another ten as Jade found herself ducking back into the tree line when security rolled by in a Humvee.

When she finally made it to a building off Cardner Road, Caleb was peering out using binoculars from one of the windows. He whirled around. He was twenty-one years old with messy, sandy-blond hair that fell just above his piercing blue eyes. It was hard not to find herself drawn to him. Known to most on the island as "Cabbie" because his old man used to drive a cab in the city, he was tall and lean, with broad shoulders and a lanky frame that suggested he was still growing into his body. His style was casual and laid-back, favoring jeans and vintage band T-shirts that he said he'd amassed over the years before the collapse of society. She rarely saw him out of his well-worn pair of Converse sneakers.

"Shit, you took long enough."

"Well, I'm here now," she replied.

"You come alone?"

She looked behind her. "Does it look like I brought anyone?"

"What about Jonah?"

"What about him?"

"Are you sure he doesn't know?"

"Oh please. If my mother says jump, he jumps. He was reading when I left."

Caleb made his way over with a certain swagger to his step that suggested he was confident in his skin. He gave her one of his wide and infectious smiles, the kind that made her feel butterflies in her stomach. "All right, let's go." He adjusted a backpack on his shoulders and they climbed out of the window, dropping behind some bushes.

"Okay, now listen up. We won't get long. We are going to have to sprint. You are a fast runner, right?"

"Faster than you."

He chuckled. "We'll see."

Jade adjusted a ratty ball cap on her head. Her dark hair flowed out of the back in a ponytail. Caleb glanced at his watch. "Any second now."

The two guards that manned the entrance point to the short causeway started heading south. "Why don't they have someone who fills the spot immediately?"

"They do. It's a Friday night. The two guys are getting hand jobs from some of the ladies over on the north side."

"Lovely," she said, frowning. "Is the admiral aware?"

Caleb smiled. "Yeah. About as aware of what we're about to do," he said before quietly laughing. "Jade, you do make me wonder some days."

She elbowed him in the ribs. "Now!" he said, grabbing her hand and pulling her out of the bushes across the road. The two of them burst into a full sprint. The causeway wasn't far, two hundred yards at the most. The ventilation building stood tall and imposing against the backdrop of the Brooklyn skyline. Its sleek modern design was a striking contrast to the historic brownstones on the island.

Darting through an archway into what could only be

described as the inner perimeter, Jade looked up at the massive structure stretching several stories high with a series of angular walls and sharp corners. It reminded her of some kind of prison. By day, parts of the clad metallic façade shimmered in the sunlight, making it stand out with an almost futuristic fortress feel. The walls however were mostly concrete. A series of large metal vents protruded from the roof. According to the admiral, they released plumes of steam and smoke into the air like a giant beast exhaling its breath into the world. But that was when there was power. Now it was still, almost too quiet.

"Whoa, this is quite something," she muttered.

It was off-limits to everyone but armed personnel. Caleb ran ahead of her, around the corner. "Come on," he said.

"You can't get in. They sealed it off," she said as she came around the bend only to find him at the top of a stairwell where a door was open. The lock was gone as if someone had taken a blowtorch to it.

"You were saying?" he replied, looking all pleased with himself.

Jade squinted at the opening that had a rough and uneven texture. The edges were jagged and irregular with sharp points. "Did you...?" she asked.

"Where there is a will there is a way," he replied, not telling her anymore before leading her inside. He shucked off his backpack and took out a flashlight and illuminated the walls.

"Hey, uh, Caleb. I don't think we should be in here."

"Says who?"

"Just about everyone on the island."

"And yet you're here." He turned toward her, shining the flashlight in her face, grinning.

"How did you know about that door?"

"As I said, not everyone on the island abides by the rules. You think we're the first to come through here?" He laughed. "You can't lock people down forever."

"It's only been seven months."

"And before that?"

She shrugged. Even though they hadn't been told they couldn't leave, it was an unsaid rule that if people left, they were on their own. No help would be coming. They would also be putting the entire island at risk of infection if they returned. How many managed to leave and return was unknown.

Inside it was dark, a labyrinth of steel and concrete. Pipes and ducts snaked along the walls and ceilings. Jade looked up at the large turbines high above them as Caleb opened multiple steel doorways and led her through like he was familiar with the route.

"Who told you about this place?" she asked.

"And throw them under the bus? C'mon, now."

"You know I'm not like that."

"No? The daughter of the chosen one."

"She's not the chosen one." Jade laughed.

"Seems everyone thinks she is. The last I heard, light shines out of her ass."

Jade slapped him on the arm and chuckled.

They had to duck down and skirt around some low ducts to make it to the next section, where a trap door led to a ladder that disappeared into a hole.

"She's trying to help. They think they could turn this around."

"Is that what they've convinced you?"

"You don't believe it?"

"I'll believe it when I see it."

"You already have," she said. "Seven months ago, I was in a coma. No one comes out of one once they progress that far. Her blood pulled me out. I have no symptoms. Nothing."

"Doesn't mean you can't get reinfected. To me, that's not a permanent cure."

"Maybe not, but that's why we're here. They're—"

"Running tests," he said, cutting her off. "Yeah, yeah, that's what they keep informing us. Every month it's the same spiel. We're close to finding a permanent cure. We're making headway. The only headway anyone is getting is the security guards on this island from all the bored and overly stimulated women."

Jade slapped him on the arm. "Why do you have to be so vulgar?"

"It's true," he shot back. "Come on. Get a sense of humor." He then motioned for her to go down.

"Down there?"

"You wanted to get off the island, right?"

"We are."

"No, Jade. I meant off the island. Manhattan."

She shook her head. "No. Hold on. I thought you were just wanting to hang out, smoke some pot, and have a drink."

"And we can but I want to show you something."

"What?"

"It's a surprise."

"I don't do well with surprises, Caleb," she said. "No, come on, let's go back."

She turned and he took hold of her wrist. "To what? The same views, the same rules? You're eighteen, Jade. In many parts of the world, you're considered an adult. Free to do whatever you want. Now I'm asking you, when was the last time you felt free?"

She stared back at him. As Jade considered his words, she could see the silhouette of his face. Although his features were shrouded in shadows, she could make out the deep furrow in his brow and the tenseness in his jaw.

He was serious.

As they huddled close together in the darkness, the only light came from the small flashlight that cast eerie shadows on the surrounding walls. The air was thick with the musty scent of old stone and damp earth. When she didn't reply, he continued, his voice low and urgent, the words tumbling out in a rush. "You attempted to leave in a boat."

"Not to go to the mainland. Just further out in the water. To fish."

"Oh, to go fishing. That's all. Sure!"

"All right, maybe to see the dock, and view the city from the water through binoculars close up, but I wasn't going to step foot in the city. That's madness. Do you have any idea what is happening over there?"

"Do you trust me?"

Jade groaned. She could sense the desperation in his tone and knew that he probably wouldn't go without her. He was relying on her to agree. The truth was she wasn't sure she wanted to leave. It wasn't about going against her mother or even rebelling. Common sense told her that there was a reason why the soldiers weren't venturing into the city frequently. And she'd heard the horror stories from Jonah of what they'd encountered on the way to the university.

There were more things to fear than the virus of the Haze itself.

"I don't know."

"I promise it will be worth it. We'll be there and back in no time."

As he spoke, his face twisted into a pained expression, revealing the depth of his emotion. His eyes were wide with wonder and determination. Jade could see the sweat glistening on his forehead under the summer heat.

"Ugh."

"Come on, Jade. Your mother won't have a clue. Live a little."

She scoffed. "Live. Yeah, that's why I'm hesitant."

Despite the danger and the darkness, Jade found herself drawn to the guy's resolute spirit. She felt a sense of safety and comfort in his presence. She nodded, and Caleb smiled, turning back toward the opening and climbing down. As she followed, she paused on a rung, thinking she heard the scuff of feet behind her.

"Jade."

"Yeah, I'm coming." She squinted one last time before making her descent into the tunnels below the East River.

2

Ten minutes later

Sex was a welcome reprieve from the mundane.

Alice rolled off Sam "The Admiral" Dawson, her body glistening with perspiration. He was no admiral — he'd never served in the Navy — but he was a commanding officer.

A former jarhead and a once-loyal soldier for GERM, he'd established himself as a leader within a core group of rebels — those hellbent on dismantling GERM and finding a permanent cure for the infection.

Some joked that he was giving Alice special attention only because she was the closest thing to achieving one of those goals. Maybe that was true. She didn't read into it too deeply.

She pulled back the sheets and paraded naked across to the bathroom. They were in what was called the Admiral's House — hence Sam's nickname. After the U.S. Army took over Governors Island back in the late 1700s, they built several establishments — Castle Williams, Fort Jay, and then abodes for the commanding officers. The Governor's House was one and then in 1843 the Admiral's House was erected, a three-story red brick building in a classical revival style with symmetrical façade and a front portico supported by bright white Corinthian columns. It was one hell of a place. It had a large entrance hall, a formal parlor, a dining room, and multiple bedrooms. It featured high ceilings, ornate plasterwork, and large windows that drew in natural light.

"Damn, you are something else," Sam said, eyeing her.

She smiled, glancing over her shoulder. She would have been lying to say that she didn't appreciate his remarks, especially when most days she felt less than. Everyone did. While they had found ways to stay clean and had amassed a good supply of hygiene products, life was far from glamorous. She no longer wore David's Forest Service Ranger shirt, and she didn't exactly go out of her way to make herself look good. That required effort and when death was forever at the forefront of her mind, it seemed meaningless.

"I expect you said that to the last woman that warmed your bed." Alice scooped up her clothes.

"Come on. Come back to bed," he said, patting her side of the mattress before reaching for a pack of smokes and tapping one out.

"I'd love to but I have to get back."

"How many times have I told you? They're safe. You're on an island protected by Uncle Sam's finest."

"Yeah, but for how long?"

He gave a confused expression.

Wearing only panties and a long shirt, Alice ambled back into the room as she did up the buttons.

He continued. "We've been here two years and seven months. No one has breached the island."

"That was before people knew about me," she replied.

"Who knows?"

She cocked her head and raised an eyebrow. "You know word travels fast."

"And?" he asked. He lit his cigarette, leaned on an elbow, and blew out smoke.

"Sam. How much did you see before you abandoned your post with GERM?"

"Enough," he replied.

"Well then you know people are desperate."

"No one knows about you."

"You all did."

"Because we had people on the inside. Like your sister and Jonah's father."

"Yeah. Well. With so much misinformation out there, who knows what people might do."

"More reason for you to stay on the island where I can protect you." He reached for her hand but she pulled it away.

"I don't need protecting. Remember, I made it two years through this before meeting you."

"Right, you were a Marksman and a U.S. Marshal. I get it. You can handle yourself. That doesn't mean I can't watch out for your best interests."

"Is that all it is?"

"Why wouldn't it be?"

Again, she cocked her head.

Sam sighed. "Sure, my interest in you is multi-layered. But have I put you on the operating table the way Robert Weston wanted to?" He paused. "No. That's right. There's always another way."

"What if there isn't?" She paused and he simply stared back at her. "Erika said there would be people here who could help."

"And we are. But it takes time. You're different, Alice."

"Don't be condescending." Sam groaned and stubbed out his cigarette in an ashtray as she continued. "You've run tests for seven months. Besides getting a select few out of comas and seeing others clear of infection, we still don't know if that's made them immune. If my blood is a permanent cure, we've yet to see if someone who receives a blood transfusion from me can be reinfected. We need to test that. If they can be, it's not permanent."

He sat up in bed, a serious expression forming. "Listen to me. Before you were discovered. We were checking blood types. Matching them up with people. That was a challenge right there. Once we found matching blood types, we could do a blood and plasma transfusion and it would provide a temporary treatment. First-line therapy. A means of reducing symptoms for a while. Not a permanent solution. People who received the matching blood type within three to six weeks needed another transfusion or they would make a steady decline back into the thick of infection. We did this as a way to give people time with their loved ones, to avoid some falling into a coma or dying. However, for all our trying, it never worked with those who were in a coma. Your blood is different. It brings them out. No one else we've found can do that. Those you have given blood to have not only come out of comas but they haven't declined back into infection. Jonah and Jade are proof of this. It's been seven months since both of them received a transfusion from you. Your Rh-Null blood saves lives."

"But we still don't know if it can prevent them from being reinfected. You haven't exposed either of them or any others."

"Because we are still monitoring. Give it a year or two and..."

"Sam, we don't have a year or two. Hundreds of thousands are already dead. Maybe millions. There are many others in comas, still dying, still suffering, still dealing with trappers, scalpers, and the consequences of that." She paused. "Robert Weston and my sister said that this was neurological. That the answer to it could be found in the brain."

He stabbed the air with his finger. "Could. Big difference. Do you want to take that risk based on a... could?"

"I want to live. Let me be clear about that but if they are right—"

He cut her off. "They don't know for sure. They didn't know back then. Hell, they didn't even know what your blood would do until they gave it to Jade. Much of what we are dealing with here is unknown. C'mon, Alice. You know that this was something created in a damn lab by a biotechnology company using your sister's research into finding a cure for neurological disorders like Alzheimer's, Parkinson's, Huntington's disease, schizophrenia, and bradyphrenia. They then turned it around and used it as a biological weapon just like..."

"Operation Sea Spray, Big Buzz, Project 112, Big Itch, Drop Kick, and the others. Yeah. Yeah. You're preaching to the choir."

"Then you know that putting you under the knife is like playing Russian roulette. Maybe we get lucky. Great. But what if we don't? If we lose you, we lose our ability to bring people back from this infection."

She sighed, getting up.

He continued, "You know it's the truth."

"Not everyone can live on an island. If it's not

a *permanent* cure and people get reinfected — what then? Keep giving them my blood? C'mon! We have to run a test on someone who has received my blood and see if they get reinfected. If they don't then we know my blood ends this. If they do get infected, then we are back at square one trying to find a permanent solution."

He leaned back and blew out his cheeks. "Best of luck finding someone willing to take that chance. Especially when we don't know if we can bring them back out of it a second time with your blood."

There was a lot of risk but that was the history of humanity. Through time, humanity had encountered all manner of life-ending viruses, natural and man-made. Solutions were often found on the back of thousands of lives lost. Alice tugged on her boots. "Just give it some thought. Maybe we put it out there. You never know who might step up to the plate."

As she made her way around the bed to head out, he took hold of her wrist and pulled her down for one more kiss. "You should move in here with me. Then we can stop doing all this back and forth."

"It might save us time but I can't imagine it would stop people talking," she said.

He smiled as she walked out.

Outside, Alice breathed in the salty air.

Seven months had been a long time to live on an island when she was so used to the freedom of Washington, the mountains, and the surrounding forest.

Still, safety was the island's strong point. It was hard

to attack a place when they could see a threat coming. The last time she felt this safe was when she was living in the fire tower back in Washington. Her thoughts went back to that time — the months after David and Lucas died. Those were painful days. And yet even then she found a rhythm in the madness. She smiled at the memory of Dog. The jet-black Cane Corso that had come into her life and drawn her out of her misery, protected her at night better than any soldier walking the perimeter. And Ed, the old man that Dog eventually chose to stay with.

What had become of them?

Alice waved to a few individuals she saw. The island had a population of just over six hundred. Everyone contributed in one way or another whether it was working in security, monitoring the health of everyone, or simply keeping the place running through menial jobs. In some ways, she wondered if that's what would become of society — reduced to living on islands until a permanent cure could be found.

"Hey, Jonah," she said, entering the two-story brick house, one of many on Comfort Road. She tossed her keys down and crossed into the kitchen. She'd expected the kitchen to be a mess. A collection of plates or bowls. Leftovers from supper. The house was quiet. She lifted her eyes to the ceiling, expecting to hear the two of them moving around. Alice crossed to the stairs. "Jade? Jonah?"

Her pulse picked up a little as she took the steps two

at a time, making it to the top and pushing her way into Jade's room. It was empty. She backed out and knocked on Jonah's door. No answer. Pushing it wide, she saw he was gone too. "Okay, don't panic," she told herself while crossing to her room. It was there she found the answer.

A note resting on her bed. *You were right. She's gone to meet with him. I'm following.*

"Shit!"

Alice turned and raced out into the night.

~

JONAH'S COVER was blown somewhere between the Waterfront District and Brooklyn Heights. He'd kept his distance. Never getting too close but not letting her out of his sight. That was until Jade and Cabbie ducked into an abandoned pizza joint.

The door had been kicked in. Tables overturned. Windows smashed. It was a shithole. Every second he was out on that street, he wasn't worried about being spotted by them but by those who lurked in the shadows. Marauders were everywhere. Reports had come in over the last seven months of all manner of weird shit taking place.

Trappers were those who lured people into traps, then hooked them up to a human juice machine. They didn't waste time finding blood type matches. You were snatched, hooked up, and drained of every drop they could get out of you.

Scalpers weren't much better. Thoughts of his time in Washington came rushing back. Alice saving him from death or rape had haunted him since. Scalpers were a heartless group. They auctioned people off to the highest bidder. What currency they were paid in was anyone's guess, but they could get what they wanted as they could guarantee buyers the right blood type. In many ways, they were selling hope - blood slaves that would extend life for another three to six weeks and then again and again.

And of course, who could forget the beaters, those nasty bastards who went after both trappers and scalpers or anyone they believed was in cahoots with them? Beaters were like damn vigilantes out to get justice for their loved ones who had been stolen off the streets and drained of blood. It was a vicious circle.

Oh, Jonah, why did you agree to this?

He knew why.

Alice had asked him to keep an eye on Jade. She'd caught wind of her antics since Jade's escapade off the island on the boat. Since then, she'd found out that Jade was seeing Cabbie.

Still, that wasn't why he was helping. Oh no, in his mind it was a way of repaying Alice.

Guilt had plagued him since Seattle. He felt at fault for leading her back. Being used by Robert Weston like a pawn in a game of chess. So many lies. He'd told so many. And not only had he lost his father but Alice had lost her sister.

Now he'd lost her trust.

Creeping through the dark store, he peered into the back, taking out a flashlight to shine it down a corridor that led to the rear. The door was open. "Shit."

He hurried for it, expecting to see them running, but instead, he found himself landing hard on his knees.

Cabbie appeared from the darkness. Cracking up laughing. "Oh, you should have seen your face. Wah!" he said, impersonating the noise he made after being tripped.

"Asshole!"

"What are you doing here, Jonah?" Jade asked, arms folded.

He brushed off the dirt as he got up. "I could ask you the same. You were told not to leave the island. Either of you."

"And yet here we are," Cabbie said, leaning against the wall and picking his teeth with a toothpick.

"Go home!" Jade said. "And you better not tell her."

"Nah. Ease up, Jade. He's here now. Let him stay."

"But I thought it was just us."

"Well, it was. But we can't let him wander these streets alone. Dangerous out here," Cabbie said, picking at his teeth as a grin formed. He was finding it all a little too amusing.

Jade grumbled. "All right. But if you fall behind or anything happens to you. Not my problem."

Cabbie put his arm around Jade and they exited out the back.

In some ways Jonah was pleased. The thought of traversing the streets alone was intimidating. He scuffed his feet on the way out. Jade rolled her eyes at him. "I can't believe you followed me."

"And I can't believe you would put Alice through this."

"That's right, you're my mother's pet project."

"I'm nobody's pet. Or project."

"No? Seems every time she asks you to do something, you do it."

"And?"

"And it's a little weird. But I get it. You remind her of him. Lucas. My brother who died."

"He does?" Cabbie asked, glancing over his shoulder.

"But let me tell you something. You might look like him but you're not him. You will never be. You're just an outsider. Got it?"

Jonah shrugged. "Whatever."

The animosity between the two of them had been there since Jade had recovered. She'd had questions. Lots of them. Who was he? Why was he there? Why did her mother treat him like a son? It was all perception. He never felt as if she treated him any differently than the day they first met on the shore of Mowich Lake. Some days, he honestly thought she wished he was gone. But that might have just been his thoughts.

"Where are we heading?" Jonah asked.

"None of your business," Jade answered.

"Brooklyn Bridge," Cabbie replied as they got closer to it.

"Why?"

"You ask a lot of questions, little man."

"Ignore him," Jade said. "Works for me."

Jonah held his tongue. He wanted to ask her why she was so angry toward him but he thought it would only stir up the waters and create more trouble. He'd already created enough of that. He didn't want to give Alice another reason to doubt him.

~

A HARD WIND howled as the sky threatened to empty. On top of a brownstone building a raggedy, hooded stranger eyed the three through a high-powered night vision monocular telescope, stopping only to unsnap his radio from his belt. "Three. Unarmed."

"You sure?"

"Can't be positive. What do you want to do?"

"Follow them."

3

The Brooklyn Bridge was an iconic landmark.

Even at night, Jonah couldn't help feeling awestruck by its grandeur. The towering suspension cables stretched across the East River, seeming to disappear into the distance. The closer they got, the more he could pick out the intricate lattice of steel and wire and the tall stone towers that held it all in place. While many buildings on both sides of the river had been reduced to rubble in the almost three years since the event, the bridge remained untouched, a masterpiece of engineering and architecture, a true testament to human ingenuity.

As they walked cautiously across, their footsteps echoed in the silent darkness.

Jonah noticed the faint outline of the Manhattan skyline on the other side, illuminated by a dim, eerie glow that came from fires. The scent of smoke and ash lingered, carried along by a howling wind. It was a reminder of how the Haze had swept across the city, leaving it devastated, barren, and seemingly desolate.

A Boeing 747 that had gone down had cut through a section of the city, leaving only an engine behind as a reminder that it had been there.

People who hadn't died immediately because of the delay in physical and mental response succumbed to the infection, much like those who had experienced the epidemic of encephalitis lethargica back in the early twentieth century.

"Where are we going?" Jonah asked.

"Nearly there," Cabbie replied.

As they crossed the bridge, they could see the remnants of the past, abandoned cars, and debris scattered along the way. The bridge was mostly empty, with no other living soul in sight. He couldn't help but feel a sense of despair and loneliness, wondering if they were the only ones left in a hundred miles.

"You think everyone abandoned the city?" Jade asked.

"Yes and no. This place would have been madness when the Haze spread. A hive of chaos. But not everyone would have exited."

"Why not?" Jade asked.

"Habit. A false sense of security," Cabbie replied. "But you would know that. Remember when it happened in Seattle?"

Jade exhaled hard. "I don't have much recollection of those times."

"You were caught in a storm," Jonah said without thinking.

It was post-traumatic amnesia. Jonah had overheard a doctor tell Alice that it was a common stage for many after emerging from a coma. While he assumed Alice would have brought her up to speed on those final hours, it was clear now she'd purposely left out some of it. No doubt to protect her from further pain.

Jade looked back at him trailing behind. "My mother never told me that."

Jonah glanced at her. "I thought... she had."

"No. She said that my father and brother had died but she didn't say how."

"And you never asked?"

"Of course. She said it didn't matter now."

Jonah nodded. In light of all that had happened, how people passed was of little consequence. Survival. Staying mentally strong. These were key.

"What do you know?" she asked, now showing more interest in him than she ever had since she came out of the coma.

"Ah, maybe Alice should tell you."

"No. I want you to tell me."

Jonah was reluctant.

"Please," she said. It was the first time she'd ever used manners.

He nodded.

"You were out celebrating your father's birthday in Tacoma when the Haze hit. A storm followed after, a hard storm that devastated the landscape and brought down trees." He paused for a second. "One of those trees came down on your father's car, and your brother died en route to the hospital. My father..." He paused again. "He was working as an EMT at the time. He was on shift that day. He knew your aunt. Erika. After the accident, you called her."

"I never phoned my mother?"

"No. Anyway, they pulled you out of the vehicle."

"Your father did? What was his name?"

"Eric."

"He's..."

"Dead," Jonah said before she could finish. "All of you were exposed to the Haze at some point. You went into a coma. Your aunt kept you at the university until they transferred you to a Canadian Air Force base on Vancouver Island."

There was silence between them. All that could be heard was the groan of metal as a hard wind blew across the river. "And my father?"

"He died after."

"Alone?"

"No, your mother reached him before he passed."

Jonah felt bad telling her without Alice's permission but what was he supposed to say? They had walked for what felt like hours, with nothing but their thoughts and fears to keep them company.

"Here we are," Cabbie said. They'd reached the halfway point. They stopped. In the silence, Cabbie shone a flashlight on the bridge. "Back in the early 2000s, couples began attaching padlocks to the bridge as a symbol of their love and commitment to one another. They came in all colors and sizes. Some had the couple's initials or a special message engraved in them. Eventually, the city removed them for safety reasons."

"Safety?"

"The weight. It posed a threat to those on the lower deck. At one time there were thousands attached. I guess they followed suit to what the folks did in Paris after a portion of a railing on the Pont des Arts bridge collapsed."

"Then what are these?"

"Posters of the missing. You know, when the World Trade Center went down, there were hundreds of posters plastered to chain-link fences, stapled and tacked on community bulletin boards, on schools, church walls, you name it. Some were typed, others handwritten or drawn with crayons. A name, a picture, a description, or a simple have-you-seen? question."

Jade crouched and looked at them. Some were in 9-by-12-inch plastic sleeves. Those not in plastic had torn away, others were flapping wet or nothing more than a corner. "God, that is sad."

"Sure is."

"Why would you bring her here?" Jonah asked, baffled by his train of thought.

"To show her what she hasn't seen. You might have seen a lot. But since the event happened, she's been locked up on that island, hidden away from reality. This is the reality. Lives lost. People gone too soon. Others missing because some trapper, scalper, or beater has them. Or worse — a cure was kept from them."

Jonah caught the animosity in his voice. If he wasn't mistaken, Cabbie was angry.

A few tears streaked Jade's cheeks. She didn't know these people. There was no attachment to them, however, after learning about her father and brother's fate, this must have unearthed deep-seated emotions.

"You sound like it's personal," Jonah said.

"Isn't it for everyone?" Cabbie replied. "My old man is dead because of this shit storm. However, unlike you two, if a cure had been available, or if Alice had been on hand, he would still be here."

"Well, sorry to piss on your parade, she's not the permanent cure," Jonah said.

"Yes she is," Jade spat.

Cabbie grinned as if he was privy to some inside joke. "She's damn near close to it." He glanced down and pulled away a sleeve from the railing. "This. This was my father," he said, holding it up.

"But you said he was dead, not missing."

"Dead, missing, it's the same thing now." Cabbie

stared at the image, clutching it tightly. There were no tears but anger was evident.

Jonah looked off in the distance toward Manhattan. His brow furrowed as he squinted. There was movement. He took a few steps in that direction, squinting again. It was a group of people making their way toward them. He could have thought nothing of it, assumed they were just another band of survivors on a supply run, but traveling through Washington, he never encountered that. As he watched, he began to feel uneasy. There was something off about this group. They moved with a sense of purpose that suggested they weren't just aimlessly wandering. From where they were he couldn't see if they were armed, but he expected they would be.

"Um, guys."

Cabbie was still rattling on about his father and the state of the world and how all the testing on Alice had led to nothing when Jonah piped up again. "Hey!"

"What?" Jade asked.

"We should get going," he said, motioning with his head toward the group coming their way. It was hard to tell how many there were but they were outnumbered. Fear gripped him at the thought of facing a hostile situation. Adrenaline shot through Jonah as he turned back toward Brooklyn, keeping his head down to avoid drawing attention.

That didn't last. Fear got the better of him.

"Don't run," Cabbie said. "It might just give them a reason to come after us."

"Well, I sure as hell am not going to walk," Jonah said, picking up the pace from a fast walk to a jog. Jade was right beside him.

They were a good distance from the group but it didn't mean they were out of the woods. They still had a long trek back to the tunnels. "I hope this little trip was worth it," Jonah added.

At the far end of the bridge, Jonah glanced back and could see the group running.

"We need to book it, now!" Cabbie yelled, leading the way and breaking into a full sprint.

"Oh, now you think it's time," Jonah said out of frustration.

Heading south along one of the many streets, Cabbie took a left and headed east.

"Where are you going?" Jonah shouted, pointing ahead of him. "The tunnel is south."

"We won't make it." Cabbie pointed and that's when Jonah's stomach dropped. Up in the distance was another group. They were closing in on them.

It was a trap.

Panic set in.

The reality that they might not make it out came crashing down on him, hard and heavy. With every labored step, Jonah could feel stomach acid in his throat, that familiar burning in his chest. At that moment, he was right back in Washington, feeling exactly what he had when he and Alice encountered beaters in the forest.

Like cornered animals in a maze, they darted one way only to see more coming.

"In here," Cabbie said, darting into a six-story red brick building. It was an apartment block, one of many sandwiched together with others and spread out throughout the neighborhood of Brooklyn Heights.

"Where are you going?" Jonah asked.

He received no answer. Flight-or-fight was in full swing and they had opted to flee. They darted down a dark corridor toward a back door only to find it locked. Cabbie turned and headed into a stairwell.

"Please tell me you brought a gun?" Jonah said.

"Nope," Cabbie shouted.

"Are you kidding me? Why not?"

"For the same reason you don't have one."

It was a good point. As no one was meant to leave the island, weapons weren't required. The only ones sporting them were the soldiers. However, that hadn't stopped Jonah from snagging a butterfly knife. He fished it out of his pocket to have it on hand just in case. It wasn't ideal but it would have to do.

"I hope you know where you're going," Jonah yelled, his voice echoing in the stairwell.

"The roof. We stand a better chance of crossing from building to building via the walkways than staying on the ground."

As they burst out onto the roof and started bolting across the top, it began to rain.

"Are you kidding me?!" Jonah cried out.

Nearby a bright flare shot up into the air, arching over them and leaving a stream of smoke behind. It was an odd sight. Why was someone firing a flare? As he looked out, he noticed several more streams of smoke. It was as if they were using them to alert whoever was in pursuit of them to their location.

Then.

Above, Jonah heard the sound of rotor blades. That meant only one thing, either GERM was closing in or...

Thump, thump, thump.

A helo from the island soared over, sending down a pocket of air. Their coats flapped; their voices were lost in the noise. At that moment, all that mattered was staying one step ahead of their pursuers.

Parallel to Remsen Street, the majority of buildings were joined to one another.

Others had wide gaps and were joined by walkways that people had moved into place. An unstable bridge of plywood and steel was the last thing he wanted to step out onto but he had no choice.

Jonah looked back and saw the door burst open.

Gunshots rang out.

"Shit!" Jonah yelled, instinctively ducking and zigzagging.

"This way," Cabbie shouted, pressing on as if he knew the area.

They had made it to the top of 24 Remsen Street before Cabbie darted out across the wide divide that separated it from 27 Grace Court, the building to the south.

"I hope you know what you're doing," Jade said.

High above them, the helo circled back around, this time dropping down to a nearby adjacent building and landing.

The doors slid open.

Alice jumped out along with multiple soldiers.

Jonah felt a wave of relief flood his chest.

The soldiers opened fire on the group on the other side, pushing them back into protruding fire escape doors or behind large steel air vents. The staccato of gunfire was deafening.

Alice didn't waste any time crossing from one building to the next.

"Come on!" she shouted, urging them over one at a time.

That's when it happened. Cabbie buckled. He hit the roof hard, grasping his leg. Jonah reached down to help but he waved him on. "Go!"

There was no time to argue, rounds were snapping past their heads.

Alice, who'd been on the other side of a walkway, rushed across to help.

"Get in the helicopter. Now!" she shouted as she moved past them to assist Cabbie. Jonah kept moving, his eyes glancing back for but a second more as another soldier surged past them to help. He saw Alice trying to help Cabbie to his feet and figured they would be following momentarily.

He didn't see what happened next but he heard it.

"What are you doing?" Alice cried out.

Jonah turned back to see the walkway that bridged the two buildings was now gone. He didn't hear it hit the ground but he knew Cabbie was to blame by the way Alice pushed him out of the way. Cabbie stood behind her, seemingly unaffected by his injury.

As Alice peered over the edge of the building — and before she could react — Cabbie came up behind her and stuck a needle in her neck.

She fell back into his arms.

"Alice!" Jonah shouted, jumping out of the grounded helicopter and rushing back to where the soldier was. He'd dropped to one knee and was taking potshots at the approaching pursuers.

"Cabbie? What the...?" he shouted as Cabbie dragged Alice back toward a doorway where he was met by others.

They took over, taking hold and dragging her into the building.

Cabbie looked back; a grin formed as he lifted a hand to show fake blood before he gave a salute and disappeared into the stairwell.

A steady onslaught of gunfire pushed them back.

They had no other choice but to leave.

Several soldiers were injured, and two were dead.

Jonah gritted his teeth as he snatched a rifle from a dead soldier and unleashed a barrage of gunfire at those closest. But they were no longer interested.

They got what they wanted.

Like rats they disappeared over the edge of buildings, some down fire escapes, others into emergency stairwells.

All he knew was Alice was there and now she was gone.

The look of utter shock and despair on Jade's face said it all.

4

It was far too dangerous.

The few remaining soldiers on board the helicopter refused to go back to search despite Jonah's imploring. As they soared high over the East River, questions circled, fury rose, and blame was shifted.

Jade's guilt was evident. She never looked at Jonah once on the ride back. As much as he wanted to chew her out, it was clear there was nothing to be gained from it. She'd have to live with the consequences, as would he. After touchdown, they were abruptly marched from the helo over to the Admiral's House.

Sam Dawson was pacing in the living room. He'd already heard the update over the radio, now he just wanted to hear the reasoning.

One thing was sure, Jonah wasn't going down in flames with her.

Before the admiral could tear into them, Jonah beat him to the punch.

"Alice asked me to keep an eye on her. That's the only reason I was out there."

Standing by his side, Jade fiddled with the rings on her fingers, her face downcast.

"You should have told us. This could have been prevented," he said.

Jonah eyeballed Jade. "I didn't think they were stupid enough to go that far."

"No one stopped you from turning back," Jade blurted out defensively.

Sam shifted from one foot to the next. His anger and anxiety were evident from his clenched hand and continual pacing. "Hey! You will get a chance to say your piece," Sam said. He turned back to Jonah. "What happened?"

"It was Cabbie. He was a plant. You should have vetted him."

"And how do you expect us to do that?"

Jonah shook his head. He was seething at the betrayal. "I should have known after seeing those flares. The whole drawing of Jade out to the bridge was just a ploy. Whoever he is aligned with knew that Alice would follow. The flares in the sky were simply to draw the helo to the right spot. Cabbie led us there. Everything was a setup. The walkways from one building to the next. The fake blood. He had it all timed out perfectly. Alice went across to help him. Figured he was injured.

We all did. We were distracted by the attack, and he injected her neck with something that put her down. There wasn't a chance in hell of us reaching her." Jonah dipped his head and then looked at Sam. "Why did you let her leave the island?"

"Don't you turn this on me! I didn't even know Alice got on that helo," Sam replied.

"Well, she did and now she's gone. So we need to get out there and search for her."

"And we will but right now it's dark and it's too dangerous. We have no idea where they have taken her. It would be like trying to find a needle in a haystack. We've already lost multiple soldiers. I won't lose any more."

"Then kiss goodbye whatever hope you had of curing this... whatever the hell it is."

Silence fell over the room. All that could be heard was the pop and crackle of wood in the fireplace. "So? What do you have to say for yourself?" Sam asked Jade.

She didn't try to deny it. What could she say that would justify her reasons for breaking the rules of the island?

"I'm sorry."

"It's not me you have to be sorry to," he replied.

"If I had known, I would have..." she trailed off.

"Would you?" he asked, a hint of doubt shining through.

A door slammed and a soldier appeared. "Admiral. The ventilation building will need to be secured. Seems a blowtorch was used to remove the lock." That only confirmed what Jonah had said about the whole thing being a setup. From the moment Cabbie arrived on the island, he was grooming Jade for this purpose. He had to take his hat off to them. Who would question a teenager? He'd been on that island for close to four months, taking his time and working his way into Jade's life, buttering her up with compliments and encouraging her to rebel. From there it was a simple matter of waiting until the right time when he had her in the palm of his hand, and when he knew the routine of the island, before implementing the plan.

"Do you want us to do a flyover?"

"No. They will have gone underground. They won't show their faces. Thank you, corporal."

The soldier exited and Sam let out a heavy sigh as he walked over to the fireplace and leaned against the mantelpiece, staring into the blaze. "You are both free to go," he said.

Jade immediately turned and exited. Jonah remained.

Sam looked back at him. "What is it?"

"Is that it?"

"For now."

"We need to be out there."

"And we will but nothing is to be gained from charging into the unknown without solid intel. We need to know where she is. Once we learn that, we'll go get her."

"And how do you expect to find that out?"

He smiled at him. "Jonah. You're just a kid."

Jonah stepped forward, stabbing the floor with a finger. "Don't give me that. I've survived this long."

"Because of Alice. Don't forget that. If it wasn't for her, you would be in a coma or dead. Now go. I want to be alone."

Jonah remained for a beat longer before he exited. Jade was waiting for him outside, leaning against the pillar. He walked straight past her without saying a word.

"Thanks for throwing me under the bus back there," she said.

"Oh please, you threw yourself under the moment you decided to leave the island."

He kept walking and she fell in step.

"I didn't know. Okay?"

"Oh, that makes everything better."

"Look, screw you."

"No. Screw you, Jade," he said, turning on a dime and jabbing a finger at her. "All she asked of you was to follow a few simple rules and you couldn't do that."

"From what I hear, you couldn't either when you first met her. Let's be clear. This whole act that she's your mother is bullshit. The only reason you are here is because you got on that plane. If she had her way, she would have left you behind."

"You don't know that."

"No? You want to point the finger at me for lying? You lied long before I did."

"That's not what I heard," he said, turning away and continuing to cross the Parade Ground back to the house.

"What's that supposed to mean?"

"You act like you are close with her but let's call a spade a spade here, you phoned your aunt the day shit went south. You didn't reach out to her. Now I don't care what kind of issues you had with your mother but that's very telling. So don't act like you were close." He stopped and stared at her. "You're just pissed that she and I got close through this thing and that she trusts me more."

"You're dreaming."

"Am I? Did she ask you to watch out for me?"

"No, but that should tell you something," Jade said. "She doesn't care what happens to you. I'm her flesh and blood. I always will be. That's why she came to find me."

"Then I guess that makes you all the more disappointing."

Jade twisted around and slapped him across the face. It stung but not half as much as he thought it might. He grimaced, clenching his teeth. "Jonah. I'm sorry... I..."

"Yeah, you keep telling yourself that. Maybe someone will believe you." He walked off, leaving her alone.

Five minutes later, he entered St. Cornelius Chapel, a limestone structure with a massive tower, nave transepts, and a chancel along with a side chapel. Despite all that had occurred throughout the event, those on the island tried their best to make life seem as normal as could be. That included faith. Services were held on Sunday. A priest led each one and was available throughout the week to speak with anyone that was struggling. In the first few weeks after arriving, Jonah had gone there trying to come to terms with the grief of losing his father and the guilt he felt from having lied to Alice.

Jade was right. He had lied. Numerous times. But it was all done to survive.

In his mind that was the difference.

Jonah pushed open the creaky doors of the chapel. He was met by an eerie silence, broken only by the soft shuffle of his sneakers against the stone floor. The dimly lit space was illuminated by candles. It smelled of dampness and old wood, and the air was thick with a musty scent. Making his way down the center aisle to the front of the chapel, drawn to the beauty of the altar, he sat down on a pew, contemplating what to do.

He wasn't sure how long he was there before he heard the sound of footsteps approaching. Turning, he saw the tall, imposing figure of Reverend Charles Baker making his way toward him. "What brings you here so late?" the reverend asked, his deep voice echoing in the empty chapel.

Jonah hesitated for a second before speaking. "I… I

just needed a quiet space to think," he said, his voice barely above a whisper. The reverend nodded.

"I'll leave you be then."

He turned to walk away when Jonah spoke up. "Reverend."

"Yes, my son."

"Do you think it would be okay to go up to the tower?"

"Of course. You know, Jonah. You don't need to ask each time."

"Yes, I do."

He smiled. "Just lock the door on the way out and put the key in the box."

"Will do."

The reverend set a key down on the bench and exited. Jonah sat there for a moment longer before he collected the key and went through a doorway, his mind still consumed with thoughts of Alice. He needed to do something, but he wasn't sure what. He felt lost and helpless. A feeling he hadn't experienced since the early days of the event.

Making his way up a stone staircase, Jonah reached a ladder that took him up through a trap door to the tower. He gasped as a hard wind blew against him and he looked out across the water surrounding the island. The moon cast a soft glow on the rippling surface, and fires in the city glimmered in the distance.

He glanced down at a box in a corner of the tower. He lifted it and felt a wave of relief. It was still there.

Unsure of what might become of him in the days after their arrival, he'd taken precautions, stealing a gun, night vision binoculars, and two smoke grenades. He gathered up a compass and a map of the city and filled a backpack with food, a flashlight, and matches. There was a poncho scrunched up and tucked through the handles. He unzipped it and pulled out the Glock 22. Feeling it in his hand again brought back memories of Washington.

He also had a box of ammo and two magazines. He'd taken it from a soldier and buried it all until he found out from the reverend that no one ever went up to the tower. He never planned to use it. He could have collected it on his way out to Brooklyn that night but it would have taken him out of the way and he had made a point to keep a close eye on Jade out of fear of losing sight of her.

Rising to his feet, he peered out, taking the binoculars and glassing the area. He could see soldiers walking the perimeter. The islanders would awake the next day to the bad news that Alice was gone. Unless, of course, the admiral wouldn't tell them in the hope of finding her at first light. But best of luck with that. As he said, she was a needle in a haystack, somewhere out there in the concrete jungle. Without a lead, without... he squinted, bringing the binoculars back to the docks down at Yankee Pier.

The island residents had several boats at their

disposal. Fast patrol vessels were used for fishing and getting soldiers to and from the island.

It wasn't the boats that caught his interest, it was who was speaking with one of the soldiers.

Sebastian Harris. He had arrived just a few days after Cabbie and was by far the closest friend that he had. It was rare to see them not together.

What are you up to? he thought.

If he wasn't mistaken, they exchanged something before Sebastian turned and walked away. Jonah stood there a moment longer, following him until he disappeared out of view, heading up Division Road. He brought the binoculars back toward the lone soldier who rejoined another group standing near a vessel.

"Huh."

Call it a hunch, a gut instinct. Jonah collected his bag and headed back down the tower and exited the chapel. He took off at a jog toward the apartment Sebastian stayed in.

Building 333 was a historic three-story red brick structure with a flat roof. It reminded Jonah of a Harvard dormitory, full of beauty and a rich history. It had soaring arched windows and ornate stone carvings that adorned the exterior. It was tall and imposing, its stark brick façade weathered and worn by the passage of time. It had been used for military barracks during the war. In the years after, it had been repurposed as a storage facility, a research lab, and even a temporary prison for enemy combatants. After that, it became a cultural center drawing those searching for a glimpse of its storied past through art exhibits.

Jonah ducked in, shrugging his backpack off. He took out the Glock and double-timed it up a flight of steps and down a corridor until he reached his apartment. The door was slightly ajar. He could hear movement inside. Sliding his arms through his backpack and tightening it, Jonah held the gun at his side and entered, quietly.

There, he found Sebastian hurrying, filling a bag with clothes from a closet.

"Going somewhere?" Jonah asked.

Like a kid caught with his hand in the cookie jar, all the color in his face washed out. "Oh. I…"

"Didn't close the door," Jonah said as Sebastian fumbled over his words. He was a lanky kid with a lean build that suggested athleticism. His hair was a deep shade of brown with natural waves that fell gently around his eyes. He straightened up, releasing his grip on a T-shirt. He was wearing a grey hoodie with denim jeans and a pair of Converse sneakers.

His eyes drifted down to the gun in Jonah's hand.

"Where did you get that from?" Sebastian asked.

"Never mind that. Where are you going?"

He didn't reply.

Jonah smiled. "How long did you know?"

"I don't know what you're talking about."

"Your pal, Cabbie. What he did tonight."

"I'm sorry. I'm confused. I'm just moving to a different apartment."

"Really? Is that why you paid off that soldier down at the pier? Let me guess, you've arranged a ride to the mainland. Perhaps to meet up with your butt buddy."

"You are out of your mind. When the admiral hears about this..."

"Sure. Let's go tell him. Shall we?" Jonah said, stepping to one side and gesturing for him to head out. As quick as a flash, Sebastian darted toward the window.

"Where are you going?" Jonah said, crossing the room as Sebastian opened the window and looked down. "Go ahead. Jump. You'll save me beating your ass." Jonah pistol-whipped him across the back of the head, knocking him to the floor. Next, he grabbed him by the collar and pulled him up, keeping the gun jammed into his throat. "Go on. Just give me one reason."

He tossed him on the bed like a rag doll and pointed the gun at him.

"Where did he take Alice?"

"I don't know what you're talking about."

"Then perhaps this will jog your memory." Jonah snagged up a pillow, put the gun into it, and squeezed the trigger, shooting him in the leg. The pillow muffled the bark of the gun.

"The next one goes in your skull. Now, where is she?"

5

The truth came at a cost.

Jonah kicked open the door of the Admiral's House and shoved Sebastian forward, bloody and beaten. He slid across the hardwood floor, grimacing in pain. Sam emerged from the living room, shock masking his face.

"What the hell is—?"

"Tell him what you told me!" Jonah barked. "Go on."

Sebastian looked up at him. "I don't know what he's talking about, he shot me and—"

"Oh, you son of a bitch," Jonah said as he rushed him only to be shoved back by Sam.

"Enough. Stay back," Sam hollered. He unclipped his radio. "I need a medic over here immediately," he said before clipping it back on his cargo pants.

Jonah wasn't done. "It seems Cabbie wasn't the only one

involved. This asshole was packing his bag, about to leave the island and join him. It seems he paid a soldier who is going to take him over to the mainland tonight by boat."

Sam looked at Sebastian.

"It's not true."

"You piece of shit," Jonah said.

"What soldier?"

"Aaron Wilder."

"Well, we can clear this up fast enough." Sam got back on the radio and requested Aaron be brought to the house.

"They're taking Alice north," Jonah said. "There's a group that plans to use her."

"GERM?"

"No. He won't say. But I think we can get it out of him," Jonah said, kicking him in the leg.

"Jonah, stop. Now how did this happen?"

"Beats me."

Sebastian was quick to clarify. "The lunatic shot me."

"With what? No one has access to guns."

"Exactly," Jonah said, feigning innocence and shrugging.

"He's dumped the gun," Sebastian said.

"Tell the man the truth," Jonah insisted. "You shot yourself."

"That's bullshit," he replied, grasping his leg and grimacing in pain.

"Yeah, and everything coming out of your mouth is truth."

"Jonah?" Sam said in a firm and measured tone.

"All right. I gave him a beatdown when he tried to turn a gun on me."

"He's lying."

"Shut your mouth. No one cares what you've got to say. What matters is he knows who has Alice."

"Is that true?"

Before he could answer, Jonah tossed a bag over to Sam. "Look inside. The proof is in there."

Sam lifted his eyes for a second then unzipped the bag. He pulled out some clothes and then a map. He opened it and he saw the areas that had been circled and directions for reaching Brooklyn via the ventilation building. There were Xs on parts of the map to indicate where Cabbie had led them.

"Explain this," Sam said. He was now seething.

"He's lying. That's his map," Sebastian said.

"Oh, sure. I'd create a map and come up with some story for what?"

Sebastian couldn't answer that.

A medic came rushing into the house, dropped down, and began working on Sebastian's leg. As he was doing that, Sam got up and pulled Jonah aside, holding tightly to his arm. "Where's the gun, Jonah?"

"Back at his place on the floor."

"Are you lying to me?"

"You're asking if I'm lying? That piece of shit over

there was involved in the abduction of Alice. Wake up and see what has happened. People have infiltrated the island and played you like a fiddle. Alice tried to tell you but you wouldn't listen."

After he said that, Aaron arrived with two other soldiers. "You asked to see me, Admiral?"

"You know this kid?" Sam asked.

Aaron looked down at him. "Not personally."

"What did he give you at the pier tonight?" Jonah asked.

"You must be mistaken. Besides seeing him on the island, I've never talked to him."

"Bullshit," Jonah said. "Both of them are lying. They are taking her north tomorrow. We need to act now. She's being held over in South Williamsburg then they are taking her over to Lower Manhattan where they will be heading north."

"Do you have a location?" Sam asked.

"Only for Williamsburg."

Before the Admiral could respond, a loud explosion rocked the room, causing the windows to rattle. It was followed by one more. Jonah and the Admiral looked at each other in shock before rushing outside to see what had happened.

In the distance, they could see smoke and flames rising from the location of the helicopter pad. Sam got on the radio for an update. The report came back fast, followed by several more explosions down near the water. "We're under attack," a voice cried over the radio.

"The helicopter has been taken out. Boats have been destroyed."

Jonah whirled. "It's him. I'm telling you."

"Stay here!" Sam barked.

"No, we need to get to Williamsburg."

"That's going to be a little hard if they've taken out our transportation," Sam said, going back into the house. Jonah lingered for a moment as soldiers ran in every direction, and a siren rang out alerting those on the island. He'd heard it a few times when they ran drills.

"Jonah." Jade came running toward him.

"I know where they're keeping her," he said, taking off across the green to collect his bag. Jade glanced toward the Admiral's House for but a second before following him.

"What? Hold up. Where are you going?"

"To find Alice."

"You heard what Sam said. We can't leave."

"Look around you, Jade. We have no other choice now."

"Whoa. Just stop and tell me what is going on."

"There's no time. The clock is ticking. You want to come with me. Fine. But if you slow me down, I'm not hanging back." He crossed into a grove of trees and collected his backpack that he'd left there earlier. He slipped his arms through it and shrugged it high on his back, pulling the cords tight.

"Please. Just tell me what is happening."

Frustration got the better of him. He knew if he didn't bring her up to speed, she would be pestering him all the way there. "Sebastian. A soldier. And many others were involved. Everything was planned out to take your mother. She knew it was coming, Sam wouldn't listen. They were too busy running their tests, and she and I were so busy keeping an eye on you that we didn't think of how they would ambush her. Right now, she's over in Brooklyn until the morning. We stand a chance of reaching her before they move her but we need to go now."

"Are you crazy?"

"You want to get your mother back?"

"Of course, but you saw what it's like out there."

"Yeah, and I expect it to be worse. So, if you want to stay, I'd understand. But I'm going."

With that said, he turned and broke away from the tree line, heading for the Hugh L. Carey Tunnel Ventilation Building. It was only when he made it to Fort Jay did he look back and see that she wasn't there. He couldn't fault her. He didn't expect her to come. Any logical person would have waited, reassessed in the morning, but one look at the flames coming from the pier and the helicopter pad and it was clear that these people had no intention of letting anyone follow.

The window was closing.

He wouldn't have been surprised to find out that the tunnel was blocked.

That's why he was leaving now before daylight broke and Alice was gone.

Reaching the ventilation building was a lot easier this time because every soldier that was on the island was busy dealing with the attack. It was bullshit. They had gone seven months without anyone managing to reach the island. If the helicopter and boats were up in flames, then it had to have been an inside job. They were the only ones that could get close enough to plant any explosive material.

Following the same path he took before, Jonah hurried into the darkness of the ventilation system and began to make his descent into the tunnel. He'd just made it to the bottom when he heard Jade. "Jonah!"

He shone a light upward to see her coming down the ladder.

"Wait for me."

As much as he didn't think it was a good idea that she came, he had a feeling she wouldn't turn back now. He took a seat on the curb of one of the roads that sliced through to the other side until she emerged from the darkness.

"Did you tell anyone?" he asked.

"They were a little busy," she replied, adjusting a pack on her back before they headed off into the chaotic world that lay high above the ground.

6

The world came back into view like emerging out of a dark tunnel into a pinprick of light.

Alice slowly blinked her eyes open. Her head was pounding and her vision blurred. As the room came into focus, she realized she was lying on a bed, her ankles and wrists held down by leather restraints.

Panic set in as she tried to move, but the straps held her firmly in place.

Her mouth was dry and she felt nauseated like she'd had too much to drink. She tried to speak but all that came out was a croak. Alice concentrated despite the room looking like a kaleidoscope of images and colors before it slowly solidified for just a short while. The faint smell of antiseptic lingered in the air. She tried to remember how she got there, but her mind was fuzzy and her memories were fragmented.

A helicopter ride.

A building.

Gunfire.

Something pricking her neck.

That's when it all came together, a jumbled series of memories slowly falling into order, moving back into terrifying reality. As she looked around, Alice noticed the room was dimly lit by candles. It reminded her of her grandmother's home. Doilies covered well-made furniture, drawers, and a side table. Lifting her head from the pillow, she caught sight of her reflection in the mirror, that's when her heartbeat increased and her breathing became labored.

A tube snaked away from her arm, draining her blood.

Fear crept in at the understanding of what was going on, mixed with confusion as to who was behind it. She'd been abducted. But was it only for blood? Her heart raced as she began to struggle against her restraints, but it was no use. She was trapped.

Time passed with what felt like hours. Her fear turned to anger and frustration. She cursed herself for being so careless.

Her fourth time off the island, she'd gone with the soldiers simply to prove to some key figures that she was the real deal. Skepticism was high and rightly so with people only seeing a temporary solution.

That outing led to the death of multiple soldiers. It was a costly mistake but a valuable lesson.

Then the whole thing with Jade changed it all.

She should have told Sam before leaving but it was her daughter, and she knew that Sam would have had his guys go alone so she lied. Lied to the pilot. Lied to the soldiers. Convinced them that the admiral had given the all-clear. Now she was kicking herself. The only satisfaction she had was that Jade and Jonah were safe. At least she hoped so. Her world had turned black before she saw the helicopter rise.

Alice heard movement then voices. It was coming from down below.

Finally, after what seemed like an eternity, the door creaked open, and a shadowy figure entered the room. Alice strained to see who it was, but her vision was still blurry.

"Who are you? Why am I here?" she demanded to know.

"I think you know why."

The voice was familiar but she couldn't pinpoint it. The figure moved towards her, keeping his distance, checking the tubes and equipment before making sure her restraints were still tight.

"Caleb?" She blinked hard. "Let me out of here."

"After all that I went through to get you here? Sorry. Not happening."

"Where am I?"

"In Brooklyn for now but tomorrow we go north."

"To where?"

"You'll find out," he said, moving toward the door.

"Please. I need to use a washroom."

He returned to the bed and reached down to produce a steel bedpan. "You know it will have to be me that unzips you, we don't have nurses on hand."

"Fuck you!"

He smiled and then fumbled with her belt buckle and zipper. "You know, I've always had a thing for older women and you really are quite the looker," he said, running his hand over her thigh before squeezing it. He reached up and began to undo his shirt buttons but he'd only managed to get a couple undone when he heard someone call his name.

"Huh. Now that's some shit timing. But hey, you just sit tight. We'll resume this later."

He turned and headed toward the door.

"Unhook me from this," she said, struggling again.

"I'm afraid I can't do that."

"Why are you doing this?"

He paused and looked straight at her. "You're going to save my father and then from there, I don't give two shits what they do with you. But trust me, I think they will drain you dry and perform the surgery that you should have done months ago. If you had, maybe my father wouldn't be clinging to life."

"Are you with GERM?"

"GERM?" He laughed. "Please give me some credit. They are nothing more than an annoying fly on the shoulder of the people you are about to meet."

"Caleb. Please. I'll help your father but don't do this.

Let me go. Whoever forced you into this doesn't have to control you."

"Who said anyone's controlling me? I know that shitbag Jonah screwed you over. But this isn't like that. No, I purposely put this in motion. It was my idea and look at how well it worked."

"You don't know what you're doing."

"Months of watching them run tests on you. Seeing you give blood to others. Oh, you learn a thing or two," he said, about to close the door. "Now you just sit tight. You're going to need your strength."

With that said, he shut the door and she screamed, "Let me out!"

7

The night was their ally.

Slipping back into Brooklyn enveloped by darkness was easy. They had the chaos on the island to thank for that. Whoever was behind the coordinated attack had created a distraction that was second to none. Jade hadn't said a word since they left. Jonah assumed she was feeling the weight of guilt and the potential consequence of living with it if they didn't find Alice.

He would have been lying to say he was comfortable going back to the city so soon. No, he was intimidated by what lay ahead but sitting idly by and expecting the situation to improve would have been far worse. The admiral would have wanted meetings, discussions, and endless votes on what they should do. By then Alice would be long gone. Dead even.

At least now, Jonah felt a sense of control.

He preferred it that way.

"Why are you doing this?" Jade asked.

"I told you."

"To get her back. I get that. And I understand why I'm here. She's my mother, and it's my fault, but you... you don't owe her anything."

"You're wrong."

"Okay, she allowed you to go with us to the island."

"She did more than that," he said as they ambled along the street, gazing up at the windows and roofs for threats. "She saved my life multiple times."

Jade offered a puzzled expression.

"She didn't tell you much, did she?" he asked.

"I guess not."

Jonah contemplated Alice's reasoning for that. All he could notch it up to was an oversight, or a way to shield her from the worst, or... Jonah looked at her. "What did she tell you about the days leading up to us finding you?"

"Only that my father and brother died in the Haze."

"And after?"

"That eventually she found me."

"Huh," he replied. "She was living at a fire lookout for two years, working as a Marksman and trying to find a man with a blue scorpion on his hand. That was the only lead she had on who took you. Turned out that man was my father."

"Huh. Was it Tolmie Peak Fire Lookout?"

"That's the one."

Jade sighed. "My father used to take us there. I always said if anything ever happened and we were separated that I would go there." She shook her head. "Two years of searching?"

"Every day. According to her."

"I didn't know."

"How could you? You were in a coma."

"Still, why didn't she tell me this?"

"That, you'll have to ask her."

"And you, how did you meet?"

It seemed crazy to think that they hadn't had this conversation over the past seven months but they hadn't. Jade had to go through months of physiotherapy to improve her motor skills and stimulate her brain function. Even though she'd recovered from the effects of the Haze, it still had done a number on her system. So, that's where the focus was. Not conversations with him.

"She pulled me from Mowich Lake, saved me from some assholes in a town, a handful of beaters, a city full of scalpers, and all manner of shit after that."

"But that's because she needed you to find me."

"Yeah. Look, I was infected on purpose by Robert Weston to draw out those who were working against him. He believed my father was leading the resistance against GERM who had turned to killing innocents."

"And was he?"

"He was a part of it but not the leader. If everything had gone to plan, we would have arrived at the university and gone with my father, you, and your mother to the island. I had to get your mother to believe I didn't want to go and then lead her back. When I did, Robert Weston was waiting and had my father killed for his betrayal. After, they took us from Seattle to Vancouver. Like you, your aunt gave me a blood transfusion using Alice to save my life, otherwise, I would have fallen back into the thick of the infection."

She nodded with a better understanding now of what had occurred.

"So, your lies were... to save yourself and others."

"Yes, but it never came out that way. I told your mother so many lies. So... getting her to trust me again, well..."

"That's why you do everything she says."

He nodded.

"And that's why you're here."

"I owe her my life, literally. Heck, her blood is flowing through me."

They continued in silence for a few minutes, crossing the main road and heading toward the neighborhood of Carroll Gardens. Then Jade asked, "Is your mother dead?"

He scoffed. "I was told many things. That I was given up at birth through to they died in a car crash. The truth is, I never got to know my biological parents."

"Then the whole foster system was a lie?"

"No, that part was true."

"Just the rest was warped."

He smiled at her and nodded. "So she did tell you a few things."

"A couple."

"Why did she bring that up?" Jonah asked as he eyed a large public school up ahead.

"I guess she wasn't the only one that noticed I was ignoring you."

He laughed. "Yeah, you were kind of obvious."

She summoned a half smile.

"Look. I'm not trying to be your brother or her son. I just appreciate what she's done and wish to repay her. If that's even possible."

Jade had been looking at him for but a moment when her eyes widened and she grabbed his arm, tugging him toward the school. Jonah glanced in the direction she'd been looking just in time to see a ragtag group emerging from a tree line that surrounded a baseball diamond.

A rush of adrenaline shot through Jonah as they darted into the large, four-story school with ivy crawling up the walls. Most of the windows were boarded up, and some were broken, allowing the wind to whistle through the empty rooms.

"Did they see us?"

"I don't know," Jade replied, standing at a heavy oak door with a large brass handle and looking out. The handle was rusty. Jonah took out his night vision binoculars and peered out.

The baseball diamond they'd seen the group coming

from was located directly in front of the school. It was overgrown with weeds and tall grass, and the bases were barely visible. The bleachers were rusted and falling apart, and there was no sign of life on the field. Long gone were the days of being able to determine the upscale and rundown parts of the city. It all looked the same, ransacked, destroyed, and weathered by a lack of attention or too much.

"Jonah?"

"Hold on. Still looking." Abandoned cars were dotted around the school. The only sign of life was the occasional stray dog or rat scurrying across the pavement. He recalled how sneaky the individuals were back in Pierce County, Washington. Trappers and scalpers were careful not to show their faces. It would have made the capture of people much harder. If anything, those wandering the streets were either marauders or other survivors trying to get from one building to the next. He glanced up at the makeshift walkways leading from one building to the next all over the city.

"Can't see any movement but it doesn't mean they aren't out there."

Jade breathed a sigh of relief, placing both hands on her knees. "I thought they spotted us."

"You know it's going to be like that all the way and probably worse. There's still time to go back if you want."

"No way." Jade shone a flashlight around the foyer that was once grand and elegant but now was covered in dust and debris. The tiles on the floor were cracked, and the walls were peeling.

"Come on, we'll exit another way," Jonah said, cautiously making his way further inside. The air was musty and the smell of decay filled their nostrils. Above him, Jonah heard the sound of creaking floorboards.

"You hear that?" Jade said.

"Wind. The temperature's causing the wood to change."

"Or it could be a group inside."

"I think they would have made themselves known with all the noise we made entering."

They went down the hallway to a set of double doors but they were locked by chains and a huge padlock. Many of the rooms on the lower floor were locked. That might have been the usual for when the school was closed or it might have been done to keep intruders from entering during the Haze. Jonah felt like a rat being fed along inside a maze under the watchful eye of a scientist just waiting for them to take a wrong turn.

"We could break into one of the lower classrooms and exit through those smashed windows but that's liable to draw attention to us. So, it's out the way we came or..." He turned in the hallway.

"What is it?"

"Nothing. Um."

"Jonah."

"We came that way, right?"

The building was huge. In the day it would have

been easy enough to get lost inside but now it was pitch dark and every corridor looked the same. "Yeah, we..." Jade pointed. "It's this way."

Turning back into the corridor, they noticed the main doors they had entered were closed. Sealed tight from the outside. "Are you sure this was where we came in?"

"Positive. Look, there's the baseball diamond," Jade said, straining to look out the window by going up on her toes.

"Then who locked the door?" The hairs on the back of his neck went up. Instinctively Jonah turned as if expecting to see the same group behind them. But no one was there. Tightening his grip on the Glock 22, he inched his way back to where the corridors intersected and a stairwell went up to the second floor. He said nothing but motioned with his eyes.

Jade nodded and he led the way, keeping his back pressed to the wall and holding the gun high. Their footsteps echoed off the walls. As they crept up the stairs, Jonah scanned for any sign of danger. The second floor was much like the first, all the doors were locked. It was only when they reached the third floor that they found several open rooms.

Jonah motioned to one that read "Chemistry Lab." The door was slightly ajar. He used the tip of his boot to cautiously push it open and began to investigate.

The room was dark and the air was thick with dust. The walls were lined with shelves filled with test tubes, beakers, and chemicals, all covered with a layer of grime. Many of the lab tables were littered with papers, notes, and broken equipment. Chairs were overturned and missing legs. At the far end of the room, there was a large chalkboard covered in equations and formulas. The writing was faded.

As he moved toward a second door on the far side to exit, Jonah nudged a table and a stack of books tumbled to the floor. He bent down. He scooped up some of the paperwork and shone the light over it. It was dated before the event. As Jade looked around the room, she noticed a storage room.

"Jonah."

He turned and walked back and under the glow of the light saw multiple bodies stacked high. Many were now nothing but skeletons, their bones picked clean by the passage of time. Were they students or wandering survivors who had been herded into the school only to be drained of blood and discarded like garbage?

The sight was beyond disturbing.

As they quickly backed out of the room, they heard the faint sound of a voice.

Jonah froze, clasping Jade's top to make her stop. In the darkness and silence, they listened. Someone was coming up the staircase.

Moving as quietly but as fast as they could, they made their way past multiple rooms before finding another unlocked. Entering that, they were met with an atrocious smell. The room was filled with more decomposing bodies, some of them so badly decayed they were unrecognizable. Flies buzzed around the carcasses. The stench was unbearable.

One thing he noticed was how young the dead were. No more than teenagers.

Again, out they went, trying not to make any noise.

They knew they needed to get out of the school as soon as possible but every noise they heard only pushed them toward the far north wing.

Jade checked doors on one side while he did the other until they found a classroom open. They entered, glad to see that it was clear. Going to the far back, they got into a storage room and closed the door. Slats on the door gave them just enough visibility.

The voice grew louder. It was hard to hear what was being said.

Waiting felt like agony, then they heard.

"Wasn't this door locked?" a voice asked.

After a few minutes, the footsteps faded away, and the two of them breathed a sigh of relief. Still, they waited, expecting the stranger to return.

Unable to stay there any longer, Jonah quietly ventured out and made his way across to the exit that led back into the corridor. He peered out. It was clear.

"All good," he whispered before stepping out.

As they made it further down the corridor, they heard the most ungodly muffled scream. The two of them froze again. Jade tapped his back and told him to keep moving. They continued, making it back to the room where they'd seen all the bodies inside.

Jonah stopped abruptly.

"What is it?" she asked.

Another scream followed.

"Where is he?" the same voice they'd heard grew louder.

Jade skirted around him to get a better look.

Inside the room, all they could make out in the dim light was a figure looming over someone sitting in a chair. They were doing something but couldn't tell what. Whatever it was, it was causing untold agony.

Jonah nudged Jade to keep moving but another scream changed her mind.

"We need to do something," she said.

"Yeah, get out while we can," he replied, his voice a mere whisper.

The scream sounded like a young kid as it was followed by tears. Before Jonah could protest, Jade took the gun out of his hand and entered the room holding it up. Her entry was noted by the hooded individual turning.

That's when Jonah saw what had been done.

A young boy no older than ten was strapped to a chair, his shirt removed. All over his skin were knife marks.

"Put it down!" Jade demanded.

8

"You've got this all wrong!" the stranger muttered.

It was a hard sight to take in. An unthinkable horror. Jade moved a few feet forward, nudging the gun at him as Jonah remained in the doorway, watching the corridor for any other threats. This was what life had become, an endless slew of terror and horror forced upon others by those who wanted people for one reason or another. There was no one to stop them. The world had become a shell of its former self. Law enforcement had retreated to save their own families, the military struggled to keep hold of quarantine zones, and so cities became the abyss for the sick and depraved.

"I won't ask again," she said.

The boy wrestled in his restraints. He'd been sliced multiple times down his chest, face, and arms. These weren't superficial wounds but deep cuts made to inflict the most amount of pain and damage.

"Jade, wait!" Jonah said.

She glanced at him for but a second. "Why? Look at him."

"I know but not everything is what it seems," he said, thinking back to those who were beaten to death in Washington. He thought they were innocent people only to find out they had kidnapped people and drained them of blood.

"Listen to your friend," the stranger said.

"Shut the hell up!" Jade shot back.

"Did you kill all these people?" Jonah asked.

"Sure did."

"Why?"

He snorted. "Why? You're asking me, why? Where have you been?"

"Just answer the question," Jade demanded, annoyed that they were even allowing the stranger to continue holding that blade.

"All right. Because someone has my brother."

The stranger lifted a hand and pulled back his hood. He was a black kid who couldn't have been much more than twenty. And he was equally as slashed as the boy that he was working on. He turned his face from side to side as Jonah shone a light on his face.

Jonah squinted. "Who did that?"

"Who do you think? These little bastards."

"But he's just a kid," Jade replied.

"A kid? Is that what you think? I don't know what stone you two crawled out from underneath but you aren't from this city. This place is crawling with these little fuckers. They will slash you from ear to ear or take a baseball bat to all your joints then leave you to bleed out."

"But he's just..."

"Small? Alone? Sure. But you'd be surprised at the damage they can do in groups. That's how they travel. Together. In packs. You never heard of ransackers?"

Jade glanced at Jonah. "Yeah. Erika told us that the Haze was evolving, affecting younger groups. Making them more violent."

"It's not just the young. Others too. Glad to see one of you isn't stupid."

"Watch your mouth," Jade replied.

"Look, are you going to shoot me or can I go back to slicing him up?"

"Put the knife down."

"Jade," Jonah said. "Let's go."

"I'd listen to your friend if I was you. However, word of advice. Probably best to wait until morning. These little fuckers are everywhere at night. Like rats out of a sewer, they emerge to wreak havoc."

"Sleep inversion," Jonah said.

"So, you do know about it then."

"A little. The Haze was meant to affect people in different ways, for some it caused sleep inversion."

"Sleeping in the day, awake at night. You got it. Look, the name is Malik Davis. And you are?"

"Getting a little tired of you not listening," Jade said.

"All right. All right. But I warned you," he said, dropping the knife on the floor and stepping back with his hands up. Jade passed the Glock to Jonah.

"Keep that on him. If he moves, you squeeze the trigger."

"Oh, don't worry about me, darling. You worry about yourself. You're about to get a rude wake-up call."

Jonah stepped forward, extending a precautionary hand. "Jade. Don't get close."

The two of them were wearing N95 masks and gloves but the chance of infection was still high.

The boy groaned. His head dropped ever so slightly, blood dripping down and creating tiny pools on the floor. Jade moved in. "Hey, it's all right. We're going to help you."

She went behind him and looked down at his restraints.

Malik shook his head. "Um. I wouldn't do that if I was you."

"Jade, listen. Maybe we should—"

Before he could finish, she undid the boy's restraints around his wrists. He pried the gag out of his mouth and then it was like letting loose a crazed animal. He lashed out at Jade, knocking her back. His ankles were still restrained to the chair, causing him to collapse on the floor. With all the prowess of a snake, he slithered forward, the chair clattering behind him as he clawed the floor with his fingers going for the knife.

Jonah acted on instinct and fired a round into his skull.

Jade, still on her ass, looked on, shock taking hold.

Silence fell over them.

A moment of quiet prevailed before Malik shrugged. “Ah, he wasn’t going to give me an answer anyway.”

Jade blurted out, “What the fuck?! What the...”

“I told you not to do that,” he said like it was obvious. “This shit affects the brain.” He looked at Jonah. “Is she wet behind the ears?”

Jade bounced up and flew at him, bringing the knife up, but before she could do anything, Malik grabbed her arm and used her forward motion to put her back on her ass.

“Let her go!” Jonah barked.

“All right, Casanova. Ease up. I wasn’t the one that attacked her. I gave you forewarning.”

He removed the knife from Jade’s hand and flipped it around and handed it to Jonah without any fear. It was clear why he’d managed to survive; the question was for how long?

Jade scowled as she rose to her feet.

“How long have you been out here?” Jonah asked.

“Here or in the city?”

“Both.”

“I only come here when I snag one of these assholes. But I’ve been in the city since the beginning. I used to live over in Brownsville with my little brother until we got separated. I've been searching for him since. Figured he was caught, infected, and was running with these pieces of shit."

"What were you planning to do if you found him?"

"Put him out of his misery." He dipped his head. "It's not like there's a cure for this."

Jonah glanced over at Jade who was back on her feet, brushing off dirt from her jeans. After what had happened with Cabbie, he figured that word had spread about Alice. "What if there is?"

He laughed. "Trust me. It's been almost three years. If it existed, we would have heard of it by now. No one comes back from this. Once exposed, you only have a few options. Blood transfusion — best of luck finding the right match — or death. Of course, there is the third, which is what you see here."

"A variant."

"If that's what you want to call it."

"So, they don't fall into a coma or die?" Jonah asked.

"No, but they might as well be dead. It fucks up the brain. Neurological shit. You know what I mean." He peeled off his blue latex gloves and put a new pair on before he reached into his top pocket and pulled out a pack of smokes. "You smoke?"

"No."

"Nah, neither did I until this. I figured there are worse things I can inhale, right?" he said before bringing down his mask to put one in his mouth. He lit the end and blew out smoke, gazing back at Jade who scowled before making her way over to the door.

"What if there is a cure?" Jonah said.

"There isn't."

Jade tugged on Jonah's jacket. "We should go."

"Like I said, I can let you out but you'd be safer here tonight."

Jonah nodded. "We have to go. A friend of mine. Her mother is out there. Someone took her."

"What a novelty," he replied, blowing smoke and stretching out his arms all theatrical. "Let me save you some time and hassle. If she's gone. You won't see her again. This city is too damn big. Trust me. I've spent two years scouring it for my brother and haven't even come close. One night. You think you'll find her in one night?" He laughed as smoke came out his nostrils. "You'll be dead or infected before you make it one block."

"We made it more than that so far," Jade said, folding her arms.

"Is that right?" He smiled, jabbing his finger at her. "I like you. All spunk and grit."

She stuck up her middle finger and he chuckled. "She really is a firecracker." Malik slipped off a table and went over to a window. "Come. Let me show you something."

Jonah hesitated.

"If I wanted to kill you, I would have done it by now. Come on. If you want to go out there, you should know what you are dealing with."

Jonah went to cross the room but Jade pulled at his jacket. He shrugged her off and went to see. Malik pointed. "You see those fires dotted around the city? Think of that dead kid, now multiply that by a thousand or at least a few hundred. They tend to stick to groups of about ten or a few more, but you never know what you're going to run into. Then, of course, you've got your regular trappers out there whose traps you're liable to walk into. And if they don't get you, you have your scalpers who will sell you off to the highest bidder. Then of course we have beaters."

"Yeah. I'm familiar with them all."

"Oh, you are? Yeah, they are sweet little bastards. I mean not little as in young, but they sure know how to get their jollies. And believe me, no amount of pleading with them changes their minds. If they think you look like the person that took a family member, your number's up." He walked away from the window. "But hey, it's your funeral."

"We have to find her."

"Doesn't everyone."

"She's different."

"Isn't everyone." He chuckled.

Jonah hesitated for a second then said, "She's the cure."

Malik stopped in his tracks and looked back at him before bursting out laughing. "The cure? Oh, that's hilarious."

Neither Jade nor Jonah was smiling.

The smile faded from his face for a second. "You two are bat shit crazy." That only made him laugh hard until his laughter trailed off. "Are you serious?"

"Maybe not a permanent cure but she's the key to it."

"Let me guess, she convinced you or someone sold you a line."

"No. We're alive because of her."

He frowned for a second, then took a few steps back, bringing up his mask. "You're infected?"

"Were," Jade said, still standing at the door and blocking the way. Malik backed away.

"She was in a coma. Her mother's blood brought her out."

"Bullshit. No one comes out of these comas."

"I did," Jade added.

"And I was infected," he said, bringing down his eyelid and shining a light into it. The panic on Malik's face was very real. "We're not infected anymore."

"People get transfusions and show no symptoms for three to six weeks. You've got this wrong. You're just not experiencing..."

"It's been seven months," Jonah said. "I haven't gone backward and I've been in contact with lots of uninfected people and they are fine."

His eyes darted between them. "Look. Just go." He reached into his pocket and took a set of keys and threw them over. "The red one opens the door you came in through. Just leave them behind after you're gone."

"I'm telling you the truth, Malik."

"I don't give a shit. You should have told me you were infected the moment you saw me."

"Well, you were a little busy slicing up a ten-year-old," Jade said.

"He was twelve."

"Oh, that makes all the difference." Jade rolled her eyes.

"I don't care if you two think this woman is the cure. You're clearly out of your fucking skulls and with all the neurological shit that I've seen over the past two years, including these assholes, I wouldn't be surprised if what has happened to you both is just another variant."

"Come on, Jonah. We're wasting our time," she said, stepping out into the hallway.

Jonah scooped up the keys and crossed the room but paused at the doorway. "If we're infected, would we be wearing gloves and masks?" he asked Malik before shaking his head and walking away.

They made it all the way downstairs and to the exit. Jade was unlocking the door when Jonah glanced over his shoulder to see Malik standing there.

"You really believe she's the cure?"

He hesitated for a second before replying. "Yeah, I do."

"And uh. Do you think her blood could help my brother?"

"That would rely on finding her and your brother and it sounds like you haven't had much luck."

"But you know where she is?"

Jonah glanced at his watch. "For now. If we stay here until dawn, no."

Jade unlocked the door and pushed it open. "Are we going or not?" she asked.

Malik shifted his weight from one foot to the next. "If I help you reach her, you have to promise to help me find my brother."

"If he's alive," Jonah said. "Her blood brings people back from the brink of death, not death itself."

"And who's to say we even need your help?" Jade asked.

"Darling, I know if looks could kill, you could probably take out an entire flock of ransackers but I've been at this far longer than you. You decide. Trust me. Or trust yourself."

Jonah glanced at Jade and shook his head to indicate for her to back down. She had every reason to hate the guy after what he'd done to that kid but that was because she had been protected since the day she'd gone into a coma. Malik. Him. Alice. They'd been in survival mode. Doing whatever they could to survive. Killing whoever they had to if it meant seeing another day.

"We good?" Malik asked.

Jonah turned back to him and nodded.

"Where is she?"

"Williamsburg. The Dime Residences."

"All right. But we'll need to wait a few more hours."

Jonah shifted forward, stabbing a finger at his watch. "We don't have time."

"You said dawn. That's not for another nine hours. Trust me on this. You don't want to be out there right now. You asked me how I've survived this long. This is how. By making smart choices and moving only when it's safe."

"We can't wait for dawn," Jonah said.

"And we won't. But for now, we have to stay put."

"This is a bad idea," Jade said, closing the door and locking it behind them. There was no telling if he could help or if this was just a ploy to give him hope when in reality, his brother was probably dead. But with enough against them already, Jonah figured stacking the odds in their favor was wise.

9

Screams rang like alarm bells throughout the city.

Their departure from the school would happen sooner than expected.

Before Malik took them up to the roof to give them a better view of Brooklyn, he entered a science room where he collected an M4 and two SIG Sauer P226s. "You always stash them here?" Jonah asked as he watched him fill a bag.

"Rule number three of surviving this shitfest. Never put your eggs in one basket. No, I've stashed buckets of ammo and guns all over this city. I figure if I run out of ammo, I know where there is more."

"Where did you get all of this?"

"Some of it I found in buildings. The M4 I snagged from a dead soldier. There's a lot to be found out there, you've just got to be willing to risk being spotted."

Jonah glanced over his shoulder. Jade was perched on the edge of a table. "She could use a gun."

"Does she know how to use one?"

"Could you be any more condescending?" Jade replied.

"She's pretty good," Jonah said coming to her defense.

"All right. Well, you'll need one."

"You say that as if it's a given that we'll have to use them," Jade said.

"You will," he replied, rising to his feet and strolling over to hand her the gun. She went to take it but he kept it just out of reach. "What's the magic word?"

"Um, let me think. Is it, would you like to keep your testicles?" Jade shot back.

He chuckled and handed it to her before zipping up his bag.

"What have you done for food and water?" Jonah asked.

"Oh, I just hit up the local Burger King. You know, get myself a Whopper and a big shake. It's a little on the stale side, but you can't be picky nowadays." He laughed as if the question didn't need an answer. It was clear from one look at him he hadn't gone without. They'd seen others arrive at the island as thin as a rail. "Nah, you just need to know where to look," Malik added. "Food is scarce but after the infection spread, a lot of folks were distracted searching for blood for loved ones or they left the city. My brother and I were already used to living from hand to mouth. In many ways, this opened up the doors for us to stock up."

"You stole?"

"If you want to call it that. I call it surviving. C'mon!" he said, shrugging the pack over his shoulder and leading them out.

"So where are your parents?" Jonah asked.

"Dead."

"They died in the Haze?"

"No, and yes. My father passed away from cancer three years before the event. Our mother died on the day of the event. She was in a car accident. It was just before I turned twenty-one."

"You're twenty-one? I thought you were..."

"Younger? Yeah, most say that." He sniffed hard as they double-timed it up the stairs to the next floor. "Anyway, Tyrone, my brother, was going to be put into the foster system so I petitioned the court for guardianship of him."

"You can do that?"

"It's 100 percent legal. At least it used to be."

"And so they just agreed?"

"Not exactly. Tyrone didn't want to do it at first but then he changed his mind after he found himself living in an unsanitary and abusive environment."

"Who was he staying with?"

"Aunt and uncle. They didn't give a shit about him. They just wanted him for the government checks. You know, the handouts they give you to help. Anyway, it worked out in the end."

They kept moving up the stairs until reaching the fire escape, which led out onto the roof. Outside the air was thick with tension and uncertainty. The sky was darker than normal, with no stars, only a faint orange glow of fire in different neighborhoods. As Jonah moved closer to the edge, his eyes adjusted to the darkness and they were greeted by the view of the surrounding neighborhoods. There were no streetlights. Every so often they could hear the crackle of gunfire, and screams, followed by the shattering of glass as the city continued to descend into chaos. The howling wind added an unsettling atmosphere, creating an ominous feeling of impending doom.

"You always come here?"

"Not always. You have to stay moving to survive. Stay in one spot, they eventually will sniff you out."

Jonah looked at him.

"Figuratively. Here, look," he said, taking a night vision monocular and handing it to him. "See that apartment block over there? The one that's lit up by those little lights strung along the wall. Some guy moved up there a week ago. He's hooked into those solar panels. Pretty smart, right? He gets to use the sun to charge up whatever he needs. I've seen him cooking food over there. He thinks he's safe on the roof."

"He's not?"

"No. I mean, sure, chances of them finding him are

low but all it takes is for those little bastards to reach the roof of any one of those apartment blocks and they'll find him in the night. He's survived so far but the mistake he's made is relying on those solar panels. He collects water from the rain and goes down into some of the apartments, I'm assuming to find food as I have seen him return with cans. But… look," he said, nudging the monocular to the right.

Jonah squinted. The apartment blocks directly adjacent had young kids running across the tops of the roofs, rolling and jumping like they were doing parkour. "If he's lucky, he'll survive one more night. But just like over there, they will eventually find him. That's why I only pick buildings like this. No surprises that way."

"So, they haven't searched here?"

"Oh, a few have, until I started locking the doors. Ransackers are opportunists. They take the path of least resistance. Unlike scalpers. They will hunt you down if they know you are nearby. Trappers are just lazy. They set traps like a hunter and then return a day or two later to collect. That's how I caught that kid. He'd fallen into a trap. Was hanging upside down. A quick whack to the head and he was easy to get over here."

"And the others?"

"Similar. Depends on how I feel. There are days I become the hunter."

Jonah nodded. "Your brother Tyrone. You think he's still alive?"

"I don't know. But I won't give up until I find out."

Jonah continued peering at the man on the apartment block. He was middle-aged, reminded him of a banker. He was still wearing the remnants of a suit, a torn-up one but a suit nonetheless. He could only imagine him working on Wall Street or at one of the upscale businesses in Manhattan. He probably knew just enough to stay ahead of the crowd.

"We should warn him," Jade said.

Malik laughed. "No," he said, turning and walking away.

"He could die out there."

"As could we if we make ourselves known to him. You don't get it, do you? Maybe that guy is a survivor. Someone like me, trying to stay alive long enough to find his loved one or maybe he's a scalper, a trapper, or a beater. They have many ways of getting people." Malik walked back and pointed at the man. "But here's the thing. Look at how he's dressed. That should tell you something. If he was a survivor, he would have shed those threads by now and gotten into something a little more comfortable. No, he's still wearing the same shit that he had on the day this event started. Which tells me, he was nabbed and made a deal with the devil. Trappers. Scalpers. I don't know. Maybe they have his wife or kid. And they've offered him a deal — bring in X number of people in exchange for them. But you want to know the clear giveaway?" He breathed in the smoky air. "The radio. He's been up there a week. If he was communicating with someone, he would have met up with them. No, he took to the high ground to spot people. He's a point man."

"A what?"

"A scout. Someone who radios back to the others what he sees."

"Shouldn't we find out?" Jade asked.

"No. I don't interfere with others unless they interfere with me."

Malik walked away.

"Who's to say you're not one too?" Jade said. He looked back at her, then his gaze bounced between them.

"She has a lot to learn."

No sooner had he said that than they heard the sound of glass breaking down below. Malik rushed to the edge of the building on the east side and peered down. "Oh shit."

"What is it?"

"We have company."

He hurried back into the building. Jonah followed almost in his shadow.

"Who is it?"

"The rest of that asshole's group."

"The kid you killed?"

"Don't say it like he didn't deserve it. Had his feet been free, you may have well been on your ass along with your pretty friend," Malik said.

"So how do we get out?"

"Third floor. Let's just hope we reach it before those

coming up do."

Jonah could hear a screaming sound that cut through him. He'd seen the way that kid had gone nuts and he was only one person. By the sounds of the ruckus below them, they were dealing with more than a handful.

Malik stopped running. "Shh," he said, peering over the stairwell. He reached for a dangling piece of rope and tugged hard. "Wait for it."

"What are we waiting for?" Jade asked, panic setting in fast.

As they stood there, they heard what sounded like thirty or forty people hurrying up the steps.

"Malik," Jonah said.

"Wait for it," he said, raising a finger. He looked as if he was counting in his head. Then he reached into his pocket and fished out a Zippo lighter. He grasped it tightly in his hand, feeling the weight and running his thumb over the smooth metal. With a quick wrist flick, and a snap of his thumb down on the lid, it sprung open, exposing a flame. He glanced at Jonah and smiled as if this was just another day for him. Then, he tossed it down.

They heard it clatter followed by the largest whoosh.

Malik swept his arm around them and forced them back into the corridor on the third floor at the sound of an explosion. The explosions happened one after another as though the entire first and second floors had been rigged to ignite. "Go. Go!" he yelled.

“Where?” Jade asked, looking like a chicken with its head cut off.

“Fourth classroom to your right.”

They darted down the corridor and ducked into there. Below they could hear screams and several loud pops. Malik tucked a chair behind the door and then darted over to a window. He slid it wide. “All right, you first.” He handed Jade a long piece of rag that was wrapped around a carabiner so someone could slide down it like a zip line.

Jonah looked out to see rope anchored to a ventilation system on a building on the other side.

“Oh, hell no!” Jade said, taking a few steps back.

“It’s either this, or you go up in smoke. This place is going to be an inferno in a matter of minutes.”

Jonah urged her. “Go.”

She grimaced and climbed out of the window onto the ledge. She held the material with both hands. “Hold on tight,” Malik said before giving her a push. She let out a yelp as she flew away from the window, sliding down toward the next building at an astonishing speed. Jade landed hard, rolling across the roof before gripping her ankle.

“You’re up,” Malik said, getting another carabiner ready.

Jonah looked down, his heart racing with adrenaline. They were high above the ground. Behind them, they could hear frantic voices.

Just as he was about to climb out onto the window

ledge, he heard the slam of a body against the door behind him. He turned to see the intruders trying to find a way in. Their voices were muffled, their faces hidden by smoke and fire.

They had to move quickly.

"Go!" Malik shouted.

Jonah didn't hesitate. He looked down for but a second at the dizzying height below then launched before his nerves could falter. He plummeted towards the building. As he tore away, he could hear the sound of the door finally giving way, and a chorus of gunfire.

Then it all faded in the rush of wind.

Jonah landed equally as hard as Jade. Even though he lifted his legs in the last part, his body slammed into the ventilation system.

"Malik!" Jade shouted but it was no use.

A second later, the line was cut. They watched it collapse.

"Shit." Jonah saw numerous faces through the glass, looking down at them. None of them were Malik. Jade tapped Jonah's arm.

"Come on. We need to move now."

"But..."

"He's dead."

As they turned and ran toward the nearest stairwell that led down into the apartment block, Jonah heard the shattering of glass coming from a window behind them. Suddenly, hope rose in his heart at the sight of Malik further down. He was in a different classroom.

"Jade."

She looked back and he pointed. A moment later, Malik burst out of the room and came sliding down on a separate line, except he landed on a different apartment roof.

"Malik!" Jonah shouted, pointing to others that were following him down. Malik turned, extracted a knife, and cut the rope just as those that were pursuing him were suspended over the divide between the school and the apartment. The rope went limp and three fell to their death.

Malik turned and headed for the stairwell.

"I'll meet you on the ground!" he shouted.

They didn't waste another second. The two of them hustled, racing down the steps past multiple apartments. Most doors were locked. Some were open. An ever-growing sense of dread crept up in his throat at the thought that they could get attacked just trying to make it to the ground.

Fortunately, for now, they were safe.

They reached the ground and waited in the darkness for Malik to emerge before joining him. They shared a moment of elation, knowing they had just pulled off the escape, but it was short-lived. They couldn't be out in the open long.

"This way."

They took off into the night.

Even though they had survived, they knew that it was only the beginning of the danger that awaited them.

10

Adrenaline kept them alert, fear kept them awake.

An hour and a half on foot. That's how long Malik figured it would take to reach the Dime Residences in Williamsburg if they didn't stop. But that was when the world was normal and every moving thing wasn't a possible threat. Nothing was normal now. Brooklyn neighborhoods had been turned into a war zone. It was every survivor for themselves.

"How did you manage to escape?" Jonah asked Malik.

"Ever heard of a contingency plan? I had several."

"Like rigging that place."

"Amazing what you can do with enough gasoline and a small amount of C4. Of course, I had exits in most of the rooms, sections of drywall cut out but covered by furniture. I couldn't be stuck, right?"

"Right."

He was pleased to have someone guiding them through the city who had survived this long, but realistically, how many contingency plans could one person create out in the open air? Jade turned on her flashlight and Malik snapped.

"Turn that off!"

When she didn't act fast enough, he grabbed it out of her hand and bashed it against a wall. "You want to alert everyone that we're here?"

"It's dark."

"Yes. It is. And it needs to remain that way if you want to make it the next few blocks." He handed back the flashlight or what was left of it. The bulb and glass up front were gone, all she had was the shell and batteries.

"Thanks." She tossed it and it clattered on the ground.

"Are you serious?" Malik said, facing her again.

"What? Huh? What now?"

"Keep your voice down. Geesh! Why don't we just start a marching band?" he said.

"Or smash a flashlight against a wall," she shot back, pointing out that he'd created noise doing that.

"Hilarious."

"Why are you such an asshole?" Jade asked. Jonah shook his head.

"Because it's what keeps me alive, princess."

"Don't call me that."

"Then don't act like one."

Jade stopped walking and Jonah turned back. "Come on, Jade."

"Not with him. I'm done."

Of course, Malik found this amusing. "Oh, did I hurt your feelings?"

"Screw you."

"Come up with something original. Seriously, I somehow get the feeling that no one tells you what a pain in the ass you are. But I'll be more than glad to."

Jade refused to be the brunt of his joke. "And I get the feeling that..."

"Stop!" Jonah said. "Okay. This back-and-forth bickering shit is getting old. We just need to reach the location. You, stop winding her up. And you, show him some respect. The reason we're still here is because of him."

"Thank you, Jonah," Malik said, acknowledging the nod in his direction and then smiling at Jade.

Jade narrowed her eyes at him before strolling past.

"She is a wild card, isn't she."

"You don't know the half of it," Jonah replied.

It was tricky to walk incognito. They were making their way up Henry Street when Malik took a hard right and double-timed it up some steps to the door of a brownstone — one of the many that lined the street on either side. "Where are you taking us?" Jonah asked, catching up with him.

"Parts of Brooklyn are blocked off. Some areas you won't get through without a little help. We need a little."

"I thought you were the help," Jade said, teasing him back into an argument. Thankfully, Malik didn't take the bait.

"Ever heard the saying, it takes a village to raise a child? Well, the same applies now. It takes a village to get us to your destination. Some have agreements in place. Remember what I said about not getting two blocks without dying? This is what I'm talking about. And I don't mean by trappers and scalpers. Some survivors are a little trigger-happy. They'll shoot you on sight rather than put themselves at risk of infection. Some of the neighborhoods have rallied together. They figure there is power in numbers. Like tiny villages. Some lure you in only to spit you out, some block off all entry and won't let you get within spitting distance. This block, for instance, between Kane and Degraw, used to be populated by chefs, lawyers, consultants, and Wall Street hotshots."

"And now it's not?"

"Oh no. It still is. At least it was half a year ago. I haven't been down here in a while. The last time I darkened their doorsteps, I found out how much of a stickler they were for who they let through." He gave a very specific knock. A moment or two passed and the door opened ever so slightly. No one was there.

"Okay. C'mon." Malik pushed wide the creaky door.

They didn't hesitate. It was too dangerous to be out on the street.

The door clunked behind them and what sounded like multiple bolts slipped into place.

The absence of light inside, combined with the ominous silence, created an eerie atmosphere that sent shivers down Jonah's spine. They were met by a musty smell that made him wrinkle his nose. The air was stale and heavy as if the house had been shut up for a long time. The layout was typical for a four-story brownstone, with a narrow staircase that led up to the upper floors.

As they moved through the house, the creaking of the wooden floorboards echoed through the silent rooms. The only light came from the moon filtering in through areas around the boarded-up windows. They could barely see their way around because Malik made it clear that no light was to be used.

"Felix?" he called out.

"Upstairs," a voice replied.

Keeping eyes on Malik, they followed him up to the next floor. They were greeted by a figure standing by a fireplace. On the mantel was a small dome light that gave off enough light to reveal the stranger. He turned toward them, wearing nothing more than a burgundy robe and underwear. He brought a martini glass up to his lips.

Almost automatically he closed the robe, wrapping a cord around his waist.

"You brought guests?"

"Friends of mine."

Jonah heard Jade mumble something, probably related to being called a friend.

"Jonah, Jade, this is Felix Kensington."

He strode over, beaming. "The pleasure is mine," he said, shaking Jade's hand for but a second before glancing Jonah up and down like he was some sort of product. He wandered around Jonah, making him feel uncomfortable. "Not a lot of meat on him, is there?"

"What?" Jonah asked, looking confused.

Malik shook his head. "Stop playing with him, Felix."

"Oh, you do take out all of the fun." He took another sip of his drink and moved back to the fireplace, grinning.

"We need passage."

"Oh. How boring. And here I was thinking you had brought me a play toy, some exciting news, or were planning to keep me company."

"I have your drink," Malik said, turning and taking a small bottle of brandy out of his pack. Felix squealed with delight and snatched it from his hands, bringing it down to the fireplace where he held it to the light.

"It's the one you asked for."

"Had to check. A lot of folks make promises and fail to deliver."

He was an odd character, with flamboyant mannerisms and a quick wit. He turned and looked at the two of them. "Where are you heading?"

"Williamsburg."

"Why?"

"To meet up with a friend," Jonah interjected.

"And you? Cat got your tongue?" he asked Jade.

"It's my mother."

"Ah, parental reunion. I do love those."

"Are you going to help or not?" Malik asked.

"Things have changed around here, Malik, since you were last here. Not everyone agrees. I can give you passage through the first ten homes, after that, you will have to make a deal with the last four or hit the street."

"Dissension in the ranks?"

"You could call it that."

"Let me guess. The major, right?"

Felix laughed. "Little gets past you. But yes, it's the major. He had a falling out with the others. Couldn't get his way so he decided he would be a thorn in our side."

"Well, I'll deal with that when we get there."

"As you wish. Follow me," he said, taking the dome light.

"I thought we weren't allowed to use light?"

"On the street," Malik clarified. "In here the windows are boarded up and the light they use is just enough to see their way."

"And the fire?"

"To stay warm, silly," Felix said, chuckling.

Felix took them up to the top floor and down a corridor into a bedroom where he asked Malik to assist him in moving a wardrobe. Once it was out of the way, they were greeted by the sight of a large opening in the wall that went into the next brownstone.

"Why couldn't we just go via the roof?"

Felix laughed. "You can. Of course, you can. But you'll find yourself tripping over bodies. Many have tried and failed."

"You kill them?"

"Us? No. Marksmen. Trappers. Not every roof is safe to traverse," he said before beckoning them into the next room. He went with them to ensure that the owner of the next building was aware of the arrangement. It seemed that if one agreed, the rest would. And so they were taken one by one through each of the brownstones until they reached what would bring them to the major's house. "This is the end of the road, my friend. The door is open to go through but you'd be taking a big risk. The last person who tried didn't make it," Felix said.

"Where is he now?" Jonah asked.

"Um. In pieces. Somewhere across the island. In a bird's mouth. I'm not too sure."

"Malik. A moment of your time." Jonah took hold of him and pulled him to one side. "There are countless streets outside we could have used besides this way. Why are you making this more difficult? This is slowing things down."

"Slowing?" He laughed. "Oh, you have it all backward. We are making fast progress. I don't know how things worked in Washington, but here, Brooklyn and Manhattan are the equivalents of a giant maze. Ever been in one of those? You walk down one passage and find yourself staring at a leafy wall only to retrace your steps, head in a new direction and reach another dead end. The same applies here. Some roadways are blocked, others guarded, and the rest are nothing but traps that are liable to have you hanging by your ankles in the air. In some areas, we can hit the street, in others we can go by roof or using the walkways, but the rest is achieved through passages created in buildings that are joined together like this."

"But that's insane. This could take us hours."

"Yes. Like I told you… I can help because I know the route but you've got to trust me."

Jonah sighed and looked at Jade who looked equally annoyed.

"How do you think these people have survived? This is a system of you scratch my back and I scratch yours. Trading. Exchanging. Gifting. Nothing is free. You fuck them over, and well you're going to have a very bad day."

"All right. What now?"

"Well, I have to negotiate with the major."

"With what? You gave what you had to Felix."

"Some are open to IOUs if you get what I mean. Felix for instance has been waiting on that bottle for a long time. The major has his weakness. Everyone does."

"Well?" Felix asked. "Have you decided?"

Malik took a deep breath and released it. "Open the door. We'll go in."

"Brave soul. It's been nice knowing you all." He

motioned to two other men and they moved a large wardrobe out of the way. The three of them peered into the darkness. Unlike the previous brownstones that had some partial light on the highest floor, there was nothing but an empty abyss of black.

"I'm guessing this is where you could have used my flashlight, right?" Jade said sarcastically.

"I have my own, princess." He took it out and shone it into the crevice before stepping in. When Jonah was through, the wardrobe was shifted back into place. There was no going back. "Major! It's Malik Davis. I was hoping we could speak. Come to some arrangement."

A raspy voice boomed back from somewhere in the inky black. "All arrangements are off. We're no longer with them and they should have advised you of that before you stepped inside."

"They did. I can get you what you want."

"Bullshit, it doesn't exist."

"It does now."

A bright light shone on their faces, blinding them. In an instant, the three of them were overpowered by multiple individuals. A sharp jab in the ribs, a hook to the face, and Jonah's legs buckled.

"Get off me," Jade yelled.

As they were brought to their knees side by side, the light was taken off their eyes. Jonah squinted, trying to make out who was before them. It took almost a minute for his eyes to adjust. That's when he saw him, a large and imposing man in military fatigues. Jonah noted the patch on his arm. GERM. "You work for them?" Jonah asked.

"Of course not. I keep it there as a reminder."

"For what?"

"For what I plan to do when I get my hands on them."

Malik was quick to inject. "How is Sophie?"

"Don't you say her name!"

"Well, you see that's the thing, major. I can turn it around."

The major brought out a pistol and put it up to Malik's head. "Say another word and I will..."

"There's a cure," Malik said as convincingly as Jonah had told him. Somewhere between the school and here, he had become a believer or like any good salesman, he knew just what to say at the right time. "Tell him, Jade."

The major shifted his eyes toward Jade. "Sophie. Is that your daughter?" she asked.

He nodded.

"Is she infected?"

"In a coma."

"Then he's right. She can be helped."

The major shook his head. "A blood transfusion doesn't work."

"You're right. But the right one will."

"What are you talking about?"

"She was in a coma," Malik interjected. "Her mother brought her out. She's immune."

"There are no immunes."

"There is one," Jonah said. "But unless you give us passage, we can't help your daughter."

"Bullshit. This is just a lie, a means of..."

"For goodness sake, major. Show him, Jonah."

He nodded. "Don't shoot me. I'm wearing a mask for a reason." He reached up and brought down his eyelid. The major leaned in and his eyes locked on the yellow.

"So? The infection causes damage. You've had a transfusion. Is that it?"

"Seven months ago, I would have fallen back into the thick of infection if it wasn't for a blood transfusion from her mother. I haven't had one since. I'm not infected."

The major nodded to one of his guys and they stepped forward with a device to check, much like the one that had been used by GERM back when they were evaluating people in hospitals. The light blinked green.

"So, you're not infected. Doesn't prove anything."

Malik had enough. "Put your guns down. Now I'm going to stand up and you're not going to shoot. "

"Don't push your luck, Malik."

Malik rose, keeping his hands up. "The cure is out there. It exists. She was on the island until she was taken. We're on our way to get her over in Williamsburg. So what's it going to be?"

11

Sam Dawson's world was falling apart at the seams.

He regretted not listening to Alice. His ego, and his years of holding fast on the island, had made him think Governors Island was a fortress. It wasn't. The reflection of fire and smoke in his eyes revealed the truth.

No place was safe.

He should have known that better than anyone after being entrenched in the work of GERM which had him implementing quarantine zones in the largest cities across America. He'd seen how quickly those had fallen. Constraining people's movements, and rolling out rules, only caused many to hold a grudge. While most would comply, understanding the alternative was death, others began to think that the grass was greener on the other side. That no one person should have control over the masses. It was the story of humanity. Everyone wanted to be the chief, few the Indian.

Nope, safe zones were nothing more than an illusion.

Just as having an army in a country didn't mean it couldn't be invaded.

The problem was no one could deal with the unknowns, the wild cards, or check every single person that entered a country. How could anyone know if one day a person would lose their mind and take a gun into a workplace or school and open fire? The same applied to the island. In the attempt to help, they took a risk that those they helped could bite the hand that fed them.

Governors Island wasn't just safety from what lay in the city or freedom from GERM. It was so much more. They were striving to save humanity and that didn't come without extensive testing. Sure, he could have put Alice on the table and opened up her skull but what if he was wrong? What if it led to nowhere? What if Erika had been wrong? They would have essentially hamstrung themselves. As it stood, Alice could bring people back from a coma, from the brink of death itself. Sure, they hadn't tested whether someone who'd received a transfusion from her could get reinfected, but in his mind that was the closest thing to a cure and he wasn't going to lose that.

"Sir?" Johnson asked. "What do you want us to do?"

They would be looking to him, looking for answers. While they had only lost a few lives, they had lost every boat they had along with the helicopter through an act of sabotage. The two people he thought could have been responsible — that Jonah had pointed a finger at — were in the Admiral's House when the explosions occurred. There had to be other traitors among them or the bombs were on timers.

"There is nothing that can reverse what has happened." He turned away from the window. "Bring Jonah. I want to speak to him again."

"Well, about that..."

"What is it, Johnson?"

"One of our guys saw him and Jade Walker enter the ventilation building."

"Please tell me you sealed it off?"

He shook his head. "There was no time."

"So they're gone?"

"I believe so."

"And probably whoever was responsible for this went that way too. Damn it!" he shouted before throwing a glass of bourbon at the wall. He leaned against the mantel, staring into the fire and contemplating what to do. "Johnson. Where are Sebastian and Aaron?"

"Aaron went back to work. Sebastian is still in custody."

"Release him."

"But sir."

"Release him," he said, turning and scowling.

Johnson stared back then nodded. But before he left,

Sam added, "I want both of them watched around the clock."

"And the ventilation building?"

"Leave it open."

"But..."

"To catch a fly, Johnson. You have to lay a trap. If they had nothing to do with the sabotage or Alice's capture, they'll continue as usual. However, if they were involved, they'll want to get off this island as soon as possible."

"Understood."

"Keep me updated. The first sign of any change, alert me."

"Yes, sir." But he remained, looking at him.

"Johnson?"

"I was wondering. Will you be making an announcement about Alice?"

"I haven't decided."

"Very good." He turned to leave but then paused in the doorway.

"Yes, Johnson?"

"Whatever happens, I want you to know I have your back."

"I appreciate that."

With that said, he left Sam alone with his thoughts. He wasn't alone long. Ten minutes passed before Captain James Monroe entered.

"Sam, can we speak?"

"Always. Would you like a drink?"

"Sure."

Sam poured out two fingers of bourbon and handed it to him.

"What's on your mind?"

"Besides the obvious?" Monroe asked.

"I'm dealing with that."

"That wasn't what I was referring to. Johnson already told me."

Sam took a seat on the leather sofa in the living room. "You're here about Alice. Aren't you?"

"Without her. All of this is for nothing."

"Survival isn't for nothing."

"It is if people continue to die. It's not just about her saving lives, it's about giving people hope. You've seen it in their eyes. When she arrived, something shifted in our group. A new drive. Our guys out there were glad to hold the perimeter. It gave them a sense of purpose to know that they were defending something of value. Without her—"

"They'll lose hope," Sam cut him off and nodded. "I know. But the truth is, Monroe, I think some already have."

"I don't understand."

"Tonight's attack came from within. It was one or two of our men."

"How can you be sure?"

"Because no civilian is allowed near those boats or

the helicopter without authorization. But no one is going to bat an eye seeing a soldier waltz up to one."

"And that's why you're releasing Sebastian and keeping an eye on Aaron?"

"I figure if they have something to do with it, the last place they will want to be is here. The sooner they can get off this island, the better."

"And if they try? You'll kill them?"

"Kill? No. Use them. To find Alice."

Silence stretched between them.

"You want to take a team out to find her, don't you?"

He took a sip of his drink. "Do we have any other option?"

"But before, we had the helicopter, boats, a means of extraction. If we roll out into the city on foot, there's a strong chance we aren't coming back alive."

"And staying here and doing nothing will achieve a different outcome?"

There was a short pause.

Monroe knocked his drink back and stood up and walked over to the window. "You and Alice became quite close, didn't you?"

"We did."

Monroe shook his head as he looked out. "How did we get here, Sam? The country torn apart and divided and everyone at each other's throats. We've failed."

Sam got up and collected a box of Cohiba cigars. He offered him one. Monroe declined. Sam clipped the end of one, scorched it and a grey cloud enveloped his face.

"No. Helicopters and boats can be replaced. But trust, that's another thing entirely. Trust is at an all-time low in this nation. We can change that but things will have to be different. We'll get her back and then we will secure this place even tighter than before. We did it once. We can do it again."

"I don't think that's the answer."

"No? Then what is?"

"New leadership."

With that, Monroe turned and without any hesitation, he drove a knife deep into Sam's stomach. Sam dropped his cigar and staggered back even as Monroe held the knife and twisted it.

"Robert Weston sends his regards."

"You?" Sam asked as blood streaked out the corner of his mouth.

"You gave it your best shot, my friend. It failed. Now we do it another way."

Sam collapsed on the floor. Monroe reached down and picked up the cigar. He took a hard hit on it, watching as the admiral took his last breaths.

Moments later, Sam's radio cracked.

Monroe crouched down and snagged it.

Johnson's voice came over the speaker.

"Captain."

"Go ahead."

"Sebastian has been released. Aaron has been notified. I've gathered the men like you asked. When do you want to leave?"

"Immediately." Monroe released his grip on the radio, then walked to the front of the house and picked up the canister of gasoline that he'd collected before arriving. He sloshed the contents around the room, covering Sam, the furniture, and the floor and walls before he backed up to the door, took another hard hit on the cigar, and tossed it in.

A flame burst to life and began to consume the house as he walked away.

12

The restraints were tight, but her mind was free. As different strangers came and went, taking away the blood, Alice began to feel lightheaded and tired. It wasn't just the effects of whatever crap they'd injected into her body but having them take two pints of blood. Any other time she'd only given one pint. She could hear the low conversation outside the door. "That's as much as we can take right now."

"I say we take one more pint."

"If we do that, we will endanger her. You know what they said — eight weeks between."

"Whatever." It was Caleb. "Are those for her?" he asked. "You can go now. I'll ensure she gets them."

Footsteps moved away, and then the door opened and that creepy-looking asshole peered in. "Well, hello again, darlin'. Look what I brought you. Some snacks and juice, something to perk you up." He went to close the door, but not before glancing out and listening. Once satisfied, he closed the door and twisted the lock. "Can't have you passing out on me."

She knew what he had in mind.

Caleb set a tray next to the bed, then pulled up a seat. "I've got you some juice, nuts, a couple of cookies, and some smoked fish. You'll need to replenish those important vitamins and minerals."

"And how am I supposed to eat those when my hands are..." She tugged on the restraints.

"Oh, I'll feed you," he said, eyeing her body as if he couldn't restrain himself. He took some grapes and dangled them over her mouth. "Open wide," he said, teasing her by running a grape around her lips. She opened her mouth and he pulled it back then chuckled before letting her have one.

"So, what attracted you to him?" Caleb asked.

"What are you talking about?" she asked as he fed her a cookie.

"Don't be coy. Everyone knows you were banging Sam. Come on now."

She didn't reply.

"I used to watch you sneak in at night. I'd see the light come on. Do you know once I even entered the house ahead of time and slipped under the bed?" He grinned. "That's right. When he was going at it, I could hear every single moan."

Alice wanted to tell him he was a sick puppy but she had something else in mind.

"Man, I used to imagine he was me." He brought some juice up to her lips and she chugged it down, eager to get rid of feeling lightheaded. She needed her strength for what she had planned. "Oh dear, you spilled a little," he said as juice trickled down the side of her face. Caleb reached over and ran his finger up the side of her chin to her lips then brought his finger to his mouth and sucked on it like a greedy child. Everything he did made her want to reach over and strangle him but she had to bide her time. Be patient. Ensure that he didn't get spooked. If there was any other way she could get out, she would have done it by now. But they'd strapped the leather to the bed.

"The night I was under Sam's bed, I sneaked out while you were asleep and watched you both. I thought of slashing his throat. But then I thought why bother, he'd eventually get his due."

She frowned.

"Oh, that's right. You don't know. By about now. Your little fuck buddy is probably lying in a pool of blood. It was bound to happen eventually. Just a matter of time before one of your group would turn. I just never imagined it would be the captain."

"What?"

"Captain Monroe. Come on now, keep up. How else do you think I managed to get onto that island? That whole spiel he gave about finding my father and mother dead and saving me from trappers. It was all bullshit. The fact is, Monroe came to us. He sought us out. Sold us one hell of a story. A woman whose blood can bring people out of comas and back from the brink of death." He paused, holding a cookie near her lips before he slowly inserted it.

As Alice chewed, she studied his face. How could he become so depraved?

"But when he produced several units of your blood and it was used in a transfusion and we watched a woman who had been in a coma for a year open her eyes. Well. It was simple after that. Of course, there was the problem of getting to you. That fucking admiral. He just couldn't have you out of his sight, not after that close call in the city. Oh no, if he had his way you would have remained there until your death. So, that's where I came into the picture. Of course, I wasn't going to be able to convince you to leave with me. You already had a fuck buddy. But Jade," he said, smiling and running his tongue across his lips. "Oh, she was ripe pickings."

Alice chewed harder.

"I know. I know. You want to know if I cheated on you. No. I couldn't do that. I was saving myself for you, Alice. But I did come close. There were a few times I wanted to see what Jade tasted like. You know, a sample," he said, setting down the half-eaten cookie and running his hand down her leg. She felt her body shudder.

All the while he stared into her eyes.

"Jade was easy to convince. A few compliments. Spending some time with her. Saying all the right words and boom. She was eating out of my hand. Of course, you knew that, right? Having that little prick Jonah follow us around. Then I realized. What would motivate you more to leave the island? Jade or both of them? From there it was simply a case of lining up the dominoes and watching them fall." He smiled. "And here you are."

"Can you loosen these? I mean, if we're going to do this?"

A gleeful smile appeared. "You want this to happen?"

"Don't you?" Alice asked.

He narrowed his gaze. "Are you toying with me?"

"Why would I? I barely have the strength to move after giving blood."

Caleb stood up and began to unbutton his shirt, a smile forming. "I knew you would come around."

"My restraints?" she asked.

"I think it's sexier with them on."

"But there is so much more I can do without them," she muttered, feeding into his sick mind. Continuing to unbutton his shirt, he didn't take his eyes off her.

"Like what?"

"Take them off and I'll show you."

"Maybe later," he replied, unbuckling his belt and slipping off his jeans. He stood there wearing nothing but a pair of boxers. "Now it's your turn."

As he reached down to begin to remove her jeans, Alice shifted gears. She knew if she didn't convince him to take off the restraints, this wasn't going to end well. "At least let me have use of one hand. One hand so I can touch you."

"Touch me?"

She nodded. "You want to be touched, don't you?"

She could see him getting excited with every suggestion she made. "All right. One hand but that's all." He unlocked her left hand. Alice eyed a metal fork on the tray.

Caleb continued to talk, buying into her interest in him. "You know, you might even enjoy it," he said.

"Likewise," she shot back.

He stopped for a second, grinned, then released her hand. Next, he removed her jeans and unbuttoned her shirt. Then he stood at the end of the bed, marveling at her physique. "You are something else," he said. As he began to crawl on top of her and plant his lips on her belly, making his way up, Alice ran her free hand over his head. He raised his head for a second and looked at her as if checking to be sure she was into it before he went back to kissing her abdomen.

"Where are you taking me in the morning?"

"What?"

"Tomorrow. Where are we going?"

"North."

"I know but where?"

He looked up, annoyed that she was breaking the intimate moment. "You'll see when you get there."

"I don't like surprises."

"Then you won't like me. I've got one hell of a surprise for you," he said, running his hand up her leg.

"Seriously, Caleb. Where are we going?"

He groaned and met her gaze again. "After here, we're heading into Manhattan. We have to deliver your blood to my father."

"And he's where?"

"Hell's Kitchen."

"And then?"

"Hudson Highlands State Park. Okay? Now can I get back to this?"

She placed her hand on his head and forced his face down. "By all means."

As he lowered his gaze and kissed her sternum, Alice reached out in a flash, grabbed the fork, and stuck it into his neck. Caleb reeled back in excruciating pain, screaming, his eyes wide, words failing to come out of his mouth. Alice reached over and began to undo the second restraint. She had it nearly half undone when he punched her square in the face.

"You bitch!"

Like a wild animal, she retaliated fast and hard, striking him in the sternum which made him fall forward. She grabbed his head and bit his ear. He let out a howl as she tore it, then cracked him in the jaw with a left hook. Not wasting time, she reached over and continued to unbuckle the restraint.

As soon as it was undone, Caleb fought for control. She shifted gears and dug both of her thumbs into his eyes. He screamed bloody murder. She knew it would only be a matter of minutes before someone else would barge into the room.

She shoved him off the bed and Caleb collapsed on the ground, blinded and screaming.

Alice undid the restraints around her ankles and rolled out.

She didn't have her full strength back but the adrenaline coursing through her heart gave her the energy to get up. Staggering to her feet, she kneed Caleb in the face, knocking him back before snagging up the fork he'd pulled out and finishing him off by jamming it into his throat.

As he was taking his last breaths, someone came to the door. They began banging.

"Open up!"

They wiggled the handle and then tried to shoulder the door, calling out for Cabbie.

Alice took some of the blood from Caleb and scrawled a location on the window. Gazing out — it was clear she was too high to jump.

Instead, she grabbed the gun from Caleb's holster slung over a chair.

A second later, she unlocked the door and pulled back, waiting for them to enter.

The door burst open as two heavily armed guys forced their way inside.

What awaited them was fast and brutal.

She shot both of them in the back of their skulls and darted out into the corridor, only to be struck on the head by something hard. Alice collapsed, and her world faded to black.

13

It was a dire situation.

Malik might as well have just made a deal with the devil because if it didn't pan out, it would be their lives on the line, not his. Jonah had to wonder if it wasn't made as some kind of surety — an agreement to ensure that his brother ended up with the cure. If his brother was even alive.

From what he was able to glean from the conversation, if they didn't deliver a cure for the major's daughter Sophie, that would be the end of the road. Of course, the major didn't believe them. It took a fair amount of convincing.

"Think about it, major. What other reason would anyone have to traipse through Brooklyn in the dead of night?" Malik had said. "Two years you have known me. Have you ever seen me risk my neck for a stranger?" There was a pause. "If they are lying, then I was duped as much as you. In which case you can do whatever the hell you like with them but if they are right. This might be Sophie's only shot."

That was all it took.

Jonah wasn't sure whether or not the major believed them. Still, desperation could drive a person to throw out all logic if it meant saving a loved one.

Upon that promise, they were given passage through the remainder of the block. But to ensure that Malik wasn't feeding him a line, the major and two other men went with them for the remainder of the journey.

The major called it hedging his bet. It was exactly that. A way to make sure they didn't escape if it was a lie. Malik had suggested holding on to one of them but the major didn't want to do it that way. No, he wanted everyone in sight at all times.

"No funny business," he'd said.

From Henry Street to the Dime Residences was a good hour and fifteen minutes on foot, and that was extended by an extra thirty minutes. The major used his association with others where he offered a clear passage through his neck of the woods to enable them to reach their destination without issue. Of course, waltzing in there wasn't a good idea, so the major, whose name they still had not been given, had taken them into a parking lot directly across from the building to get a better lay of the land.

"These people who took your mother. You know them?"

"Not exactly," Jade replied, glancing at Jonah for a second. To admit that she had gotten close to Caleb and allowed herself to be used as a pawn must have stung.

"How many are there?"

"You're asking that now?" Jonah asked. "Are you sure you were a major in the army?"

"Jonah," Malik said.

"No, I'm serious. We had a guy at the island people referred to as the Admiral. He wasn't one. I'm just asking."

The major narrowed his gaze. "If you're lying about this woman. You're going to be the first to die," the major said, turning his eyes back to the building. The Dime Residences in Brooklyn had been a luxury apartment complex, but now it looked like a shell of its former self. Many of its windows were smashed. Still, the tall, sleek tower stood out among the surrounding debris and ruins. The shattered glass, walls covered in graffiti, and blood streaking away from the doors revealed the violence that had taken place there.

Satisfied that it wasn't swarming with threats, they exited the parking garage and jogged across the street, entering the lobby. There they were greeted by a musty, damp smell that seemed to permeate the air. The sound of their footsteps echoed throughout the space. They could hear the occasional creak and groan of the old building as the wind blew in through openings where panes of glass had once been. Shards crunched below their boots as they moved further inside.

Furniture was overturned, and debris littered the once pristine marble floors.

Ahead of them, a large reception area stood abandoned, covered in dust and rubble.

"So where did this guy say she was being held?"

"In this building. That's all I know."

The major scowled at Jonah. "You are aware of how big this building is, yes?"

"Twenty-three stories. Look, man, no one asked you to tag along. If you want to wait here while we go search, be my guest."

"I'm keeping you in full view."

"Whatever."

With the power out, they switched on flashlights and entered the stairwell, beginning the arduous and dangerous task of locating her. From the outset of arriving, Jonah was already feeling anxious. He'd seen how many were involved in the capture of Alice. He didn't expect those guarding her to be any less threatening and yet from the moment they had surveyed the building from across the street, it appeared empty.

"What if she's not here?" Jade whispered in the stairwell on the way up.

"What?"

"You must have considered it."

Jonah looked at her. "If she's not, we bolt."

"Yeah, and how do you expect to do that? They took our guns and they haven't taken their eyes off us for a second."

"What are you two whispering about?" the major asked from behind.

Jonah glanced over his shoulder. "She's just really keen to see her mother."

"As am I," he replied, chewing gum and offering back a deadpan expression.

The major and one of his guys walked behind them. The other was behind Malik who was leading the way and was also being used as a shield just in case a slew of bullets came their way.

"Do you trust Malik?" Jade said again.

"We didn't exactly have a choice. We might not have made it here without him."

"Or maybe he just wanted us to believe that."

"Look, if shit goes south, I'll make sure you get out."

"What's that supposed to mean?"

"If she's not here. Go back to the island and get Sam's help."

"I'm not going anywhere without you."

"You might have no choice," he said.

As they cleared through each of the floors, Jonah could see that the apartments had been stripped bare. Broken glass and the bones of the fallen littered the floor. The walls were covered in scorch marks and peppered with bullet holes. Before them were the remnants of a once luxurious lifestyle, now it only served as a reminder of what had been lost.

Moving up to the higher floors, hoping to find signs

of life, they encountered a few haggard and wary survivors.

On one floor, the major interrogated a small family — a father, a mother, and two small children. The father held a rifle at them but clearly by the way his hands were shaking, he was petrified.

"That tattoo you have. You serve?" the major asked.

The guy nodded. "I'm a vet."

"How long have you been here?"

"A few hours. Listen. We'll leave. We don't want any trouble."

"Lower the gun. We're not going to harm you."

The father's gaze bounced between them. He was hesitant but at the urging of his wife, he lowered it. The major continued, "Have you been to the higher floors?"

"No."

"Have you seen anyone else?" the major asked.

"I can't say we have," the father said from behind his mask.

It was a pitiful sight. Jonah knew survivors were out there. Good people just trying to make it through another day and take care of their families but to see them like this, huddled away hoping to avoid trouble, brought home the reality. It was a glimpse at what the country had become. Every state had fallen to the Haze if the admiral's reports from resistance members were to be believed.

The major looked back at the two of them with a scowl. "You better hope that's not true."

He turned and walked out of the apartment. Jonah glanced back at the family and the children for a second longer before leaving.

As they continued their ascent, they noticed many of the rooms must have had squatters living there as there were signs that people had been there recently.

With every floor they climbed, hope faded.

Three floors from the top, Jonah turned to Jade. "Be ready."

"Jonah. Don't."

As he was planning what would give Jade the best chance of escape, he heard Malik call out from one of the rooms further down. "Major!"

He turned fast and they followed him. As soon as they entered the room, they knew this was where she'd been held. A body lay on the floor in a large puddle of almost dry blood along with two more beside it. Jade pushed past them all, her eyes scanning.

"Cabbie," Jonah said in a low voice, dropping to a crouch. He would have been lying to say that he wasn't glad to see him dead.

"You know him?" the major asked.

Jonah nodded. "He was the one that took her."

"Jonah." Jade lifted a chain with a cross on the end. "She was here," she said. "This was hers. I bought it for her years ago."

"Well, that answers that," the major said. "She was here. Was. Where is she now?" he said in a demanding tone.

"How the hell are we supposed to know?" Jade snapped, growing tired of the major's attitude. As she said it, the flashlight in Malik's hand caught something on the window.

Jonah noticed. "Malik," he said, pointing. Malik illuminated the pane of glass. Scrawled in blood were the words "Hell's Kitchen. After they..."

It looked as if she was about to write something else but was pulled away.

"It has to be her."

"Anyone could have put that there."

"Alice isn't anyone," Jonah replied. "These men here. That was her doing. I guarantee you. Maybe she escaped."

"And maybe she didn't. And maybe we should just end this bullshit right now instead of being dragged along on another wild goose chase," the major said, lifting his rifle toward Jonah.

Malik got between them fast. He lifted his hands in front of him. Strangely, Jonah was surprised. Maybe Malik believed him when he said they had a cure, versus the major who seemed skeptical from the beginning. "Whoa, whoa, steady there, major. Come on now. Give him the benefit of the doubt."

"Get out of the way or I'll put you down with him."

"And what will that achieve, huh? You'll still have to return without any cure."

"There is no cure. You are talking shit."

"What the hell do you think this is?" he said, pointing at the words Hell's Kitchen on the window.

"A setup. That's what I think. What a fool. I shouldn't have come here."

"Listen. We can still find her. You heard them. They know him."

"Do they? I've seen countless bodies inside this place. I could say I knew them."

Malik looked back at Jonah. "You're telling the truth, right?"

"Of course."

"See. He's not lying, major. Okay, so just lower the rifle."

"No."

Jonah's eyes lowered as he noticed Malik take out a Glock 22 that he had stashed in the back of his jeans. He looked as if he was trying to hand it to Jonah while distracting the major and his two pals by waving his hand in front of him. "We can fix this. You had to know that she might have been moved. She is valuable. Come on, major. Would you keep her in the same place for days? Now something went wrong here. They moved her. If we go now, we can find her."

Jonah took a few steps forward and took the gun from Malik's hand.

As soon as he took it, he saw Malik make a three with his fingers, then a two, then a one.

In an instant, Malik flung himself forward at the major, forcing him back into his pal.

Jonah fired two rounds, taking out one of the major's guys before the other opened fire. In the enclosed space it was deafening. Jade had already ducked out, seemingly assuming that this was her moment to escape.

Malik was on top of the major, wrestling to get the rifle out of his hand.

Jonah squeezed the gun again but it misfired. As he went to clear the jam, the other guy with the major who had collapsed to the floor grabbed his rifle, but Jonah was already two steps ahead. He came rushing over and kicked the rifle. It unloaded, peppering the wall before Malik cried out.

"Jonah. Go. Get out of here now!"

At that moment, the major drove a knife into Malik's thigh and he let out a high-pitched wail. Jonah cleared the jam and fired a round into the skull of the major's pal. He was just about to put the major out of his misery when Malik shouted, "NO!"

It caught him off guard.

Here he was trying to help them escape.

He'd been stabbed in the leg by the major and he didn't want Jonah to kill him?

The answer came quickly. "I want to do it."

Malik fired off a right hook, delivering a jaw-breaking blow to the major's face. But he was one tough son of a bitch. He twisted the knife into Malik's leg, causing him to writhe back in agony. Every time Jonah tried to get a clear shot, Malik flung his body forward on top of the major, blocking his view.

A scream from outside made Jonah step out just in time to see Jade being dragged backward into the stairwell.

Caught between a rock and a hard place, he took off after her.

Rushing into the stairwell, he was forced back by the bark of an automatic rifle.

He retaliated with a few rounds of his own but whoever had grabbed Jade had someone else with him.

All he could do was keep putting the gun around into the doorway and firing off rounds. He did it until the gun ran out of bullets, which wasn't long. At which point he heard laughter, and then footsteps.

Jonah backed up, turning to flee down the corridor back to where Malik was.

He had only made it about ten yards when Malik staggered into view with the rifle in hand. "Get down!" he shouted.

Jonah dropped face first, his hands extended, just as Malik unloaded a chorus of rounds. Jonah looked back to see the gunman from the stairwell slide back against the wall, blood smearing the wall.

Malik dropped down, out of breath, the knife still in his thigh.

Jonah scrambled back to the stairwell but it was silent down below. "Jade!" No reply came back. "No. No. Not again."

He twisted around and scooped up the rifle and a handgun from the assailant. That's when he saw the tattoo on the man's arm of an elk skull and horns with arrows through it. He was a trapper. Jonah had heard of it through the grapevine. A new way for trappers to know each other, but it also helped the innocents know who to trust.

"Malik," he cried, rushing back to him. He gazed down at his thigh before glancing back into the room to see the major dead, his larynx crushed. "You need to be treated."

"No," he said as he gritted his teeth and leaned against the wall, his hand pressed hard against the knife wound in his leg. Jonah could see blood seeping through his fingers.

"Where's Jade?"

Jonah shook his head. "Gone."

For a minute or two they exchanged a look of defeat.

As they sat there, trying to figure out their next move, they heard the crackle of a radio down the corridor. Instinctively Jonah cast a glance over his shoulder.

"Is that...?" Jonah muttered before Malik nodded.

The two of them looked back down the corridor toward the trapper.

14

An idea struck him. It was a shot in the dark but worth a try.

Malik was older than Jonah, his voice deeper. Jonah grabbed the radio and tried to figure out who was on the other end. Initially, all he heard was silence then it crackled again.

"Come in, Red. You there?"

Malik motioned with his finger. "Give it to me."

"But..."

"Jonah."

He handed it over. Grimacing, he held the button on the side and spoke into it. "Yeah."

"Did you neutralize the threat?"

"Yeah," Malik replied.

"You sound different."

Malik groaned. "Wounded."

"Can you make it?"

"Yeah. Where are you?"

The voice on the other end hesitated for a second before answering. Jonah thought they had figured out it wasn't Red but the reply confirmed that it had worked. "The church north of 278."

"On my way." Malik gave a wry grin as he handed the radio back to Jonah. "It's all on you now," he said. "Go get her back."

"You make it sound easy. No, we need to get you treated."

"Yeah, and how do you expect to do that? I can barely walk, Jonah."

"You haven't even tried."

Malik showed him by clambering up with Jonah's help only to wail in pain before stumbling back and then collapsing. The knife was in deep.

"Shit!' Jonah muttered. It wasn't just Jade he was worried about, it was Alice. Pulled in two different directions, he knew one without the other would only spell disaster. Alice would be beside herself if she knew that he'd gone for her instead of her daughter but if he tried to save Jade and succeeded, Alice could be long gone.

No matter what he did, he couldn't leave Malik here to bleed out.

If it wasn't for him, they both could have been dead by now.

"Look, hang tight. I'll be right back."

"Where are you going?"

Jonah didn't reply. He remembered the guy from the

family several floors down saying he'd been a vet. As he hurried back down, he began to wonder if the family would still be there. They looked shaken up by their encounter with them. If it had been him, he would have moved on.

Once he reached the floor where they had met the family earlier, Jonah paused, looking around for any sign of them.

To his relief, he saw the door to the apartment was ajar and light conversation was coming from inside. He pushed it open and called out. "Hello?"

At first, there was no reply.

Jonah entered and looked around. It looked empty.

"I know you're here. I heard you. It's me from earlier. I was with the group that went up."

There was a rustling from the back of the apartment and then the same man stepped out from behind a false wall. The stranger was carrying his rifle at the ready. He was tall and well-built, with a strong and imposing presence that demanded respect. His hair reached his shoulders, it was unkempt and peppered with streaks of grey. He squinted at Jonah and ran a hand over a full beard, his piercing blue eyes full of a mixture of weariness but determination to survive. "What do you want?"

"Do you have any medical supplies?" Jonah asked.

"What?"

"You said you were a vet."

"Yeah, a veteran. Ex-military."

"You ever treated wounds?"

A smile tugged at the corner of his mouth. "A few. Why?"

Jonah explained the situation, telling the man that Malik had been stabbed and needed medical attention.

"How bad is it?"

Jonah shrugged. "No idea, that's why I'm asking you to come and take a look."

"And the others?"

"Dead. Where they belong."

"Huh. We heard the gunfire." The guy looked off to his right for a second at the sound of movement.

A young face appeared from behind a false wall. "Daddy?"

"Go back in." He looked back at Jonah. "Give me a second," he said, turning and heading back into the enclosed space. He reappeared a moment later, holding a small med kit. "Show me where he is."

On the way up, the man was curious.

"What happened?"

Jonah brought him up to speed.

"Yeah, that guy gave me bad vibes," he said referring to the major.

"What's your name?"

"Maxwell Peterson but my friends call me Max. And you?"

"Jonah."

No more was said. They arrived to find Malik grimacing in pain. Max dropped down beside him. "All right, let's see what we got here." He unzipped the med kit and began working on the wound. He had Jonah hold Malik down while he took out the knife. Malik screamed.

"The worst is over."

He then began to patch it up. "It will take a good ten days for the skin to heal, and it will have to be monitored for infection." Malik looked up at him. "Not that kind of infection," he added before tossing some bloody rags away.

Jonah's chin dipped.

Malik gripped his arm. "Like I said. You can do this. But you need to decide who to go after."

"Go after?" Max asked.

"The girl you saw earlier. She was taken by trappers," Jonah said.

"The worst kind," Malik added. "I've been dodging them since my brother and I ran into them a year ago."

"And the other?"

"Her mother. She was being held here. We believe she was taken to Hell's Kitchen," Jonah replied.

Max's brow furrowed as he stared back. "But you're just a teen."

"And?" Jonah shot back. "What has age got to do with anything?"

"Well. It's just..."

"You don't think I can handle them?"

"Look, kid, I'm not saying you can or can't. But these folks aren't playing around. One mistake and you will be hooked up for blood transfusions or dead."

He nodded. Max rose to his feet and looked down at the two of them. "Well, I should get back." He turned to leave.

"I appreciate your help. Thank you," Malik said.

Max gave a pained smile, looked at Jonah then walked off down the corridor. He made it to the doorway and shot them a look before he disappeared into the stairwell.

"Leave me here," Malik said.

"To rot? What will you eat or drink?"

"The guy on the radio mentioned the church is nearby. You'll be there and back before you know it. I can rest here."

"And if those that took Alice return…?"

"I hardly think they will. Go. Before they figure out something is wrong and leave."

Jonah exhaled loudly and sat back against the wall, looking down at the floor. He had so many questions spinning through his mind. The what-ifs, all the things that could go wrong. He felt paralyzed by his indecision.

"What is it?"

"I don't think I can do this."

Malik nodded. "Listen to me. If I knew where my family was, I would do everything within my power to get them back. You know where yours are. Do something."

"Family?" he muttered.

"They are your family, right?"

He hadn't considered that. But in some ways, they

were the closest thing to family and maybe the only ones he had now in his life.

"I guess," Jonah replied. He groaned. "I dunno if I can do it."

"Well then that's settled," Malik said. "If you won't go. Then they are gone and so is what hope I have of finding a cure for my brother."

Jonah looked at him. "You still think you'll find him?"

"If I didn't believe that, I would put a gun to my head right now and end this. What other reason would there be to live in this world?"

They sat there for another ten minutes before Max emerged. The two of them looked off toward the stairwell. "You're still here," he said, making his way down.

"He's made his decision," Malik said with a hint of frustration. "He's not going"

"I'll go with you," Max said.

"What?"

"You want to get your friend back. I'll help."

"No. You have a family. I couldn't put this on you."

"I know if any one of my family were taken, I would be glad for the help."

Malik nudged Jonah, encouraging him to take Max up on the offer. Jonah glanced up at Max. "You know you might not come back. Have you talked it over with your family?"

"I wouldn't be here if I hadn't. My wife is strong.

Every day we are here, we face the possibility of it being our last."

"Uh, I dunno," Jonah said.

As much as Jonah appreciated the offer, he understood the risk was high. He'd been on the end of a trapper's noose, figuratively of course. Held and prepared to be drained of blood to save others. It wasn't a situation he wanted to get into again but... his thoughts went back to Jade.

Malik nudged him again. "Go on."

Jonah stood up and collected one of the rifles from the major's men. He took a Glock 22 and put it in the back of his jeans, filling his pockets with ammo.

"As for you. My wife, Cassandra, will look after you," Max said.

"No. I'm good here."

"You think I'm being stubborn?" Jonah said, coming out of the room. "If I've got to do this, then you have to stay with his family."

"It would give me peace of mind," Max said. "Please."

Malik nodded and the two of them helped him up to his feet and down the stairs. Once they had left him with the family, Jonah and Max headed out.

A hard rain was falling over the city, but not even it could wash away the grime of a nation that had fallen to the Haze. As they stepped out of the Dime Residences, the darkness enveloped them. The only source of light came from the flickering of fires that burned around the city, casting an eerie orange glow across the desolate landscape.

"Are you from the area?" Jonah asked.

"The Hamptons."

He raised an eyebrow. "You owned a property over there?"

"Yeah."

"Huh. I didn't think the military paid that kind of money."

"They didn't. The job I did after did. I was in the tech industry. Creating apps for a living. Things took off. I made my money, cashed out, and took an early retirement. We figured we'd buy the house we always wanted right by the coast. Probably the worst place to be when this event occurred. Suffered a home invasion."

As they jogged along the street, Jonah noticed how the air was thick with the acrid scent of smoke and the faint sound of gunfire and screams. He gripped his gun tightly as they began heading north toward the church.

Staying in the shadows, they navigated the maze of deserted streets, their eyes constantly scanning the surroundings for any sign of danger. Now and again they would hear footsteps or voices, causing them to freeze in place and wait until the coast was clear.

Closing in on the highway, they could see that it had been blocked off with debris and abandoned vehicles. They climbed over the obstacles, careful not to make any noise.

"Why haven't you aligned with a group?" Jonah asked.

"We did. It was the wrong one."

Once on the other side of I-278, they entered a neighborhood that had been hit particularly hard. Buildings were burned out and abandoned with broken glass and debris strewn across the streets. Hanging from lampposts were numerous bodies, each one tagged with names and dates, and accusations just like Jonah had seen in the forest back in Washington.

It was difficult to see how people had turned on each other. But the loss of a family member could change a person.

As they got closer, a group of looters rummaging through the rubble of a collapsed building emerged. Jonah and Max quickly ducked behind a nearby van to avoid being seen. They waited until the looters moved on before continuing.

After that, they stopped not far from an art gallery.

"Listen up. Do exactly what I say. If I say move, we move. No hesitation. You hear me?"

"I got it."

"You want to get her back; we do things my way."

"Trust me. I'm not one to quibble."

As they got closer to the church, the streets became more deserted and quiet. They crept through the shadows, keeping their eyes peeled for any signs of trappers.

Once they made it into an alleyway, Max jumped up and took hold of the fire escape ladder. He pulled it down and the two of them began to make their ascent up the side of a six-story building. Max led the way. When Max reached the roof, he was about to climb over when he pulled back. He motioned to Jonah below to stop. Using hand gestures, he indicated there were two men up above patrolling the adjacent building to the church.

"Stay here," he whispered, passing his rifle down. Jonah slung it over his neck and clung to the ladder for dear life. He hated heights and right now staying put on a rusted-out ladder that could give way at any moment was making his heart beat faster. All he could do was wait as Max pulled a large knife from his leg sheath and climbed.

He strained to hear what was happening but heard nothing.

Curiosity got the better of him. He climbed to the top and peered over just in time to see Max execute his plan. Under the cover of darkness, he saw him crouched behind a large air vent. Two men were smoking, chatting, and walking back and forth. In an instant, Max darted out, tossing a knife at one of them while reaching for another and doing the same again.

It happened so fast.

But it was his accuracy that caught him off guard.

Who the hell was this guy?

Max crouched beside the dead men, pulling his blades out and wiping them on their clothes before slipping the blades back into sheaths. Jonah remained there watching Max fish through the men's pockets, relieving them of cigarettes, ammo, and one radio.

Jonah climbed over the edge of the building, his presence catching the attention of Max.

"I thought I told you to wait."

"Who taught you to use knives like that?"

"Don't you listen?"

"It's all clear."

Max took a firm hold of Jonah and pulled him down to a crouch behind a large air vent. "What do you see?" he said, pointing around the vent and across to the next building where there was another man. "That's why you need to listen. One mistake and you and I are dead. I made a promise to my wife to return. I'm not having you fuck it up. You hear me?" It was clear he was serious, and seriously pissed off that Jonah had ignored his request to stay put.

He exchanged a nod with Max, then waited for him to neutralize the third threat.

After that, they clambered onto the roof of the mission and church not far from Havemeyer Street and South Second Street, ready to confront Jade's kidnappers.

15

The pain was excruciating.

At the rate they were tearing into her flesh, she would be dead before dawn.

It was payback. Plain and simple. An eye for an eye, a tooth for a tooth. They wanted to kill her but they couldn't. She was too valuable. However, that didn't stop a beating coming her way.

Her shirt was torn open at the back, and her wrists were tied to an iron link bolted to a wall. Alice arched her back and let out a scream after receiving another lashing from a cat of nine tails.

The brutal multi-tailed whip had been used throughout history as a form of corporal punishment. The whip had nine knotted leather cords designed to inflict the highest amount of pain and leave visible marks on the body. She didn't even think they were in existence anymore but clearly, this group had brought it back in style.

Her torture only ended when someone came into the darkened room.

"What the hell is going on here? That's enough!" a woman bellowed. "Who authorized this?"

"Lucian. She killed Caleb and two others."

"The reason?"

There was whispering.

This was followed by silence as if the woman was contemplating.

With her head hung low, Alice heard someone approach.

The stranger crouched down beside her. "Is it true?" she asked.

With blood dripping off her body and every fiber of her being in pain, Alice nodded. She glanced over at the woman, whose face was shrouded behind a curtain of blood. A second later, the woman stood and cut her restraint.

Alice collapsed.

"My apologies. That should never have happened. Caleb was a wild card. He'd already been warned. We will speak later." She turned. "Have someone tend to her wounds immediately."

Two men rushed in and took hold of her, dragging her out, her toes trailing behind her. Alice managed to lift her head to see the woman. "Who are you?" Alice asked.

The door closed without an answer, and Alice blacked out from the pain.

16

Entry points were numerous, the dangers even more so.

The church was unlike anything he'd seen before. On the outside, it didn't even resemble one. It was contained within a six-story building, sandwiched between apartment blocks. He came to discover that the church was small, operating out of a facility on the lower floor. The rest was apartments, like many towering concrete blocks in New York.

"Are you religious?" Jonah asked

Distracted by the task at hand, Max answered without looking at him. "If you want to slap a label on it."

"Well, you're a churchgoer, right? I mean, you were?"

"Uh-huh," Max said, peeking into the stairwell that came out onto the roof.

"Must be hard."

"How so?"

"I mean to resolve all this in your mind."

"What? Why do bad things happen to good people?" he whispered.

"Yeah."

"It's called life. Can't have the good without the bad. That's how we know what's good."

"Yeah, I've never really bought into that. I think I can figure out what is good without all the bad shit in the world."

"Really. How do you know which way is up?"

"Simple."

"And which way is left?"

"That way."

"Or is that your right?"

"It's left."

"Or is that a label we've slapped on it?"

Jonah scoffed. "You make no sense."

"How do you know what makes sense without deciding what doesn't?" He looked at him. "We know what is by opposites. Up and down, left and right. Can you have one without the other?"

Jonah chuckled. "You are confusing, man."

"Or maybe I'm clear. Depends who you ask." Max grinned.

With that said, he turned and closed the door, dropping down to a crouch. "Listen up. It's going to be chaotic inside. Your job is simple. Watch my six."

"Six?"

"The hands of the clock. Watch my back."

Jonah rocked his head back. "Ah, right. Sure."

"We need to move quietly." He took the radio and turned up the volume. Chatter with a mix of static came over the line.

"Alpha, come in."

"Go ahead."

"We clear?"

"All good."

"No sign of Red yet?"

"Not so far."

Max turned down the volume. "Sounds like they bought your friend's communication. Now here's how we're going to do it. We'll clear each floor from top to bottom. Room to room. Do not fire unless you have no other choice. The last thing I want is to put the rest of these assholes on high alert. Who knows how many there are, or if she's on the lower floor."

"Got it."

Max swung his rifle around to his back, securing it in place before taking out a SIG Sauer and a knife. Then he ducked into the stairwell, pointing his gun downward as they began to make their descent. The sixth floor offered little to no sign of life. It was clear. No one was in any of the rooms. They pressed on, this time coming across two men positioned in different rooms at opposite ends of the building. They were distracted, one eyeing the main road, the other, the rear.

Everything that followed came through a series of hand gestures.

The heavy carpets masked Max's approach on the first hostile. He sliced his throat from ear to ear before the man could catch a breath. He lowered him to the floor before backing out to tackle the second. The second wasn't as easy. He must have seen Max's reflection in the window, as he turned before Max was within ten feet.

The outcome was still the same — death.

Max tossed the knife, nailing him in the heart.

The guy's legs buckled and for a split second, Jonah thought he was going to squeeze off a round. It never happened. However, he did hit the floor with a loud thump. They pressed on, moving to the fourth floor without encountering any further threats. It seemed odd that so few would be watching over Jade, but then again, she wasn't Alice. Had they taken her by mistake or was she just targeted for blood?

The Haze had placed everyone in society in a dilemma.

With the infection spreading and faced with the death of a loved one, it only made sense that people would take matters into their own hands. But at what cost? Ethics and morality didn't even play into it. At least not for those who were watching their loved ones fall into the thick of neurological infection.

On the third floor, a man was smoking a cigarette. Although his head was down, he heard Max open the door and looked their way. Max had no choice but to open fire.

Two rounds and he was down.

The radio came alive. "What was that?"

"False alarm," Max said over the radio, expecting to get the same result as Malik.

It didn't work. "Who are you?"

Max dropped the radio and they moved fast, checking each of the rooms.

With only two floors remaining, they had no other choice than to split up to keep those who had Jade from escaping. Max bolted down to the first floor in the hopes of cutting off any exit, while Jonah entered the second floor. He was immediately forced back by a staccato of gunfire from an M4.

The only upside was he now knew where Jade had to be.

He darted out into the hallway, hoping to make it to the room before they opened fire. Nothing occurred. He soon realized why. On the other side of the door, he could hear crying.

"Move it, bitch!"

Jonah tried the handle, but it was locked.

"Get out the window. Now!"

Moving fast, Jonah backed up from the door and opened fire on the lock before kicking it wide. A slew of gunfire erupted, forcing him back behind the wall. More crying ensued followed by a scream. Jonah snuck a peek just in time to see a man dragging Jade down the fire escape.

He didn't hesitate, he rushed into the apartment and over to the window, and peered out only to back up at the crack of gunfire. He couldn't just stick his rifle out the window and shoot downward, Jade would be caught in the hail of bullets and there was no way he could step outside. The fire escape was a grate of metal that would leave him exposed.

Pop, pop, pop.

Then silence.

"Jonah!" Max yelled.

He stuck his head out to see far below the guy lying dead on the fire escape. On the ground, Max was looking up with his rifle raised. "You okay?"

"A little shaken up but..."

Before Jonah could finish, he felt a blade against the side of his neck. "Drop the gun."

He didn't hesitate. It hit the carpet and he saw a boot come into his peripheral vision. The gun was kicked away. It skittered across the hardwood floor. "How many of you?"

"Two."

"Jonah! You there?" Max shouted.

"Tell him you are on your way down. You'll meet him at the door."

He felt the knife press hard into his throat and he knew the guy wasn't messing around.

"I'm on my way. See you at the door."

Instantly, he was hauled back from the window. Jonah heard the clatter of footsteps as Jade made her way down to the ground to join Max.

Jonah was forced to the floor, he felt a zip-tie go around his wrists and then tighten before he was hauled to his feet. He caught a glimpse of a raggedy guy in a mirror.

He was middle-aged, an Asian dude wearing all black.

"You fucked with the wrong people," the guy said, pushing him toward the door.

"Look, you don't need to do this," Jonah said. "I'm telling you now, it's better if you just go. I won't say anything."

"You still think you're in control."

"No. But you don't know my friend."

"Oh, there's nothing new under the burning sun. Before this night is out, your friend will be gone, and she and you will be on your way to...."

Before he could get the words out, he stopped. Jonah had no idea why. Except that they were facing a long mirror. That was the only thing that had changed. "What's your name?" the man asked.

"What?"

"Your name?"

"Why?"

The guy dug the knife harder into his throat.

"Jonah."

"Your last name."

He found that an odd question to be asked. The fact that he wanted to know who he was at all was strange but asking for a last name? "Hayes."

"Where are you from?"

"Does it matter?"

"Answer the question!" he demanded, not taking his eyes off Jonah in the mirror for even a second.

"Governors Island."

"No, I meant before that."

"Washington."

There was a short pause before he said, "Holy shit. It's you."

Jonah raised an eyebrow, looking confused. "Do I know you?"

"No. But I know you."

"How?" Jonah went to turn but was told to remain still. "Okay. Okay. Look, man. They are going to be expecting me downstairs in the next few minutes. If I don't appear—"

Before he could finish what he was saying, the guy removed the blade from his neck and cut his restraints.

"Go."

"What?"

"I said go. Get out of here."

"I don't understand."

The guy backed away, nudging him to go down the staircase with the barrel of his gun. "I'm letting you go. Take it before I change my mind." As he had taken Jonah's handgun and rifle, he removed the ammo, cleared the chambers, and handed them back. "Word to the wise, stay away from Governors Island."

"Why?"

"Because of GERM."

"They're not run by them. The group on that island is the resistance."

"Not all of them are. Stay far away from it. Even better, get out of the city."

Jonah offered back a confused expression.

"Why? Who are you? How do you know me?"

"Go."

"Please. We're looking for a friend of ours. A woman. Alice."

The stranger looked back at him. "I don't know where she is."

"You know who I'm talking about, right?"

"I've heard of her. The immune."

He nodded.

"There is a group that meets north of the city in Hudson Highlands State Park. They might be able to help. Now go."

"But—"

"GO!" he shouted.

Confused but not wanting the guy to change his mind, Jonah backed out nodding, and then hurried down the steps. Jade and Max were waiting for him in the lobby. Jade looked a little worse for wear, her top was torn, her hair a tangled mess hanging out of a hair tie but beyond that, there were no wounds on her face.

"What took you so long?" Max asked.

"I uh..." He looked back over his shoulder, expecting to see the guy but there was no one there. "I got a little lost," he said before being greeted by Jade.

She hugged him. "Max told me it was your idea." Still holding her, he looked at Max over her shoulder. She held on to him for a good minute. He could feel her heart beating fast. Max smiled at him as if to suggest that he should go along with it. The truth was, it wasn't his idea at all. If it wasn't for Max, he would still be back at those apartments wallowing in self-loathing for having let her and Alice down.

"I um... are you okay?" Jonah asked.

"A little shaken up but, yeah."

"Did they hurt you?"

"No. Where's Malik?"

"He was injured. He's alive, just back with Max's family."

"Well, we should leave. If we move now, you might have time to find her mother," Max said.

He could only hope that was true.

Jade looked genuinely grateful to see him again and to still be alive but nowhere as much as he did. As they exited the building, heading back into the night and returning to the Dime Residences, Jonah couldn't help but wonder who that man was, how he knew him, and why he had let him go. The sudden shift. It didn't make sense. As he thought back to the weird conversation in that hallway, standing in front of a full mirror, he had to wonder if the man had mistaken him for someone else.

But why ask for his second name? Or where he had come from? Or tell him to not return to the island?

If he wasn't mistaken, the look on the man's face wasn't just surprise, it was fear.

17

It was a bad sign.

They returned to find blood everywhere. Under the glow of a flashlight, there was a long streak of red emerging from the apartment and running the full length of the corridor. On the wall, a handprint and a sign that someone had dug their nails into the drywall before being dragged away. Max charged into the room.

"Cassandra?!?"

Nothing.

Not even a groan.

Jonah felt like he was intruding upon a very private family moment. He stood by the doorway, feeling awkward and out of place while Jade ventured in. Jonah shone his flashlight down the corridor and glanced behind him

"They're not here!" Max said, almost knocking her over on his way out.

"Max. Max!" Jade said, hoping to save him from the horror of what he might discover. Max continued to call out the names of his wife and children. "Olivia. Sammy!"

The two of them followed until Max saw where the blood disappeared.

At the far end of the hallway was a large window. It had been there when they left, intact, enclosing the corridor and keeping the wind out. Now a hard gale blew through, howling as the rain continued to fall.

"Max," Jade said, hurrying past him and putting a hand up. "Let us look."

In an attempt to save what was left of his fragile mind, he just stood there frozen as if he already knew the outcome. Jonah made his way to the edge and peered out. Attached to a rope strung around a beam was Malik, dangling by his feet, his throat slit, his face mangled and left to drain out. Beside him was Max's wife, Cassandra, equally as bloody. A sight that no person should gaze upon. Jonah pulled back, placing a hand on the wall to steady himself only to slip on wet blood.

Neither a scalper nor a trapper would have done this.

People were too valuable alive to waste them this way.

Blood could be used for transfusions.

No, this was something else. Vicious. Spiteful. Vindictive.

"Is it them?" Max asked.

Jonah could barely utter the word yes.

"Is it them?" he asked again, louder. Jonah cast a glance over his shoulder and nodded.

Max let out a deep guttural cry that echoed off the corridor walls before he dropped to his knees.

"But your children aren't there."

He looked up through tears, his mouth widening as he muttered, "What?"

"Olivia and Sammy. They're not there."

That spark of hope was all he needed to drive him to his feet. Max hurried back into the apartment again, calling their names, hoping, praying that perhaps his wife had hidden them before she and Malik were discovered. Jade stayed back, not wanting to see what had become of them. It was the way of the world now and yet for the past seven months she had been shielded from it. Jonah too. He'd almost become accustomed to the safety of the island.

While Max continued his search, Jonah approached Jade.

"We need to leave," he said.

"Leave?"

"Your mother is in Hell's Kitchen, at least if what was scrawled on the window was anything to go by."

"Anyone could have done that."

"Maybe. I don't think so though."

"Why are you so convinced it's her?"

He kept walking. She continued, "Jonah."

Jonah spun around. "Because the alternative is she's gone forever and I can't deal with that right now. We need to leave."

"And what about Max?"

"What about him?"

He looked back down the corridor as Max was going from room to room, calling out his kids' names. "We can't leave him," Jade said. "Not after what he risked to get me."

"That was his choice. He sought me out. Not the other way around."

"And that makes it different?"

"We don't know him."

"He didn't know me."

"Look," Jonah said, lowering his voice and getting close to her. He took hold of her arm. "I appreciate what he did. I do. But after this. After what he's lost. He's in no state of mind. Even if we stuck around. How would that help him or us? Your mother is out there. We have a slim window to find her before she's gone forever! Now maybe what was scrawled on the window wasn't done by her but remaining here isn't helping. Now I owe your mother and..." he trailed off.

"Then why did you waste time coming to help me?"

Jonah stared her square in the eyes. She studied him.

"Tell me. Why?" she asked again when he didn't respond.

"To help you."

"Bullshit. Tell me the truth."

"I just did."

She scoffed. "You're lying. Tell me the truth."

"Because if I found her and didn't bring you, she..."

"Might have blamed you?" she asked, cutting in.

Jonah exhaled hard.

Jade looked out the window. "You are willing to risk your life to find her because she saved your life. Max did the same for me."

"As did I."

"I hardly think it was all you."

"I could have left you behind."

"Then why didn't you? It would have been a perfect way to get my mother all to yourself. I mean, isn't that what you want?" She eyed him in the darkness. The glow of the flashlight illuminated her features.

"You're nuts, if you still think that's what this is about. Perhaps you should stay, and I'll see you when I get back," he said, walking toward Max who was still calling out. Exasperated, at his wits' end, Max headed for a second stairwell.

His cries turned to anguish and Jonah knew he'd found his children.

Although he didn't want to see what had become of them, he had no choice. Jonah entered the stairwell to see him peering over. Two ropes disappeared down between the stairs, they creaked from the breeze.

Jonah could only stare as the man who had been so steely, so calm heading into that building and clearing each floor, was now grasping the railing of the stairwell and sobbing harder than anyone he'd ever seen.

He had to leave.

He had to. Minutes were rolling into hours. There was no telling if Alice would be in Hell's Kitchen but if she was, it would take time to find her. There was no direction given. No building offered. It was as if Alice only knew so much.

The door behind them groaned open as Jade entered. She crouched beside Max and placed a hand on his shoulder. The tears continued to fall.

Jonah mouthed the words to her, "We have to go." He took a few steps down the staircase and Max glanced at him through red eyes. "I'm sorry. I'm sorry," Jonah said. He'd yet to meet anyone who hadn't suffered in some way.

"Go," Max said to Jade. "Find your mother."

"We can stay a while."

"No, you can't. You don't have time. I should have never left them." He shook his head looking bewildered, lost. Jade looked at Jonah. He shrugged. He had no words. There was nothing that would make this better. Max had made a judgment call, one that probably he'd made before, but now his luck had run out. Jonah could only hope that his family didn't suffer long.

"We're staying," Jade said.

"No," Max replied softly.

"Look—"

"I don't want you to. Okay!"

"It's our choice."

"No. I don't want you here!" Max shouted. Jonah took hold of Jade's arm and tugged her away. Even she knew when it made sense. No amount of saying sorry would change the situation. The fact that they had survived this long was a feat in itself.

"Max. Please. Come with us."

"For what? Everything I had. Every day that I fought. It was all for them." He paused. "Now they're gone, I have nothing." He dipped his chin, and tears streaked his face.

"You're alive. That's something."

Jonah tugged again.

Reluctantly, Jade came with him. She must have known she was in a losing battle. Max's mind was broken. On their descent to the ground, they could hear Max's cries echoing loudly. It was agony.

They had made it about six flights down when they heard a single gunshot then all was silent. Jade looked up, then closed her eyes for a few seconds before charging ahead of him. Outside, the darkness of the night seemed to close in on them like an adversary eager to steal whatever hope and light they held.

"Jade. Wait up," Jonah said as she pitched sideways

into the storm. He had to break into a jog. "Hey. Slow down."

"You should have left me."

"What?"

"I said you shouldn't have come for me."

"You're making no sense."

She turned back, her hair matted to her face as the driving rain quickly soaked them.

"Why did you have to come for me?"

"I already told you. Because it was the right thing to do."

"No, it wasn't because if it was, Malik would still be alive, those kids, his wife, and Max would —."

"So, you want to flip this around and blame me... Is that it?"

She threw her hands in the air, looking exasperated and at a loss for how to process it all.

"All right. Maybe I made the wrong choice. Okay? Maybe if I hadn't decided to help you, they would all be alive. And maybe if Malik hadn't tried to help us, maybe he would, and maybe if the major hadn't, he would, do you want me to keep going?" He cursed loudly, looking up into the sky. "Do you think I wanted any of this? Huh? Do you think I wanted to meet your mother, to lose my father, to be infected? I'm just a fucking kid." He paused for a second before stabbing a finger at her. "And so are you." He glared at her as he shook his hand. "So, forgive me if I made a wrong call and people died because of it." He lowered his voice. "We can't control the outcome of our actions. We do the best we can, that's it."

Jonah looked down at the ground as rain created mini streams across the asphalt, some of it trailing away into the sewers. "And if you must know — if it wasn't for Malik urging me, I don't think I would have gotten up off the floor. I'm as tired as you are of losing people, Jade, but I'm not quite ready to put a bullet in my skull over it." He looked off toward the east. They had a long trek ahead of them. Without transportation, he figured it would take forever to get to Manhattan, let alone Hell's Kitchen. "And if it makes you feel any better, we might be both dead before this night is over. Now if you want to stay, go back, or come with me. I don't give a shit. Do whatever you want."

With that said he began making his way toward the Williamsburg Bridge that would connect him with Lower Manhattan.

After minutes of walking, Jonah glanced back to see Jade following. She wrapped her arms around her body, shivering.

~

ONCE THEY WERE across the river, close to the other side of the bridge, they opted to go down to the street level through a door in one of the stone pillars. It also got them out of the rain that was relentlessly beating them.

"I'm so cold. I can barely feel my hands," Jade said.

"Stick them under your armpits."

Jonah would have offered his jacket but he was in the same predicament, soaking wet and slowly losing what little remaining heat he had. As determined as they were to reach Hell's Kitchen, if they didn't get out of the rain, hypothermia would kick in.

"You know I've been thinking, what if we don't find her?" Jade said.

"We keep looking."

"Or we go back to the island."

"We might not be able to."

"Why?"

He thought of what that guy had said. "I'm not exactly sure right now but... we just need to find Alice then we'll figure it out from there."

"And you think we can in this concrete jungle?"

"I'm going to try."

"How can you be so optimistic?" she asked, shivering, her teeth chattering.

"Optimism doesn't come into it. What do you want me to do? Sit around and complain?"

"Sounded like you were doing that before you came to collect me."

"Everyone needs to vent."

Their footsteps clattered against the stone stairwell inside the concrete tower that held up one side of the bridge. "Shhh!" Jonah said, placing a hand behind him.

"What is it?"

He could hear something but it was hard to make

out what it was. Jonah took out the Glock as they quietly made their way down to the ground. At the steel doorway that led to Delancey North, Jonah peered out. Taking cover under the bridge, he could just make out a group gathered around metal barrels of trash that were on fire. It was hard to tell how many there were because of the darkness. Like homeless encampments, the area was full of tents. Long before the city fell to the Haze, homelessness was rampant. Not all of them were strung-out addicts but the city had a way of wearing a person down the longer they were out there. Good people were driven to all manner of desperate acts and that was when the law was in place.

"We'll go back," Jonah said.

"No. We've already taken long enough heading this way and if this bridge is like the Brooklyn one, there will probably be someone waiting on the other side."

"We can't just go walking out there. There are too many of them. There's no telling if they're scalpers or trappers."

"Not everyone is bad, Jonah."

Without looking at her, he replied, "Max was an anomaly."

He squinted, rain running down his forehead into his eyes as he tried to see a route of passage. "Shit. Malik was right. At this rate, we'll be lucky to make it one block, let alone to Hell's Kitchen before daylight." He pointed to the slew of abandoned vehicles. "If we can just make it over to there, we might be able to—"

"That's strange," Jade said, cutting him off.

"What is?"

"There is an old saying that there's no honor among thieves. If they're trappers or even scalpers, why haven't they turned on each other?"

"For the same reason, none of us did on the island."

"Yeah, but out here, blood can buy you a lot of time, supplies, and even free passage. It's the currency that keeps everything ticking over. And their blood is just as valuable as anyone else's. Yet here they are, out in the open, warming their hands around the fire like they have nothing to fear."

"Maybe they want it to appear that way. Maybe they're infected and having one last hurrah before they kick the bucket. Or, maybe they're just waiting for folks like us to step out and make a wrong move."

"Well, if we're not going back and we can't stay here, there's only one way to find out," Jade said, pushing past him out into the open. Debris was everywhere. Cans. Bottles. Even shit where people had chosen to defecate on the ground. In the darkness, it was impossible to see it all. Jade's boot clipped a bottle, sending it skittering across the asphalt. She might as well have rung an alarm bell.

The glass bottle clattered and spun before coming to a stop.

Heads turned; eyes widened.

18

Fear held him tight.

There was no time to argue. Panic filled Jonah's mind, blocking out the blame as he took off at a full sprint. At first, he just followed Jade as she crossed a parking lot full of cars. They scrambled over the top of vehicles, using them like stepping stones. They'd been placed in the way to make escape difficult or prevent working vehicles from driving through.

They hurried between two high-rise buildings — apartments, maybe businesses. It was hard to know as they had no intention of slowing down to read the signs.

"Don't waste bullets," Jonah yelled as Jade fired behind her a few warning shots. It helped for a second or two but the thrill of the chase was all-consuming. Whatever their intentions were, they weren't good. There had been no communication.

"We might not have much choice. They're gaining on us."

"They are going to cut us off," Jonah cried, looking back and seeing the group divide, some going around the north side of a building, others going around the south. Clearly, they knew this place like the back of their hands and had done this before.

Like a pack of lions chasing wild game in Africa, the only thing that kept them ahead was fear. It ignited adrenaline that powered his legs like pistons. The two of them raced through the darkened streets, with no sense of direction, no idea of when or where to stop. Thoughts of dying or being used in blood transfusions kept him going.

They crossed Columbia Street, rushed by Hamilton Fish Park Library, and darted around the back until they saw a steely black fence that ran around the perimeter of a basketball court.

"Here," Jonah said as Jade was about to run on. "I'll give you a boost over."

"No time."

"Jade."

She raced back and he hoisted her up. As soon as she was over, he climbed a nearby tree and edged out across a large branch until he was able to swing down. Staying low, they hurried across the tennis court. For a brief moment, Jonah thought he'd outwitted the pursuers.

He hadn't.

"There they are!" a woman cried.

"Go!" Jonah yelled, firing a few rounds.

The fact was, if he didn't slow them down a little, the chances of shaking them were slim to none. He kept glancing off to his left and right, expecting to be ambushed by the others who had gone in another direction. They burst through a line of trees only to find themselves looking at an outdoor Olympic-size swimming pool. As they ran around the perimeter, Jonah heard voices ahead of them. "They're around here somewhere. Check that way."

"Shit."

He grabbed hold of Jade and pulled her back only to hear others coming through the tree line.

"We're screwed."

"Hey," a voice cried out. "Over here."

Jonah turned but didn't see anyone.

"Down here."

He diverted his eyes down to see someone in the pool. The pool had a thick blue vinyl cover that was stretched across it. There was a guy in the water, lifting the cover above his head just enough to show his face.

"What the...?" Jade muttered.

"You want to survive. Get in here now," he said.

There was no time to argue. Whether it was a bad judgment call or not, they would have to find out. Jonah raced over, dropped to a crouch, and slid his body into the cool water. Jade followed. The kid who couldn't have been much older than them pulled the tarp back, sending them into complete darkness. It was suffocating. Certainly not for the faint of heart or the claustrophobic. Treading water, they held on to a cleaning vent at the side of the pool.

Nearby, they heard voices.

"Which way?"

A few directions were tossed out before footsteps hurried past the edge of the pool. It wasn't long before they became distant and then everything was quiet. A sliver of light spread as the stranger lifted the vinyl ever so slightly.

"Are they gone?" Jonah asked.

"Stay quiet," the kid said quietly. "They are sneaky bastards."

He brought the tarp down again, sending them once more into darkness.

A minute passed or maybe three before Jade said, "Okay, I can't do this anymore." She reached up and pushed the vinyl even as the stranger protested. Within seconds, she was out on the edge, soaking wet and coughing hard. Jonah followed suit, though cautiously looking around.

There was no one nearby — at least that he could see.

It was then they got a full look at the stranger.

He pulled himself from the pool, revealing that he was completely nude. He was tall and lean and had a toned physique. His tousled hair was dark and fell slightly over his forehead. Jade took one look and then put up a hand to cover her eyes. "Whoa. Where are your clothes?"

"I took them off."

"Why?"

"Because that's what you do when you get in a pool."

She squinted behind her palm, trying to block her view. "So, you're telling me you got out of your clothes while being chased?"

"Ugh. No. I wasn't being chased. That was you assholes. And thanks for that. This place was a real gold mine before you both showed up. Now they'll be prowling around here." He grumbled as he walked butt naked over to the tree line and collected a bag of clothes and a towel.

"Who are you?" Jonah asked as he ran a hand down his shirt to drain the water from it.

"The name's Tucker," he replied as he towel dried.

"And are you in the habit of not wearing swim gear?" Jade asked.

"I didn't expect company. Who is this girl?" Tucker asked, utterly perplexed by her line of questioning.

"Ignore her. That's what I do," Jonah said, tossing Jade's words back at her.

"Noted," he replied before sliding into clothes while trying his best to cover himself.

Jonah glanced off to his left and right, making sure the coast was clear.

"Look, uh, are you from this area?" Jonah asked.

"Born and raised. And would you please keep your

voice down? You're liable to bring them back if they haven't left already."

"So, you're familiar with Hell's Kitchen?"

Tucker shrugged. "Who's not?"

"Us," Jonah replied.

He chuckled to himself. "Well obviously."

Jade had now removed her hand after Jonah said it was safe to.

"Something amusing?" she asked.

"What, besides the two of you?" He laughed a little more, then trailed off. "Oh, I don't know, maybe it's because you aren't from the area, and yet you think you can make it to Hell's Kitchen alive, or maybe it's just the plain absurdity of why I even helped you to begin with."

Jade rose to her feet. "Well, while you are on the subject, why did you?"

"I advise you not to entertain that question," Jonah said. "Trust me on that."

Jade scowled at him.

"Here," Tucker said, throwing his partially damp towel to Jonah.

"Is there one for me?" Jade asked.

"No, I didn't know I would be entertaining guests." He chuckled as he headed north toward a nearby building.

"What is this place?" Jonah asked as he ran the towel over himself.

"What are you two, foreign exchange students?"

"We came from the west."

"Really?" That made him laugh again. "Well shit, if you made it that far, maybe you can reach Hell's Kitchen."

They followed him through a set of doors into a dark building. A second or two passed before the place was illuminated by the flashlight Tucker was holding.

"What is this place?"

"The Hamilton Fish Recreation Center."

"Never heard of it."

"You two are uneducated swine." He laughed. "It's a piece of New York history. A landmark that has been here for generations. At one time folks used to fill out the pool, shoot hoops, bring their kids to the playground, and..." He trailed off as he stumbled over something in the dark. He let out a groan. "Sonofabitch!"

"How did you end up here?" Jonah asked while following him around.

"I used to get sent here for the afterschool program back when I was little. When shit went south in the country and all hell broke loose in the Big Apple, I opted to come here."

"Why?"

"Geesh, you ask a lot of questions."

"Just curious."

"Because it's familiar and they have a pool. So, I kill two birds with one stone and get clean here. Satisfied?"

"Ah, so that explains the lack of clothes," Jade said before he threw her a clean towel. "Gross. And to think I got in the same water," she said quietly but he caught it.

"Hey don't flatter yourself. I've smelled cleaner working horses than you two. Besides, had you not gotten in, you would have probably ended up being drained dry or the preference of bums on the street, used to drain others dry if you get my drift."

He didn't need to explain. Jonah caught the double meaning.

"Who were those guys?"

"Bums. Survivors. Locals out to take advantage of a few teens. The city is rampant with them. It's a colorful place full of weirdos and wannabes. Always has been. The better question is who are you, what rock did you crawl out from and why are you in my neck of the woods?"

"Your neighborhood?" Jade shot back.

"Everyone has one. This is mine."

"Sure it is. That's why you were hiding as much as we were," Jade said as she tossed the towel back at him. "Please, give me a break." Jade removed a gun from the back of her jeans. It was full of water.

Tucker chuckled. "Nice water pistol you have there."

"You didn't get in the water with that, did you?" Jonah asked.

"Well, didn't you?"

"No, I dropped mine on the grass otherwise it would be..."

"Wet. Great!"

"It might work," Tucker said. He shone his light around the room. It was full of pool tables. "If you fancy a game. Go ahead. There's a gym down the corridor, along with squash courts and…"

"Thanks. We won't be staying," Jade said, tucking the gun back into her wet jeans.

"Do you live here?"

"I have been but that will have to change now that you two morons showed up."

"Why here?" Jonah asked.

"Because it offers nothing. Apartments get checked for supplies and people, stores the same, but a recreational center? C'mon. It's not like anyone wants to do three sets and have a game of squash. It's worked out nicely for the past year."

"And where were you before that?"

"Who cares, man? I don't know you from squat and you don't know me. If you're leaving, go out the back door. People have eyes and I don't want anyone else to think someone is here. Though before you go, I would like an answer to my question."

Jade glanced at Jonah. "Screw him, let's go."

"You owe me!" Tucker said.

"Owe you?" Jade turned.

"Yeah. I'm not asking for much, just a little info."

"Why?" she shot back. "Because I mean, who cares, man, right?" she said, throwing his own words back. "You don't want to tell us about your past. That's fine. Then neither do we." She nudged her head and headed back out the door. Jonah glanced at Tucker who leaned back against a pool table.

Jonah exited. "Jade! Hey! He knows the area."

"Oh shut up. We are not bringing him along. You saw what happened the last time we did. Malik is dead because of us."

"No. Malik is dead because of someone else. We just happened to cross paths with him. Now, I told you not to run out but you did."

"Because we would have been found if we stayed in place."

"You don't know that."

She shook her head and walked on. Jonah looked back to see Tucker listening in on their conversation from the doorway. "Jade, slow down," he said, catching up with her. "We could use some help."

"I gave you help and you're griping."

"You put us in danger. We could have been killed or worse..." He didn't need to fill in the gaps. It was obvious.

"I made a judgment call, no different than you when you came to get me."

"Really? So, you're going to use the decision I made back there as a reason to justify your stupid decisions from here on out?"

"We're alive, aren't we?"

"Yeah. Because of Tucker."

She stared back at him. "Okay. Let's do it your way. Ask him. See if he wants to come. Because I'm pretty sure he thinks we brought this upon him. I hardly think he..."

"I'll go with you," Tucker said, approaching them. "I know the area. I can get you through."

"And what do you want in return?" Jade asked.

He didn't reply.

"Come on," Jade said. "There's always something."

"Yeah, there is," Tucker replied. "I want to go with you. That's it but I want answers to why you're here."

"Does it matter?

"It does. Look. Do you know how many survivors I have seen pass through this area over the past year? And I mean people traveling from one place to the next — not trappers, scalpers, or any of the assholes looking to use you for other means. Just straight-up folk like you two." He lifted a hand and formed a zero. "So that makes a person wonder. Why are you here? And why now?"

Jonah stepped forward. "I'll tell him."

"Jonah, no," Jade said. "It's not worth it."

Tucker smiled, his curiosity piqued.

"It doesn't matter if he believes or doesn't, Jade." He looked back at Tucker. "The answer to both questions is the cure."

19

A shaft of warm light pierced through a gap in a slat of the boarded-up attic.

Jonah squinted as he blinked the world back into focus. He glanced to his right across the many dusty boxes that filled the space. The other two were still asleep. The night had all but worn them down.

Dawn came with varying degrees of anxiety, frustration, and tiredness.

Tucker had taken the news of the cure better than expected. It was almost uncanny. Unlike Malik who needed to be convinced, Tucker accepted it based simply on rumors he'd heard over the past seven months and the fact that no one in their right mind would have been stupid enough to navigate Manhattan at night.

That was one of the reasons they waited until daylight.

He didn't want to, but it seemed they had no choice.

The conversation came back to him as he pawed at his eyes.

"I will take you, but we must wait until daylight," Tucker said.

"We don't have time; we still need to find her when we reach Hell's Kitchen."

"Not even with my help will you make it at night. You've seen first-hand what happens. Most of them sleep in the day. At least the dangerous ones."

"The dangerous?"

Jade was perched on a box, sipping a beer. Tucker had his own stash. It wasn't bad. It had helped calm Jade and made her less eager to head out into the night. "He's talking about the night crawlers."

Jonah waved her off. "Oh please! You make them sound like creatures,"

"Is that what they are?" Tucker seemed to get a kick out of what Jade called them, scoffing as he threw a handful of peanuts into his mouth. Jade was quick to explain. "My mother told me about them. People have given them different names. Call them what you want. Infected, crazy, violent, it doesn't matter."

"But they're people, right?"

"Yeah. She said my aunt told her about the infection evolving and that after we arrived on the island, she was privy to seeing a few — those they had captured so they could test her blood on them."

"Evolved?" Jonah asked. "In what way?"

"You remember when the Haze swept across the country, those initially exposed to the yellow dust seemed to have almost an immediate reaction to it as it attacked the nervous system and the brain. Those infected got into accidents because of a delayed response — you know — poor motor skills and mental delays. Airplanes fell out of the sky, cars crashed, and people ended up injuring themselves at home, at work, seemingly doing menial tasks. Thousands were killed in those first few days." She swallowed beer and took a breath.

"Tell me something I don't know," Jonah said.

"I'm getting to it!"

That garnered another laugh out of Tucker. "I like this chick. She's a fiery one."

Jade flipped him the bird but a smile tugged at the corner of her lips.

"Okay, as I was saying before I was cut off. Those who survived moved into the next stage where they were... you know — motionless for extended periods, had a decreased attention span and a lack of speech, as it attacked the brain. For many what followed was sleep inversion, catatonia, coma, and for others death." Jade lifted one foot on the box, wrapping an arm around her knee while her other leg dangled. She tapped the beer can against her thigh. "That was just those exposed to the initial wave. Those fortunate to have survived ran the risk of being infected by respiratory droplets or even a scratch. If they did get infected..."

"...they'd experience double vision, sore throat, high fever,

headaches, and lethargy, yada yada, right, I got that but get to the point."

"I'm getting to it. Geesh, Jonah. No wonder my mother nearly left you behind."

"Did she say that?"

"I guess you'll have to wonder until we see her again." She smirked and continued. "Anyway, so just like when the epidemic of encephalitis lethargica spread back in the twentieth century, causing inflammation of the brain, many others have been able to contract it. But this isn't the same. It's an aggressive variant of bradyphrenia and encephalitis lethargica developed by..."

"Biotechnology company Weston Sciences," Jonah said and nodded. "Yep," he rolled his hand as if to gesture for her to speed things up. Jade narrowed her eyes at him and he shrugged.

"You two sure seem to know a lot about this," Tucker said, chomping on some dried meat.

"We took the fast-track course."

"Ah," he tapped a piece of meat at Jonah. "Explains a lot."

Jade cleared her throat. "As I was saying. It's neurological. Before they discovered the effect my mother's blood has, the only known treatment to reduce the disease's activity and symptoms for some time came from antimicrobials and high doses of intravenous steroids, and blood and plasma transfusions. But as we've seen, it only reduced symptoms temporarily. Within three to six weeks, unless blood and plasma transfusions were done again, the person would expe-

rience the same symptoms and slide back into the depths of infection."

"Hence trappers and scalpers snapping up everyone to use like juice boxes at a children's festival. And there was me just thinking everyone had just gotten a little batshit crazy," Tucker said, taking another sip of his beer and then lifting a bag of peanuts to his mouth to empty it.

Jonah groaned. "We already know this. What's the deal with the night crawlers? Which I should add is a stupid name."

"I'll second that," Tucker added. "I prefer to call them assholes. It has so much of a better ring to it."

"The adolescents are called ransackers," Jade said.

"Like that kid we saw, right?" Jonah added.

She nodded. "That's part of it."

"Yeah, just a part," Tucker said, who seemed to have first-hand experience. "I've dodged the bullet numerous times."

Jade continued. "The ones who sleep during the day but are awake at night have been attacking people."

"You think they were responsible for Malik and Max's family's death?"

"Possibly. Trappers and scalpers wouldn't have done it. Unless someone had a vendetta against Max."

"Who's Max?" Tucker asked.

She waved him off so he continued. "Okay, so let me get this right," Tucker said. "The yellow shitty dust settled and killed a whack of society. Those who survived ended up in some catatonic state, a coma for many, while other survivors are seeking out people they can use for blood transfusions. And some biotech company is behind it."

"Pretty much."

"That's truly messed up."

"I would have thought you knew about this."

"How would I know? It's not like the government ran a broadcast telling us the truth."

Jonah nodded. "Point taken."

Tucker continued. "So where do the crazy young ones come into it?"

"Oh, I thought you had encountered them?"

"I have, I'm just trying to wrap my head around why they are the way they are."

"As I said, it's neurological, many end up suffering pseudo-psychopathic states. Somehow it affects the brain and causes violence. Similar to the encephalitis lethargica back in 1917, when adolescents were seen to damage property and attack strangers."

"Hence the name ransackers."

"Right."

"And the others?" Jonah asked.

"Sleepers?" Jade asked.

"Okay, now you are confusing me. You called them night crawlers."

"People give them many names because they sleep in the day and are out at night."

"Yep, all that matters is they are neurologically a mess," Tucker said.

Jonah squeezed his empty can and tossed it. "Sounds right."

"Hey, don't litter," Tucker cried. "Pick that up. Might be the apocalypse but in here, this is my house."

"Excuse me," he said, hopping off a box and collecting it. "I didn't realize you had a hard-on for recycling. Though if you're looking to save the planet, I think you're a little behind the curve." He grinned.

The previous night's memories faded as Jade stirred. She crawled out of a sleeping bag, yawning. "What time is it?" she asked, wiping drool from her jaw.

"Just after six thirty." He turned away and peered out a gap in a board that had been tacked into place by Tucker. He had to give him credit, he'd gone to a lot of trouble to secure his abode. There were false walls to hide rooms, heavy game equipment blocking stairwells, and he'd even created multiple exits so that if he came under siege, he could slip out without anyone noticing. That was the luxury of living in a place that few people had an interest in.

"Oh, you have got to be kidding," Jade said.

Jonah turned to see Tucker strolling off toward the end of the attic. He was butt naked.

"Okay. C'mon now. There is no reason why you wouldn't wear clothes at night."

"Sure there is. My briefs cut into my thighs. It's much more comfortable to sleep this way. You should try it," he said, scratching his ass and then leaning against the far-end wall to pee.

"Have you never heard the saying don't shit where you sleep?" Jade asked.

"I'm not taking a shit."

"You know what I mean."

"Chill. I rigged up a tube."

"Seriously?" Jade said.

"Well, I could be trapped in here for days. You got to think of these things. You see, that's the problem with society. They're all busy hunting down food and looking for safety on some damn island and overlooking the benefits of a place like this. A full Olympic swimming pool and...."

"You already told us this last night," Jade said, rising to her feet. "Now, please. For the love of all things holy. Put on some underwear."

Tucker ran a hand through his tousled hair. "Is she always this salty in the morning?" he said, making his way back before letting out a large fart. Jonah couldn't help but find him amusing.

As Tucker was getting dressed, he and Jade shifted the heavy game equipment that had been used to block the entrance.

"Don't be going out there yet," Tucker called to them.

"I'm not staying in here any longer. It's daylight. Time to move."

Tucker jogged over.

"I meant, wait a second." He dropped to his knees and shifted a piece of wood, then another, then one more until he could see straight down. "Okay. All good there." He moved across the room and did this four more times before he gave the thumbs-up. "All right, we're good to go. Just don't make a lot of noise. I've been caught off guard a few times over the past year when I thought it was all clear."

Exiting the attic, they quietly made their way to the ground floor.

They waited for Tucker as he gathered some dry food and snacks from his storage area and filled a backpack. He emerged holding what resembled a small javelin with a machete on one end and some contraption on the other that looked like steel prongs.

"What the hell is that?" Jade asked.

"Machete and a three-claw weeder. It's perfect for dealing with trouble from the front and behind." He demonstrated, thrusting it out then behind him in one fluid motion like he was some warrior out of *Mad Max*. "Pretty cool, huh?"

"Yeah," Jade said. "I'm sure that will block bullets well."

She shook her head as she ventured out.

"Chill. I'm carrying too. I just like to change things up. You'll thank me if we come across some of those sleepers."

"Nightcrawlers," Jonah said, correcting him.

"You say potato..." he said, breaking into the Ella Fitzgerald tune.

Outside it was quiet, almost too quiet. For a city that

at one time never slept, it was eerie walking through the empty streets, following Tucker as he led the way. It would take roughly an hour and twenty minutes according to him but Jonah thought that was being a little optimistic. One look at the landscape as they pressed into the concrete jungle and it was clear that it wasn't going to be a walk in the park. The once bustling city no longer had the sounds of traffic or people going about their daily lives.

The buildings that had once towered over them were crumbling ruins, their windows shattered and walls plastered with graffiti. The streets were littered with debris and rubble, making it one hell of a trek.

The smell of smoke and ash wafted in the air, joined by the crackle of nearby fires. Jonah glanced up at the dull grey sky with heavy clouds that looked as if they would burst any minute.

As they continued, they began to notice signs of life that had taken hold throughout the city. Vines and weeds grew through cracks in the pavement, climbing up high-rises. Small animals scurried across the streets, scavenging for food. "Three years and mother nature comes to take back what's hers," Jonah said.

"You haven't seen the worst of it," Tucker replied.

As they walked, they saw even more devastation. Burned-out cars and shattered storefronts were common; the occasional skeleton or abandoned backpack served as a grim reminder of those who had fallen either to the Haze or violence. Despite the bleak surroundings, they continued, driven by a sense of hope and determination to find Alice.

They hadn't been out there more than twenty minutes when Jonah stopped walking. "You hear that?"

"What?" Jade asked.

Tucker was a good couple of yards ahead, navigating his way over a pile of rocks.

"Helicopters. Take cover," Tucker yelled, hurrying back down and sliding under a section of building. Sure enough, a dark shadow spread over the area, and a downdraft of air pressed down, stirring up dust and grit and blowing it in their direction. The sound of the rotors cut through the eerie silence, growing louder as the chopper flew low overhead.

Jonah peered out and saw the insignia on the tail as the deafening roar reverberated through the empty streets.

"GERM." It had been a while since he'd seen one, even longer since his crash in the lake and rescue by Alice.

"You seen them much?" Jonah asked.

"Can't say I have. Not since the first year. Once people broke out of the quarantine zones, they pulled out. A few times they came back in the second year, shooting people and removing some from the city, but it's been a while. Then again, I haven't exactly ventured out this far."

"What?" Jade asked. "You told us you came to Hell's Kitchen a lot."

"Did I?"

She gave him a shove. "Yes."

"Oh. Must have been the drink."

"Tucker!"

He broke into laughter. "I'm pulling your leg. I've been all over this city. I'm the king of New York. I run this place."

"Here we go again," Jade said, rolling her eyes.

"Nah, I've needed to find supplies," he said as the helicopters disappeared. The sound slowly faded away, leaving only a faint echo behind. The city was again enveloped by an oppressive silence as if the helicopters had never been there. "You'd think it would be easy. You know — in a city this size — but it's getting harder by the day."

The three of them exchanged a nervous glance, wondering why GERM was back in the area.

20

He lived his whole life on the edge, literally.

Thirty stories above the ground in Hell's Kitchen, a light breeze blew against Dustin "Skitz" Michael's skin as he relaxed on the intricate handwoven spider web of climbing rope stretched over a street. At a head-spinning height of 328 feet, it would have given most vertigo, but for him, it was just another day. The pentagonal web was at least 100 feet away from the nearest building, a typical sight for extreme highliners, slackliners, and BASE jumpers in Southern Utah, but here — it wasn't play, it was survival.

A means to an end.

And this was better than Moab, a place he'd left years earlier after being fined for illegal BASE jumps in Arches National Park.

The canyons of concrete that made up Hell's Kitchen had become his home, his escape, and his means of survival in the world that had gone mad far below. Like a spider web spun throughout a home, he'd created his security net in the high places of the city. Unsuspected by most, a strange sight to others. Climbers' rope was stretched through a set of windows, crossing over only to exit through another and continue to another building.

While many chose to navigate the city on the ground or via numerous walkways of steel and planks of wood, he opted for even higher ground, staying out of reach.

A few had tried to get at him in the night but had fallen, unable to walk out or hold on. Others had cut the rope, but for every rope they sliced, he had another in place and another. Eventually, he was treated like a spider might be in the corner of a room, left alone to do its thing.

Nope, they didn't dodge bullets; they were the ones who fired them.

That morning he, Theo 'Tabs' West, Skylar 'Sky' Nelson, and Lee 'Levi' Cooper were eyeing movement between 53rd Street and 11th Avenue.

"I'm telling you we are wasting our talents, Skitz. We could be living in the lap of luxury if we just snagged a few unsuspecting folks and sold them off. Scalpers are making a killing," Tabs said.

"That's not what we do," he replied, looking through binoculars.

"Obviously, but come on, it's been almost three years."

"Two years and seven months actually," Sky chimed in.

"As I said, almost. And what do we have to show for it?"

"You're still alive," he replied. "That's what."

"And living off the scraps of what we find or scavenge."

"It's better than the alternative."

"Is it?" Tabs replied from behind a dirty face framed by thick dreadlocks.

"We agreed."

"Maybe for you but I'm starting to think we need to discuss this again because I think we're missing out here. I don't know about you guys, what do you think?" He posed the question to Sky, a purple-haired beauty who had cropped hair, a nose ring, and sky-blue eyes.

She shrugged.

"Levi?" Tabs asked. Levi, an Asian friend of theirs, nodded. "I think he might have a point, Skitz."

Skitz turned, lowering the binoculars. "Do I have to remind you what happened to your mother, Levi? Or your sister, Sky… and Tabs, what about your brother…"

"He left."

"Allegedly. We all know that down there you are either the predator or the prey. It's as simple as that. Now we've got the best of all worlds. We get to do what we used to do and avoid all the crap that comes from being in the gutters. I won't lower myself to that."

Tabs scoffed and shook his head.

"You have something to say?"

"You act like you're taking a moral high ground but you're no better than them."

"How so?"

"Are you seriously asking me that?" Tabs asked.

"What we do is justified."

"Well, I'm glad that you've made your peace with it."

"What you are asking for us to do is far worse."

"Than shooting people from on high?"

"Every trapper and scalper we take out is another person who gets to walk."

"For how long? One day, one week, one month? Eventually, they would have gotten themselves snagged by one of those people you think are less than us. You're not saving anyone, Skitz. Let's call a spade a spade here. The reason you do this has nothing to do with helping New Yorkers. It's about her."

"Careful."

"Why? We all know it's true."

"And that's a bad thing?"

"It is when we have to suffer for it."

Skitz laughed. "Suffer? Have you gone without a meal since this shitfest happened? No. Have you gone without clothing, a roof over your head, or anything? That's right. Now shut the hell up."

Tabs leaned in close. "Make me."

"No. I'm done having this conversation," Skitz said, rising to his feet, the web swaying ever so slightly beneath his feet.

"That's it, walk away. That's always been your default, Skitz. It's the reason we left Utah."

Skitz jabbed a finger back at him. "No, that was all you, Tabs, and your dumb ideas. So, I guess I can kind of understand you wanting to bring up another."

He turned to face him, only to have Tabs tackle him. They landed hard, causing the whole net to bounce.

"Guys. Guys!" Sky shouted.

Fists flew, Skitz blocked a couple but took one to the chin. They twisted, rolling dangerously close to the edge. "Would you two fools stop it!" Sky said. She looked back at Levi. "Levi? Would you please do something!?"

"You knew this was eventually going to happen, Sky. I say let them get it out of their system."

"If they want to beat the shit out of each other, they can do it on solid ground, not when we are this high."

The net continued to bounce.

Sky intervened, getting between them only to get cracked on the chin herself.

That put an end to it.

"All right guys, break it up," Levi said.

Holding Tabs' neck, his fist raised above him, Skitz said, "You done?"

"Oh, I'm done."

Just as he was about to release him, they heard glass shatter.

All four of them looked off to the right toward the Mercedes House, which had a luxury-tiered skyline in the shape of an S. Thirty floors above the city, it gave incredible views of the Hudson River and offered residential penthouse suites for the wealthy. Like a staircase shaped in an S, from the highest apartment to the lowest, terraces cut into the building, jutting out and giving anyone who was on one the opportunity to drop down to the next.

In that moment they saw something that was unlike anything they'd witnessed before.

A woman had burst out of the glass. She rolled across the terrace, ran, and hurdled the glass wall that separated it from the next apartment terrace below.

A chorus of gunfire echoed, then it stopped abruptly only to be followed by multiple individuals chasing after the woman. Like watching someone do parkour, they couldn't help but be mesmerized by her commitment to each jump, leap, and drop.

"Who the fuck is that?" Tabs said.

"I don't know, but she's heading for one of our lines," Skitz replied.

21

Minutes earlier

She felt like a caged animal.

Barefoot, clothed in nothing more than a hospital gown and underwear, Alice stood by the floor-to-ceiling window inside one of the terraced apartments overlooking the Hudson River. Her exposed back was raw. Multiple bloody bandages covered the many stripes she'd received from the cat of nine tails. Each one burned and stung, sending pain with even the slightest movement.

Since being left alone, she'd assessed the room, evaluating an exit strategy.

The main door was locked and from what she could

hear on the other side, even if she managed to get out, she wouldn't make it far, just like before.

The terrace on the other hand offered opportunity.

Painful opportunity but a way out nonetheless.

She'd tried the door to the terrace but it was locked. Several ideas went through her mind, none of which were good but then the situation couldn't get much worse.

The door behind her opened and the same woman she'd seen earlier stepped in, holding a plastic tray. A French press full of coffee and two mugs along with some powdered milk and cutlery clattered on top. Her face was clearer now. She carried herself with an air of confidence and purpose. High cheekbones and piercing green eyes accentuated her features. Her fiery red hair cascaded down her back like a waterfall of flames. She wore tight jeans, brown boots, and a striped shirt. Alice noted a handgun on one hip and a Taser on the other.

The thought of overpowering her faded as quickly as it came to mind.

"Quite the view, isn't it?" she said as one of her guys closed the door behind her. Alice heard it lock. "This place was built by Swedish designers. At one time it was a marvel to behold with its striking geometry of glass and steel. It stood out for all the right reasons. Now only a few of the apartments are usable. Like this one. I hope it's to your liking?"

Was this woman out of her mind? Alice thought. *To her liking?* None of this was to her liking. "I'm glad to see you back on your feet again. I'll have April come back in and change your bandages. I was hoping we could talk first if that's okay with you. I'm sure you have many questions."

"Who are you?"

The woman set the tray down, her eyes never leaving Alice.

She was cautious, she had every reason to be. Though, unlike Caleb, Alice got a sense she wouldn't make the same mistakes he did.

She kept her distance.

"Coffee?" she asked.

When Alice didn't answer, the woman poured herself a cup, dumped in a heap of powdered milk, and began to stir. "My name is Abigail Reid, formerly... Hayes. I believe you know my son."

Alice took a step back, regarding her through new eyes.

"You're Jonah's mother?" She paused for a second. "But he said he didn't know his biological parents. That he was given up at birth and bounced around the foster system before being placed in a group home for troubled teens."

"From what I hear, he told you a lot of things, some of which were untrue, to get you to Seattle."

Alice offered back a confused expression. How did this woman know that? How did she even know she was from Washington?

"However, much of that was true. The real truth is my ex-husband." She paused. "Eric. He was the one that placed Jonah into foster care. Of course, Jonah doesn't know that. He was too young. Eric would say he did it to give him something better. A real family. A chance at life. But how could he?" Her eyes darkened and her jaw clenched. "Eric stole him from me at a young age and placed him into the system anonymously to avoid me finding him."

"I don't understand. Why? And why would you allow that?"

"There was nothing I could do and I didn't know until much later." She sniffed and nodded and got this faraway look in her eyes. "He had already had me institutionalized. Said I was a danger to Jonah, to society." She took a sip of coffee and walked over to the window, looking out. Alice couldn't help but think that perhaps Eric was right after what she'd experienced. There was something odd about her and those she'd encountered.

"Still, Eric couldn't walk away. No, he wanted to hurt me. So, he kept an eye on what foster parents Jonah was with and ultimately was the one responsible for getting him out of the group home at a time when he could create a bond with Jonah that was unbreakable. That way, he became much more than a father to him; he was his savior."

"And you?"

"The Haze was my salvation, my deliverer. If it wasn't for that, I wouldn't have gotten out and had a second chance to reunite with my son again." She closed her eyes for a second. "The day I got out, I went to his home." She took out of her pocket a folded photo of Jonah back when he was fourteen, back when Alice had crossed paths with him. He was almost fifteen now.

Alice shifted her weight from one foot to the next. "If that's the case, why am I here and not him?"

She scowled. "Because shit happens."

Alice stared at her. "Jonah was meant to be taken as well, wasn't he?"

"That's right."

Alice looked out. "Then why do you want me?"

Her scowl faded. "I don't. Someone else does."

Alice offered back a confused expression again as Abigail moved around the room, keeping her eyes on her. "I believe you are familiar with him. Hell, if it wasn't for him, I don't think I would have found my son. We made an agreement. When I got confirmation, I said I would deliver you to him. Well, at least you were meant to be delivered before then but it seems those on the inside dropped the ball."

"Inside?"

"Yes. You must have thought that everyone that was on that island was against GERM. Quite the contrary."

Alice felt a knot form in her stomach. Her heart beat a little faster.

"Who helped you?"

Without missing a beat, Abigail replied, "Robert Weston."

She took a few steps back. "He's alive?"

"Very much so. He didn't want me to tell you. He

wanted to see your face when you saw him. But... that's right. You thought he was dead." She scoffed. "It's funny, isn't it? The paths life takes us on. I guess I should thank you for keeping my son safe."

"You don't know what you're doing. Weston is responsible for this. All of this."

"Then I have even more reason to be grateful."

With that said, she turned to leave.

Alice moved toward her. "You need to let me go. If what you're telling me is true, my daughter is on the island."

"I can't do that."

Feeling rage, Alice grabbed the decanter of coffee and went to crack it over her head, but Abigail turned and fired a two-prong Taser sending Alice down hard, flopping over the floor like a fish out of water. Abigail crouched nearby, out of reach, still sending volts into Alice's body. "I'm sorry, but if our intel is correct, my son and your daughter are heading this way. You'll see her again but until then you will remain here." She got up and headed for the door, pausing only momentarily with her hand on the handle. "From one mother to another, I think more than anyone, you should understand there isn't anything that I wouldn't do to be reunited with my child." Another pause. "I will send April in to tend to your wounds."

With that, she left.

Alice remained in a fetal position on the floor until her muscles began to relax.

Minutes later, she rose to her feet and began to pace, her mind spinning over multiple outcomes, none of which were good. Alice desperately scanned the room for a way out, her eyes settling on a large chair sitting in the corner

With a sudden burst of inspiration, she dashed over and lifted it, gripping it tightly. She moved to the far wall and then sprinted toward the nearest window, her heart pounding in her chest as she prepared for what was to come.

Alice took a deep breath and charged into the glass, propelling both herself and the chair through. Shards of glass flew everywhere as she tumbled out onto the terrace.

Quickly scrambling to her feet, Alice spotted the glass that wrapped around the terrace. She moved toward it and eyed the rest of the terraces jutting out below like large steps leading down.

Without hesitation, she launched herself over the edge. Her heart raced as she hurtled through the air, landing on the next terrace below. She rolled and scrambled to her feet again.

Looking back up, she heard gunfire, then shouting and Abigail's name being called. Not wasting a second, Alice took a deep breath and continued over the next glass balcony wall onto the terrace below, knowing that she was one step closer to freedom.

22

Death was imminent.

There was no way she would make it.

Many had tried, but all had failed. Highlining was an art in and of itself, birthed out of slacklining at Yosemite and eventually finding its way through California in the early '80s. For even the nimblest, balancing on a flat rope that stretched between two anchor points was hard to do, but taking it up a significant height, several hundred feet off the ground — took years to master as paralyzing fear ran through the body. It required skill, balance, and focus honed from hours, days, and months of frustration.

And that was with all the right tools.

Out here there was no typical harness, no safety leash attached to the line to prevent a fall.

It was do or die.

What didn't help was the random gunshots fired by the thugs in pursuit.

Pop, pop, pop.

"Let's stack the odds in her favor," Skitz said, turning away and stretching out his hand. "Sky. Pass me my rifle."

Tabs was all over him. "Hold on, Skitz. What are you doing?"

"I just told you," he said as Sky tossed a hunting rifle to him and he laid flat. "Levi."

"I'm on it," Levi replied.

Tabs pushed down the barrel of the rifle against the web of rope. "No. Shooting at trappers or scalpers, I get that but this...? We don't know who she is, let alone who they are. Now we've already brought down the wrath of two groups on us, you want to increase that to three?"

"Get your hand off the barrel, Tabs."

"She's not Raven, Skitz."

"I won't ask again."

Tabs groaned and lifted his hand, allowing Skitz to focus on the guy who was gaining on the woman. He squinted, put the scope to his eye, adjusted for distance and wind, and then brought the fleshy piece of his finger to the trigger and exhaled as he squeezed off a round.

The initial goal wasn't to kill but to slow them down.

Make them rethink. Hopefully, drive them back inside.

It worked. The guy scrambled for cover.

The woman looked back for a second, then out toward them.

Levi and Sky were ready for what came next, an onslaught of gunfire their way. But they had the high ground and had acquired serious firepower from downed GERM soldiers in the weeks after the Haze. They were packing M4s. They released three-round bursts in retaliation, peppering the surface of the terrace.

The woman kept moving at a fair clip.

As if recognizing them as an ally, it only strengthened the woman's resolve to head in the direction of the line anchored to one of the terraces. From above, their rope was everywhere, some frayed by time and wind, other sections newly anchored.

"She better slow down if she wants to walk out."

"I don't think she plans to walk out."

"Oh, I can't look," Tabs said, looking away.

Under his breath, Skitz cheered her on. "C'mon. C'mon. You can do it."

Like the others, he expected her to slow and balance, nope. There was no slowing for this woman. She sprinted toward the edge with little thought of safety or even if the rope could hold her weight.

Of course, it could. There was no standardized load limit; generally, it could hold up to 300 pounds but that was if a person used it as it was designed. At the clip this woman was moving, she had other plans.

"Tabs, give me the extra rope and that hangover

carabiner," he said, still focused on her, wondering if they had enough time before she launched herself. "Tabs!" he shouted, this time looking back. A moment later, he grasped the rope and connected the hangover carabiner. "Keep me covered," he said as he hooked himself to another rope that would allow him to rope jump out. It was often done off cliffs, allowing them to swing out on rope into the middle of a canyon where a line was anchored from one side to the other. With the need to disappear at times after taking out trappers and scalpers, they had rigged up multiple lines, allowing them to swing out and then slide down. It was second nature to them.

To her, he could only imagine it must have looked terrifying.

And yet whatever she was trying to escape, it must have been far worse as she didn't hesitate in launching herself off the side of the building. Skitz nosedived off the net trusting the connection he had, formed from doing it time and time again. He swung down while hearing gunfire from above as the other three offered support.

"Hold on. I'll come to you!" he said as the line went taut and he swung back and forth until he came to rest out in the middle. From there he hooked up another line, using a carabiner and additional rope in his backpack. In what must have looked like a performance out of Cirque du Soleil. He dropped backward, his body rushing down to her only to have the line tug him.

Upside down, he extended a hand.

"Can you pull yourself up?"

She was hanging from a straight line of rope and trying to bring her feet up but failing miserably. It was to be expected. It must have looked easier than it was.

"Trying," the woman cried out. "Give me a second."

"Oh, don't mind me. We have all the time in the world," he said sarcastically as he looked back up to see his friends laying down cover. Within seconds, she managed to get a leg over the rope, and with a little bit of coaxing, he clasped her one hand. "All right. Now you're going to have to reach up into my backpack."

All the while the flat rope beneath her moved as she tried to balance.

"For what?"

"Trust me. Keep your breathing steady and..."

A sudden burst of gunfire aimed in his direction came scarily too close. He heard the snap as a round whipped past his head. The woman nearly lost her balance but he kept his grip.

"Tabs!" Skitz cried out.

"I'm on it. Hurry up!"

Skitz cursed under his breath and then redirected her back to the backpack, aware that her weight and his would put a strain on the anchors but there were few other options. "I'm not going to be able to reach it."

"You don't have much choice. If we weren't under fire, you might be able to walk it or pulley yourself across but—."

Pop, pop, pop.

She realized the situation was only getting more dire by the second. All it took was one good shot and it was over. Using the rope beneath her and him as a support, she strained and reached up, snagging the yellow rope from his backpack.

"Now hook that onto the rope beneath you, wrap the other end around you, and slide toward that window," he said.

Above them a chorus of gunfire continued, holding back the tide that wanted to take them off balance and send them down into the depths.

"I got it."

"It's all you now!" he said.

Just like that, she released her grip and dropped off the rope she was balancing on. The line connected to it went tight and then the slight angle of the rope allowed her to slide toward the building on the other side and a window that no longer had glass. Skitz didn't stick around to watch if she made it, he was already making his fast exit.

On any other day, they might have BASE jumped from this height but he wasn't wearing the bag with the parachute. Instead, he simply connected himself to one of the many ropes anchored between the buildings using a carabiner and slid his way across to the other side. The landing was hard inside the abandoned building. Dust and grit went everywhere. Based on where he went in, he knew he was two floors above where the woman had entered.

As soon as he unconnected himself, he hurried for the stairwell, adjusting his backpack and keeping his eyes peeled for more trouble. When he made it down to the floor she came in on, he found her lying face down, her exposed back revealing numerous bandages that had peeled off.

"Hey, hey," he said, dropping to a knee and tapping her face. She groaned. Her eyes blinked. He slipped an arm underneath. "Come on, I got you."

As he lifted her, in one smooth motion the woman snagged his SIG Sauer from his thigh holster and backed up. "Stay back."

Skitz put his hands up. "Whoa! Whoa! Look, I wasn't going to hurt you. Hell, I just risked my life to help you."

"Back away."

"Fuck." He shook his head. "All right. Just ease off that trigger."

They rotated in the room with her moving around him and Skitz moving backward, keeping his hands up. "Look, I don't know who you are or why you are running, and frankly, I don't care but I'm not the enemy. There is far worse out there. Now you look as if you could need a friend," he said.

"I don't need anything."

"You sure about that?" he said, noticing how unsteady she was on her feet.

Movement off to her right caused her to turn her

head but she wasn't fast enough. Tabs used the butt end of his rifle to crack her in the jaw, knocking her out cold.

"Really?" Skitz said, hurrying over to her, his brow furrowing.

"Fine! Next time I'll let you get shot," he said, shaking his head.

Sky and Levi emerged from behind him, jogging into the room. "Hey, we should go. They'll be looking for us."

"Give me a hand," Skitz said, wrapping an arm around the woman.

The others looked down at him but didn't take a step forward. "Come on. Give me a hand."

Sky tried to reason with him. "Skitz, you know our rules."

"She needs help."

"No, you do. Mental help," Tabs shot out.

"Fuck you. Just give me a hand."

"She's a liability," Sky said.

"Yeah. A dead weight," Tabs was quick to add.

"All right. All right. I'll do it myself," he said, struggling to lift her. He'd used nearly all of his strength to hold her out on that line and make his way back. He was strong, which came from years of slacklining, but even he had his limits. He stumbled and Levi stepped in to assist.

"Thank you."

"They're right, brother. This is a bad idea," Levi said as Tabs and Sky went ahead to make sure the coast was clear. On the other side of the building, they all slid down a construction chute into a large dumpster full of garbage. There wasn't one area within Hell's Kitchen they didn't know. They'd taken care to get familiar with it and make changes that would help them. Rarely did they venture out of the neighborhood. This gave them the advantage of not being caught off guard or pushed into a corner.

They ambled over to the nearest manhole cover and ventured down into the darkness. While they rarely used the sewer system, it was still a viable way of getting from point A to point B without being seen.

As they navigated the narrow tunnels, they heard the steady flow of water rushing past them, the voices above, and the occasional scurrying of rats darting out of their path. Skitz hated coming down there. It wasn't just that the air was damp and musty, and the smell of sewage was overpowering, but he was claustrophobic.

"Once we send her on her way, we need to talk," Tabs said.

"Whatever, man."

"No. Not whatever. We have put this off far too long. Things need to change around here. If we're to survive, for however many years are ahead of us, we need to rethink what we are doing. "

"And you know what to do," Skitz said, trying not to lose his footing as Sky illuminated the way with a flashlight.

"You're not the only one with ideas around here."

"Never said I was," Skitz replied.

The conversation with Tabs was long overdue, it had been coming to a head for quite some time. It wasn't just what they were doing but who was calling the shots that pissed him off. He wanted to make the calls on where they went, what they did, and what mattered.

"But you imply it."

"Geesh, Tabs. You want the reins. They are there for the taking. But you don't take them."

"Well, maybe I will."

"Good for you. Sky, we'll head to the apartment above the convenience store," he said, trying to shift the conversation. Skitz looked over at the woman who was still out cold. She certainly had a lot of courage. He couldn't help but chew over questions in his mind. The who, why, where, and what.

The light from Sky's flashlight bounced off glowing patches of bioluminescent bacteria that illuminated the walls, giving the underground an otherworldly feel. He spotted clusters of colorful graffiti art adorning the brickwork, evidence of the city's vibrant underground subculture that had only gotten bigger since the event.

After what felt like hours, he spotted a faint light in the distance.

It grew brighter as they drew closer to a ladder. They emerged from the sewer system to find themselves in a completely different area of the city, several blocks away from where they started.

There wasn't one place in the neighborhood they didn't utilize. It was easier for the four of them to travel around using the rope linking buildings together but with the woman, they had to go another route.

Sky lifted steel shutters, shouldered a door and they piled in before she closed and locked it from the inside. Working off memory, Tabs wandered into the darkness, then a glow emerged as he lifted an inflatable solar lantern. There was a small button on the top of each one. They would leave them in windows and on roofs to charge throughout the day. They were perfect for the inside, as they never gave off a bright light but were more than enough to see.

Skitz and Levi set the woman down on an old beat-up mattress.

Under the glow of the light, they all stared at her. "They went to town on her back," Levi said. "Who do you think she is?"

"I don't know but I intend to find out."

23

It was a terrifying sight.

Like a pack of wolves descending on prey, the grim outcome was inevitable. There had to be at least twenty or more chasing after three strangers through Tompkins Square Park. Their attackers weren't ordinary. At least if their bald heads and pale skin were anything to go by. Bare-chested, donning only pants and boots, they stood out as deranged, an anomaly among all they'd seen to date. Some of the weirdos wore darkly tinted thick goggles, others bandannas.

The screams mixed in with the hooting and hollering caught their attention as they moved north along Avenue A. With shutters on many of the businesses, and doors locked, they'd had no choice but to climb up a fire escape to avoid intersecting with the chaos.

Five stories high above the street, hidden by the lip

of the roof, they bore witness to a new form of insanity that had spread throughout the city.

"Stay down," Tucker said as they peered over the edge. Since leaving the recreational center in Lower Manhattan, they'd been fortunate to not encounter any threats until now.

Far below between the trees, one of the three being chased was a middle-aged man. He was armed and firing a pistol. Even when rounds hit their mark, the wounded seemed to bounce up with little regard for the pain.

"How the hell are they getting back up?"

"PCP. They're all drugged out. Delusional. Trust me, they can die. I've killed a couple. Nothing unusual about these people. They bleed like us. They are us."

"Then how?"

"It's not a kill shot. It's not that it isn't painful, they just don't pay attention to the pain, injury, or any of the normal physical and psychological cues a regular person would because of the drugs."

Within minutes the armed survivor was swarmed from three sides. Like a pack of wild beasts, they drove the man to the ground.

All Jonah could do was watch as the victim was dragged across the asphalt and then held down on a grassy knoll.

His shirt was torn open and someone lit a portable blowtorch and lowered the blue flame to the man's chest. His cries were brutal to hear, cutting through the air.

With so many swarming in to be a part of his final moments, it saved them from seeing it.

Jonah's eyes bounced to the other victims: two women who never stopped to see what happened to their friend. Perhaps they knew? No, fear drove them on. A pure will to survive.

"They won't make it," Jade said, watching intently as the women made a desperate sprint for the road. Jade brought up her gun but Tucker placed his hand on the barrel and lowered it.

"Don't."

She continued, "We need to help them."

"You do that and you will bring that entire group down upon us. You want that?"

She stared back at him. Her jaw clenched before she pulled away, realizing he was right.

The two women never made it out of the park. The exit was cut off by more of them, some coming up through manholes as if they'd anticipated where they would run and planned to cut them off.

Swarmed. Encircled. A frenzied attack. The women cried out. One of them swiped a machete at the pale group before being grabbed from behind in a chokehold and brought down. They suffered the same fate their friend did.

Scorched by blowtorches.

Jonah thought he'd seen it all but it couldn't be

further from the truth. He was starting to think that reaching Hell's Kitchen was an impossible feat. Washington was bad but it had nothing on this place. Malik was right. Unless you knew the right people, navigating the maze of concrete was wishful thinking.

"I don't get it. Why would they do that?" Jade asked.

"A pack mentality. Territorial. In all fairness, they did those people a favor."

"A favor?" She looked at him, disgusted.

Tucker got up, ready to leave. "Yeah, they often infect them. You know — expose them to one of the infected. And man, that is a slow and painful death."

"Why?"

Tucker sighed. "Because they believe this event is the best thing that's happened to this world. The day that the Haze spread, it leveled the playing field. No rich, no poor, no status in life matters. It brought millions to their knees and elevated those who had crawled on theirs for years."

"Who are they?"

"The mole people."

"The what?"

"Lower your voice."

"Are you serious? What the hell is a mole person?" Jonah asked.

"You've never heard of that?"

"No."

Tucker looked back into the park full of lush green trees. "It was a term given to the homeless that lived below Manhattan in the tunnels. Long before the event, it was believed there were more than two thousand of them down in the sewers and forgotten subway tunnels. That was the low end. There were many more."

"Why are they so pale?" Jade asked.

"Darkness. A lack of sunlight. Even more so since this event. That's why they wear those tinted goggles. At least I think it is. Most used to spend their days riding the subway, begging, sending out only a few to garbage dive, collect cans and exchange them for money and food."

"So why shave their heads?"

"Yeah, that I'm not too sure about. I think it's some kind of whacked-out version of what their belief system is. I know it wasn't like that before the event but hey, cult groups aren't exactly the most logical people, right?"

"A cult?"

"Uh-huh," he said, replying as they crossed the top of the roof to the other side. Fortunately, the block they were on had all the buildings joined together so they were able to put some distance between themselves and the freaks below.

"Hold on a second. Back up the train. You're saying they're some kind of cult?"

"Yeah. Something like that. They've adopted some type of ideology that worships the infected and the outbreak. They see it as some kind of gift from above, a leveling of the playing field, so to speak. Anyone from above ground, survivors, you, and I are seen as something blasphemous in their eyes. And so, they either get you to join, or you die by their hand or from them exposing you to the infected."

"That's kind of sick," Jonah said.

"As I said, cults aren't logical. And those folks down there lost their marbles a long time ago. Have you ever tried to reason with someone on PCP, a drugged-out individual who spends their days living in the darkness among rats? Best of luck."

"So, who's in charge of them?"

"I'm not sure. I've never stuck around long enough to ask them that," he said, a grin forming. At the far end of the block, still on the roof, Tucker turned. "Look, we're probably going to have to take a few different turns. The route I had in mind may not work."

"Oh, hold on a second," Jade said. "Might not? I thought you knew these streets like the back of your hand?"

"I do. But this is an evolving situation. Dynamic. It's not like I have the schedules of freaks like those folks back there."

"But you know how to steer clear of them?"

"Mostly."

"Mostly?" Jade shifted her weight from one foot to the next, narrowing her eyes. Jonah had seen it before. It was usually before she began to go on a rant.

"Jade. He's doing his best. We could be doing a lot worse if he wasn't here."

"Yeah, especially if you'd opened fire back there." He

shook his head. "Seriously, for someone who has survived this long, I have to wonder." He began to climb down. "Oh, and, when we make it to Hell's Kitchen." He pulled a face. "You'll be on your own from there." He continued his descent.

"What?" Jade replied. "Hold up."

Tucker looked up.

"You didn't say anything about that earlier. You said you were going to help us find her."

"And I am, by getting you to Hell's Kitchen. I'm just not going through that neighborhood."

"And why might that be?" she pressed him further. Jade wasn't going to let him off the hook that easily. And to be fair, Jonah was furious himself.

"It's bad news."

"And this is not?" she asked, taking a step back.

"Call it history. I prefer not."

"Well, that's not cool."

"Take it or leave it," he said, continuing. Jade looked at Jonah and he shrugged, climbing over the roof's edge and following Tucker down. He heard Jade let out a frustrated groan before following. Jonah noted the way Tucker had been elusive about his past but then again, they hadn't exactly offered up much in the way of truth.

To say there was a high amount of hesitation in dropping back to street level would have been an understatement. However, they had no other choice.

THE TIMING WAS BEYOND BAD, it was downright ironic. Abigail stood on the helipad, joined by Lucian and six others awaiting the arrival of Robert Weston. Few people knocked her off balance. Robert was one of them. She wasn't sure if it was his association with GERM and the consequences that could come from failing or the thought of being sent back to some psychiatric institution. Days felt like years in that hellhole, surrounded by the worst of society. She wasn't supposed to be there but with her ex's father being a lawyer and her former mother-in-law a doctor, it became very easy to make others believe she had lost her mind.

The truth was far from it.

She'd had an emotional breakdown. Some would have called it postpartum depression, others, working too hard. Whatever it was, it took her to a dark place, one that clouded her judgment and for a brief period left her unfit to be a mother.

So, to have a chance again to prove herself meant a lot.

"He's not going to be happy," Lucian said.

"We stick to the story."

"And when he finds out it's not true?"

"By then you will have found her. The teams are out there, yes?"

"As we speak."

"Good."

"And if he doesn't buy it?"

"He must. Remember, it's your neck on the block as

much as mine," she said, glancing at him. Lucian had been a thorn in her side since Weston had assigned him to assist her after numerous attempts to bring Alice in had failed.

Where his loyalty lay was unknown. She assumed she would soon find out.

A tiny dark dot in the distance grew larger on the horizon as they waited for the military helicopter to arrive. The sound of the rotors got louder and louder, drowning out all other noise. As it came into view, she could see a sleek, black exterior and the distinctive GERM emblem emblazoned on its side.

Abigail squinted as the wind from the rotors whipped her hair around her face. She could feel its powerful downwash blowing against her skin as the chopper descended and the pilot expertly brought it close to the roof until it touched down on the helipad.

As the blades slowed, the noise wound down, and the dust settled, Abigail felt her heart pound in her chest. She knew Weston would be eager to see Alice — and wasn't going to be pleased to find out that she was gone. Her group waited anxiously for the door to open; her hands were clasped tightly behind her.

Finally, the door of the chopper slid open, and several GERM soldiers stepped out wearing red biohazard suits, black helmets, and oxygen tanks on their backs, all connected to a self-contained breathing apparatus. They were armed with MP-5s.

They fanned out, guns at the ready, expecting trouble.

Weston emerged between them, wearing a similar breathing apparatus but dressed in a suit. He removed his helmet and handed it to one of them before moving at a fast jog toward Abigail.

She smiled outwardly to convey confidence but inside she was unraveling.

"Mr. Weston, glad to see you again."

He looked ecstatic but then again, he should have, the last radio update had given him exactly what he wanted — hope. Hope of seeing Alice again, hope that his tests could continue and his work with the Haze would progress.

He'd sold her on the cure. A permanent solution to the hell they were in and she had bought it because it came as a package deal with her son's whereabouts.

The trouble was connecting with Jonah.

With GERM having all but fallen by the wayside, its ranks splintering, and many joining resistance groups, it had taken longer than he expected to find Alice and Jonah. From there it was a simple matter of planting the right people among them. Loyalists, he called them. Those who would appear to have turned their back on GERM but were working both sides of the fence to gain intel. She came to learn that GERM wasn't only interested in the cure but in squashing those who would seek to control the narrative of the nation since the event.

It was a precarious time in which the former world would be lost if authority fell into the wrong hands.

That's where she came in.

Whereas she was simply seeking information on her son, Weston had other ideas.

Now, after her conversation with Alice, she was beginning to wonder what was true and what were lies.

Was it his intention to cure people or control them?

"Sir," Lucian said. Weston patted him on the shoulder which garnered a broad smile from Lucian.

All the people around her were connected to Weston. They either worked for him or served GERM in some facet. After getting out of the institution, she'd sought out Eric, hoping to find him or Jonah, but instead, her efforts led her to the university in Seattle. She'd spent weeks there, trying to piece together what had happened. Had it not been for the arrival of GERM and the collection of data stored at the lab, she might never have found out the truth. In some ways, she saw that as a sign from God.

Weston fell in step as they went inside, and the door was closed behind them.

"I must say I am pleased with how quickly this worked. I'm sorry to hear that your son wasn't brought in at the same time."

"Not everything goes to plan," she replied. She'd hoped that might lessen the blow of what was to come, but it wouldn't

"I'm glad to see you're still optimistic."

"It worked once, it can work again."

"Right."

"I imagine you are tired from your trip. We have prepared a room for you."

"It won't be necessary. I don't plan to stay long. Take me to her. I'm eager to see her."

And there it was, the request she knew was coming. Abigail cut Lucian a glance. He smiled as if just waiting to see how Weston would react.

"I'm afraid that won't be possible."

Weston stopped walking and turned abruptly. "I beg your pardon?"

"I mean, she will be here later. There were a few people that needed her blood. Key people that could help the cause."

"Then take me to where she is."

"It's too dangerous. You would be better to stay here."

"Why do I get the sense that I'm not being told the truth?"

"Because you're not, sir," Lucian blurted out, his eyes bouncing to her with a look of betrayal. "She's gone. She escaped. We're looking for her but right now we have no idea where she is."

His eyes narrowed and went dark.

"Mr. Weston, I'm sorry. I..."

Before she could say any more, he turned and swiped her across the face with the back of his hand. Abigail landed hard on the floor. Weston loomed over her like a dark shadow, his teeth gritted, his hand balled as if preparing to unleash a beating. "Lie to me again and it will be your last."

He turned back to Lucian. "By God, I hope you have something."

"Yes, sir. She was seen with a group. That's the only lead we have right now."

"You better hope she's still in this city. Find her!" he shouted.

24

The world came back to her as a kaleidoscope of sound and images.

It was followed by a dull pain in her jaw.

"Hey, guys... she's stirring."

Alice blinked, hearing someone's voice in front of her as she rubbed her face. At first, all she could see was the outline of dark figures behind the fog of her mind, but then it solidified.

There before her was a purple-haired woman, she couldn't have been more than thirty-five. She was sitting cross-legged on a web of rope that formed a makeshift hammock. As her vision cleared, Alice realized she was inside an apartment.

Two other people stepped into her line of sight; another was by the door.

That's when her fight-or-flight instinct kicked in.

She scrambled to get up, only to feel dizzy and off balance.

"Whoa, we've got a live one!" someone said.

Laughter erupted.

The same guy she'd seen hanging upside down over the wide gap between two buildings got closer. He was good-looking. His hair was up in a man bun, he had a hard jawline with lots of facial hair. He was wearing the kind of comfortable clothing that climbers would wear, form-fitting, nothing that would get in the way. "Yeah, sorry about that. You'll have to forgive my friend. He thought you were going to kill me."

"Who are you?"

The stranger in front of her turned and pointed. "The guy by the door — that's Tabs."

"The good-looking one," Tabs added, leaning back against the frame and smoking.

"And full of himself," the purple-headed woman added. "Hi. I'm Skyler but people call me Sky."

Another of them gave a nod, picking at his teeth with a knife. "Levi."

"Oh, and I'm Skitz."

Alice rubbed her head. "Where am I?"

"Safe. In Hell's Kitchen."

"That's where..." She went to get up but stumbled again.

"Yeah, you're going to have to take it easy. You took one hell of a crack to the jaw and by the looks of those whip marks on your back, I'd say you've been through the wringer." Levi approached with a bowl and gave it to Skitz, he set it down in front of her.

"Why don't you have something to eat?"

"What is it?"

Tabs laughed. "Well, it's not filet mignon, darlin'. What is it? That's a funny line. Like we have choices now."

"It's noodles," Skitz added.

"I don't want it," she said, swiping at the dish and knocking it over. Liquid spread across the floor as she tried to get up again. "I've got to get out of here. I've got to find my kid before..." This time Skitz let her move, putting his arm out at the others to leave her be. She didn't make it far. A few steps, and she had to support herself on a table in the kitchen. A moment later, she bent over and threw up.

"Oh geesh, c'mon!" Tabs said. "Are you serious? I was just about to tuck into my food. Sky, can you..."

"Why do I have to clean it up?"

"I'll get it," Levi said, rushing for a mop.

Skitz moved in close to Alice. "Look, lady. I get it. You don't trust us. I wouldn't either, especially after all the shit that's happened but if it wasn't for us, you probably would be lying on the sidewalk with your brains out or back with those people who were after you." He paused to catch a breath. "Incidentally, who were they?"

Alice coughed hard, spat on the floor then wiped her mouth with the back of her sleeve.

"People I don't want to see again."

"Yeah, well, join the club. Now because you're here, I've got to ask. Why were they after you?"

Alice chuckled as she continued to wipe acidic muck from her lips. "Your guess is as good as mine."

"All right. You don't want to tell us. Fine."

"You wouldn't believe me if I did."

"Try me," Skitz said.

Alice waved him off. "Maybe another time." Without knowing them, she didn't want to just throw it out there that her blood was rare and she held the key to a permanent cure. Hanging that kind of information out there hadn't exactly served her well. For all she knew, they could make a deal and hand her back over in exchange for more noodles or whatever the hell they wanted.

She thought the guy would pressure her but he backed off. "You know, the wounds on your back are bleeding pretty bad. I used to be a medic."

Tabs coughed then chuckled. "A medic?"

Alice glanced over. Tabs was quick to correct himself. "Oh yeah, I forgot you did that." He smirked and she could tell it wasn't true.

"Anyway, I think I have some bandages out back. I'm sure Sky can wrestle up some new clothes while I do that, can't you, Sky?" Alice looked at him and then the others. She had a good sense that they didn't mean her any harm. If they had, she would have been hooked up to a transfusion machine or in the grave by now.

Sky nodded and disappeared out the window, balancing across a rope until she vanished out of sight.

Alice followed him into the next room where he pulled out a chair and asked her to take a seat so that she was facing the back of the chair. He took a bottle of water and emptied it into a bowl, then collected some clean rags and a small medical bag. He got behind her and began to peel off the bandages. She let out a groan.

"Sorry. Probably best I just tear these off fast rather than do it slowly."

"Do it."

She gritted her teeth as he removed them one by one, each one stung as much as the last.

"Wow, this shit is gnarly. Those people back at the Mercedes House. They do this to you?" he asked as he cleaned the wounds, dabbing each one gently. She grimaced with every touch.

Alice nodded.

"You know they did this to Christ. He received thirty-nine lashes because forty could kill a man. Can you imagine that?"

"You religious?" Alice asked.

"Religious? That depends on what you class as religious. Do I believe in God? Yeah. Did I hang out in churches week after week? Nah. It wasn't my thing. Naw, my church was hanging out under the open sky; shooting the breeze with people over a beer, spreading love. You know?"

She smiled. "I guess."

"You don't believe?"

She shrugged.

"You don't look very convinced."

"Well, I haven't seen much around lately to convince me."

"I hear you. So, your faith has changed since this event?"

"It's made me have doubts. Look, forget I asked. The last time I had a deep conversation with someone over faith, it ended in an argument. Probably best we avoid it."

He listened while continuing to dab each wound. "That's too bad. I mean that we have to be so divided and opposed to one another. In my mind, we're all the same. Stuck on a rock, looking out of this fishbowl into space, wondering who put us here and why."

"Sure is a mystery."

"You'd think we could all just get along."

Alice snorted. "Gotta dream, right," she replied.

Sky reappeared, climbing back in through a window and holding an armful of clothes. "I found these. You look about my height. There's a couple of options there," she said, tossing the clothes on the floor beside her. With that said, she went back into the room behind them.

"What's the deal with all the rope?" Alice asked.

"Oh, that."

"A little odd."

"What can I say, we're a kinky bunch."

She glanced over her shoulder and he chuckled. "Naw, we're just slackliners. I did it for a long time before the event. Traveled. Entered competitions. We visited different places and would set it up over canyons, between trees, heck even buildings."

"I noticed."

"Wild, huh! Who would have thought Hell's Kitchen would look like this." He snorted.

"You from here?"

"No. I ended up getting busted several times for illegal highlining in Utah. Ended up moving to New York. Tabs, a friend of mine, was born and raised here. We figured we would do something locally; you know, start a school to help other climbers interested in it, but then the event happened." He paused for a second or two as if reliving it all in his mind before continuing to tend to her wounds. "Anyway, after the looting started, and people were dropping like flies, I didn't think it was a good idea to stick around. You know — down here — what with people breaking into homes to get supplies when the stores were running out. We decided to use the newfound freedom to um... decorate... you might say." He tossed a bloody rag on the table, got up and emptied the water, and refilled it again. "In the chaos, you'd be surprised what you can find in the city and even more surprised what you can get away with. We collected as much rope as we could and began anchoring up in different places."

"Like the steel and wooden planks."

"Yeah. Initially, it was to get from one building to the next in a pinch — our way. Not a lot of people can balance on them so the chances of being followed are slim. And having them high, well, let's just say people tend to change their minds when they look out."

"But they can be cut."

"They can and they have." He stopped.

"You lost someone?" Alice asked.

"Hasn't everyone?"

She nodded.

"What about you?" he asked.

She shrugged. "Not much to say really."

"That's fine. You don't need to tell me."

She found it refreshing that he didn't push it. Others would have. Especially after seeing what they had. As he quietly worked on her back, she opened up. "I'm from Washington."

"That's a long way from here."

"Yeah. Been here seven months."

"Family bring you out here?"

"Something like that. Safety, mostly. I guess. Now that I look back, I think it was the only option available. We left in a hurry. Everything else..." she trailed off thinking back to that night, her sister, the escape, the plane ride out of Vancouver to another location in Washington before changing into another ride that took them the rest of the way. "Anyway, it looked safe but..."

"It wasn't." He tossed another rag. "I hear you there. It's getting worse out there by the day. We try to help from time to time, you know, picking off some of the trappers, scalpers, and stopping the beaters."

"You try to stop them?"

He looked at her as he walked back with some bandages to start patching everything up. "Sometimes they get it wrong. They pick the wrong person. Someone who looked like..." he trailed off.

"You lost someone to them?"

He dropped his head for a second.

"Who was she?" Alice asked.

"What makes you think it was a woman?"

"Instinct, I guess."

There was a short pause before he answered. "Her name was Raven. My fiancée. They uh... took her to get back at us for taking in someone. We got separated. They cut the line and the next time I saw her, she was hanging from a noose, her body beaten..." he trailed off and she heard him take a deep breath. "Anyway, that was then, this is now."

Alice arched her back.

"I'm sorry for your loss. I lost a husband and a child. It doesn't get any easier."

"But you have one more?"

"A daughter. Yeah. She's supposed to be heading this way if what I was told is correct. That's why I have to get out there. She can't..." Alice went to get up but he placed a hand on her shoulder.

"Whoa. You're not done yet."

"Sorry. I'm just worried."

"I can see. This daughter of yours have a name?"

"Jade."

"Chances are…" he paused. "I just realized I don't know your name."

"Alice. It's Alice Walker."

"Alice. All right. So, your daughter was where?"

"Governors Island."

He stopped working on her. She twisted around. "You familiar with it?"

"You could say that. Look. Chances are Alice, if your daughter is heading this way, she's going to have a hard time finding you. This is a farm of haystacks and you're a needle. Now we can go out and see if we can spot her but…"

"You run the risk of being seen by those who were after me."

"Exactly. But we can do it." He paused. "You know, I realize you don't know us, but it would go a long way if we knew why they were after you."

"I wish I could tell you but…"

"You don't trust us."

She got up and he didn't prevent her this time. "How's it looking?"

"It's done. Pretty much. I got most of the bad ones."

Alice turned. "Dustin."

"Skitz," he said, correcting her. "Always preferred it."

"Skitz. Okay. Why do they call you that?"

"It's used to describe a mental state. Some of the highlines I've walked have made people wonder if I'm a little…" He brought a finger up to the side of his head and swirled it around while whistling.

"Makes sense." Alice scooped up the new clothes. "Well, Skitz. I appreciate you helping me. I do. But I need to get out there and find my kid before they do."

"An impossible feat."

"I've done it before."

He nodded, rising and heading over to a radio. Skitz sat down and donned a pair of headphones before turning the dials. "I don't doubt it. However, you might be biting off a little more than you can handle. You might not be able to find her but I think I know some people who might."

25

Taking a shortcut through Union Square Park was their downfall.

A place that had once been a bustling hub of activity in New York City was now nothing but a desolate wasteland of broken concrete and overgrown vegetation.

Mother nature had come to reclaim what man had stolen and in a very short time, she had covered much of the ground. Its once-manicured lawns were now overrun with weeds, and many of the towering buildings that surrounded it on four sides were crumbling ruins.

Fire combined with the pull of nature had wreaked havoc on the historic intersection located where Broadway and the former Bowery Road met. Now it was framed by 14th Street to the south, 17th Street to the north, and Union Square West and East on either side.

"Are you sure about this?" Jonah asked.

"I'm not sure about anything," Tucker replied. "But it should shave off at least ten minutes, and what's that saying... time is money, right?"

The two of them gave him a confused expression.

Jade rolled her eyes. "I think that term has lost its meaning."

"And the saying doesn't apply as we're not after money," Jonah added.

"Well... English wasn't exactly my strong point." He grinned. "Look, maybe you don't know this city, but I do. There is a bad element running through these streets during the day and at night. Most are restricted to certain areas by choice, others because they don't have a choice. I'm doing my best to avoid the worst."

"Like the mole people?" Jade asked, trying to make a point that had it not been for the other survivors, it could have easily been them attacked.

"Hey, they've broadened their reach. They weren't supposed to be near Tompkins Square."

Jade grumbled. As they made their way through the overgrown brush, they could hear the rustling of leaves and the faint sounds of wildlife in the distance. The air was thick with the scent of decay and the ground beneath their feet was soft and damp.

Suddenly, without warning, the ground gave way beneath them.

Jonah felt his stomach lurch up into his throat as he lifted. But it wasn't the ground, it was rope. The three of them found themselves trapped in a net, suspended in the air. They struggled to break free from the tangled mess of rope, but the more they fought, the tighter the net became.

Even if they could cut their way out, they were at least thirty feet high.

Jade cursed under her breath as she looked down at the ground far below them. "What the hell is this sick trap?" she yelled, unable to hold in her frustration. Jonah and Tucker were equally stunned, their eyes wide with fear.

It was like being a fish in a deep-sea fisherman's net. All they could do was hang there, helpless as the sound of footsteps approached. A group of armed marauders emerged from the brush, their faces twisted into cruel sneers.

"Well, well, well," one of them said, grinning wickedly. "Looks like we've caught ourselves some fresh meat."

Even though they were armed, they were outnumbered. There had to be at least thirty of them. If they opened fire, it would have been a slaughter. Like shooting fish in a barrel.

"Trappers!" Jonah said.

"Oh, no, far worse than them," Tucker replied, his eyes fixated on those below.

"Worse?"

"Beaters."

His thoughts went back to Washington, to the young teenagers he and Alice saw in the woods that day, and all the bodies strung by their necks with placards hanging from them with the names of victims. "Well, this should be a breeze, we haven't taken anyone," Jonah said. "Right?"

The two of them looked at Tucker and he dropped his chin before cutting them a glance.

"Please tell me you haven't met these people."

Before Jonah could get an answer, they squirmed as the net trap was lowered. Almost immediately they were set upon by their captors. Gun barrels jabbed in their faces as others took them out and disarmed them. "All right. All right. Get off me." Jonah was shoved to his knees and quickly restrained with zip ties as were the other two.

"Hold on a second." One of their group burst into laughter. "Oh, Dante is going to love this," he said. "It's Tucker. Well, well, well, Tucker. Who would have thought our paths would cross again? Man... karma is a bitch!" He roared with laughter.

Jonah and Jade glanced at him. Tucker's head remained low. Jonah's heart sank, realizing they were in deep shit.

"You know this guy?" Jonah asked.

"Know us? Oh, Tucker used to be one of us. At least until he decided to go AWOL. Joined with those highliners, isn't that right, Tucker?" The guy looked at them all.

"Shit. Where are my manners? I'm Kai. An old friend of Tucker's. Let me guess, Tucker, this is a new group you've joined or did you convince them that you know this city?"

"You piece of shit," Jade said.

Kai laughed. "Oh, don't you worry, he has a habit of turning coat on those he runs with. I'm assuming the high-flying act over in Hell's Kitchen tossed you out or did you double-cross them like you did us?"

"That's why you didn't want to go through Hell's Kitchen?" Jonah said.

"It's not like that."

"Oh, it's like that," Kai said, waving a baseball bat around. He pursed his lips together. "You poor bastards. Because of this asshole, you're probably going down with him. But hey, who cares right? You're just more meat." He got close to Jade. Ran his finger over her lips and then stuck it in his mouth. "Tasty meat. Maybe Dante will let me keep you."

Jade spat in his face. "Fuck you!"

"Oh, sweetheart. If that's what you think riles me up..." He laughed. "You and I are going to hit it off really well. I love a fiery woman. Someone who knows how to play rough." He rose to his feet. "All right, let's rollout. Orion, reset the trap. I'm thinking we might be on a winning streak this week. That's the sixth one we've bagged. Let's see if we can nail some others tomorrow." As he walked away, they heard him say, "Man, I love taking trappers' tools and putting them to good use."

As they were led out of the park across the empty street towards the Daryl Roth Theatre, Jonah soaked in the outside. "What is that place?"

"Used to be a bank, now it's a theater," Tucker said.

"Shut the hell up," one of their captors said from behind, nudging them forward with the butt of his gun.

The theater was a large, ornate building with a grand entrance and tall stone columns. It reminded him of something gothic. The walls were adorned with intricate carvings and statues of angels, adding to the eerier atmosphere.

They were quickly ushered inside, and the smell of sweat and blood hit him like a brick wall. The air was thick with the stench of unwashed bodies, and the sound of a frenzied crowd. Cheers echoed through the cavernous space. They were forced into a main auditorium which at a glance could have held over 300 people. The floor beneath them pitched down towards a large stage with velvet curtains on either side. Throughout the room, people were engaged in all manner of shenanigans. He spotted couples sucking each other's faces, others eating, or shooting up while some danced in the aisle. A few faces turned as they were led down.

Someone threw a paper cup of liquid at Jonah and it splashed all over his face. Instantly, he knew what it was — urine. Laughter followed.

His heart sank at the sight of what was happening on stage.

Several people were hanging by their necks from the

rafters, their bodies limp and lifeless. A group of men was taking turns beating them with baseball bats, their faces twisted into a frenzy of bloodlust.

"Knees, or ribs?" one of the men shouted, beckoning for an answer and reveling in it.

The audience responded with sickening glee, shouting their requests and cheering with each bone-crushing strike.

"Look, I think you've made a mistake," Jonah said, trying to sway his captor. "We haven't taken anyone, no blood transfusions, nothing. We're not trappers or scalpers."

"Shut up. You'll get your chance to plead your case."

Case? Jonah thought.

Like cattle being led to the slaughter, they were brought to the front and made to wait off to one side and watch as others were murdered. It was horrifying. Truly terrifying to witness. He'd heard rumors of beaters, groups of people intent on seeking revenge for the deaths and disappearances of loved ones, and he'd encountered them, but he thought it was just a fringe minority. A few in Washington looking to strike back at a time when so many felt hopeless.

The madness had spread. In some ways he understood. With no law or order, people were snagging humans to be used to temporarily reduce symptoms of the Haze. But that didn't make it right.

He'd escaped them before but now he was face-to-face with the reality of the horrors these people were capable of.

"Please. Please. I didn't take anyone. No!" The final person on stage was brutally beaten into silence before being cut down and dragged out to be hoisted up for all to see. Just like in Washington, it was a warning. It was meant to get trappers and scalpers to rethink taking innocent lives, but it wasn't working. Before Alice was taken, she'd told him that it was rampant in the city, every lowlife and freak of society was out there trying to work an angle. For some, it was simple survival. A need for supplies to last another month. For others, it was to have another month with a loved one. To talk to them like they had before. To bring them out of the hellish symptoms that the Haze inflicted.

Jonah felt a hard whack to the middle of his shoulder. "You're up, asswipe!"

Tucker went before him, he followed after, stumbling up a series of steps. Jade was in his shadow.

Almost immediately, people began jeering. Jonah squinted as he looked out at the audience while bright lights shone on their faces. This was a new form of Broadway. Live, savage entertainment.

Food, drink, and all manner of objects were thrown at them.

He glanced up to the steely black metal rafters that crisscrossed the room, full of lights

Kai stood before them smiling, mostly staring at Tucker before he turned. "Silence!"

Down before them in the front row of seats was an Asian guy with a full head of hair, in his mid-thirties, maybe early forties. He had his arm around some woman and she was laughing as if he was telling her a joke.

"Dante!"

The guy glanced his way, to which Kai stepped out of the way and pointed at them.

Dante's gaze fixed upon Tucker, his jaw dropped and a smile danced on his lips as he rose from his seat. The room went quiet and it was clear that he was leading this shit show. He hopped up onto the stage and that's when Jonah got a better look at him. There was this gnarly scar down the left side of his face. He ran his fingers over it and walked straight over to Tucker and, without saying a word, unleashed a right hook to his ribs.

The crowd cheered.

Tucker doubled over and Dante took hold of his hair and brought a knee up, knocking Tucker back on his ass. "Get him up!"

While they were doing that, he prowled in front of Jonah and Jade. "Anyone recognize these two?" he yelled out. Jonah expected people to reply with a yes but they didn't, which was a surprise to him but more so to Dante.

"Look at that. You know, we get a lot of people coming through these doors each day. They don't leave. Most are recognizable. But you two. No one knows you.

Now, on any other day, I might have cut you loose and sent you on your way with my apology but..." He pointed at Tucker who was now back on his feet, coughing hard. He spat a glob of blood on the stage. "You are with him. Fucked by association, isn't that the term, Kai?"

"I believe so," he said, smiling from ear to ear. Oh, he was loving this.

Dante moved back to Tucker. "You are either stupid or are very unlucky showing your face again. Why would you come here?"

"We weren't here last time, Dante," Kai said.

"That's right. We weren't. Huh. Shit. All that alcohol must be dulling my memory. In which case, that would explain why you're here." He paused and cocked his head. "Why are you here? And where are those high-lining freaks you chose to align with?"

Tucker said nothing.

That only garnered another hard hook, this time to the face.

"When I speak. You answer. Why are you here?"

Tucker finally piped up. "Well, it's a bit like the old joke. Why did the chicken cross the road? To get to the other side," Tucker said. Jonah couldn't believe he had the nerve to attempt sarcasm at a time like this. Dante smiled for a second before unleashing a violent beating on him, this time he kicked out his legs and began stomping on his body.

"Hey! Hey! Stop!" Jonah shouted.

Dante looked at him with a menacing expression.

"He was just trying to help us."

"Is that so?" He walked over to Jonah. "And you are?"

"Jonah Hayes."

Dante looked at Jade and for a brief second, Jonah held his breath hoping, no, praying that Jade wouldn't say something that would piss him off any more than he already was.

"Jade Walker."

He breathed a sigh of relief.

"And how did you meet this piece of shit?" he said, referring to Tucker.

"He helped us."

"Ah, okay. I see now. Yeah, Tucker has a way of doing that. That's how he got hooked up with us. Isn't that right, Tucker?" He said it with a hint of disdain. "Back when you were useful. Back before you got one of us infected."

Across the room, there was a commotion.

A woman thrust her way through a knot of people. "I want to see him. Get out of the damn way!" She hurried down then leaped up onto the stage, dropping down beside Tucker. She looked up at Dante. "Really? Did you have to do this?"

Dante tapped the side of his face where the scar was. "Oh, that's nothing compared to what I have planned for him."

"You're such a bastard."

"Nova. Do I need to remind you what he did?"

"It wasn't his fault."

Dante laughed. "Right, right. I guess the saying is true. Love is blind. Well, old love may not die. But people do and these three — whether it's shit luck or fate — are going to die."

26

It was a matter of life and death.

Jonah's father had always told him that when confusion and doubt set in, sometimes all a person could do was throw everything at the wall and see what would stick. He had every intention of doing that.

"We're here because of your friend," Jonah spat out as Dante looked as if he was about to rough up Tucker some more.

Heads turned, including Jade and Tucker who had no idea what he was talking about. In all truth, he didn't know either but he'd paid close enough attention to connect the dots. Sure, he ran the risk of being wrong but he had a feeling he wasn't.

"What did you say?" Dante asked, still bent over Tucker, fist raised.

"You asked him why he was here. I'm telling you. It

was to help your friend."

Dante looked confused. He glanced at Tucker and then back at Jonah.

Jonah heard Jade whisper, "What are you doing?"

He ignored her and continued. "Your friend is infected, right?"

There was a pause. It was possible that the person could be dead as he had no idea of when Tucker was last here. It was a shot in the dark and he'd taken it knowing that either way the outcome was likely to be his neck on the chopping board.

"And?" Dante asked.

"We can help."

A smile formed and he chuckled. "First, you don't know if you're the right blood type. Second, if you're offering, forget it. It's too late. She's fallen into a coma." He turned to Tucker. "Thanks to you."

"We can still help."

His brow furrowed. "No one can help once they are in a coma. Blood and plasma transfusions only work for those who haven't reached that stage."

"That's where you're wrong."

As Dante looked back at Tucker, his anger evident, Jade leaned into him and whispered, "Jonah, what are you doing? You're not immune."

"We have her blood in us."

"Yeah, but she's the only one that can help."

"I know."

"So, we don't know what would happen."

"What are you whispering about?" Dante asked, rising to his feet and approaching them.

"She was just reminding me to tell you how she came out of a coma."

"You came out of a coma?"

Jade looked pissed off and she had every right to be. All testing on the island over the past seven months had only involved Alice, not those who were brought out of infection. They didn't want to chance infecting others even though those who received a blood and plasma transfusion from her were showing no symptoms. Additionally, it was unknown whether or not someone who received Alice's blood could be reinfected. They were dealing with unknowns and to date, Alice was the only one known to have brought people out of the coma state.

"Yes."

"Bullshit."

"It's true."

Dante smiled, his face turning away for but a second before he lashed out, swiping Jonah across the face with the back of his hand. He fell to the stage floor and Dante was on him, grasping him by the back of the neck. "Do you think I'm stupid?"

"No."

"Do you think you can talk your way out of this?"

"Damn it. Listen to me. What I'm telling you is true. Her mother is immune. We were based on Governors

Island. She brought her daughter out of a coma and then gave me blood."

"You are infected?"

He stepped back as did many others. Not that it would have helped them had he been infectious.

"Was. That was seven months ago. No symptoms. I can help."

Dante stared. Jonah could imagine the cogs of his brain turning over, contemplating, questioning if he was lying or not. "Look, what do you have to lose? Chances are your friend is going to die if they don't get a blood transfusion."

"We already tried. It didn't work."

"I know. Blood and plasma transfusions from matching blood types only work if they aren't in a coma because it doesn't deal with the root cause of the infection. The patient needs to be exposed to blood from an immune."

"So what? You're immune too?"

He glanced at Jade and she shook her head ever so slightly, a last-ditch effort at advising him not to say yes. But he'd already come too far and said too much. "Yeah. I am now." The truth was he didn't know. Sam hadn't run the critical test which involved trying to reinfect him. "Look, what have you got to lose? Hook me up, take some units of blood, and give them to your friend and see."

"And watch her die if you're lying?"

"She won't die."

"No, she won't because I'm not that stupid. First off, even if you were immune, you might be the wrong blood type. Blood compatibility is critical. Even you should know that."

"Her mother has a rare blood type that allows her to donate to anyone."

"Even if I believed you and I don't. That's her mother. Not you."

"What do you think we were doing on Governors Island? I have her blood running through me. So does she," he said, looking at Jade.

Dante smiled and looked back at Nova. "I told you their lives would be decided by us. They've decided it for themselves. They are with GERM."

"GERM?" Jonah said. "You're wrong. We're with the resistance."

Dante walked over to Jonah again and got close to him. "How naïve you are. But here's what I'm going to do. If you truly are immune, you'll show no symptoms when exposed to the infected. We'll test your theory then if you're telling the truth, we'll take blood after. Until then, I guess you get to live, Tucker. For now." He paused. "But if your friend is lying. Well, I think you can figure out what comes next. Take them into the next venue."

As they were led away, Jade said nothing. Even though he could tell she wanted to scream for them to stop. She must have known if she spoke up, that it would throw more doubt into the mix and Dante was already skeptical.

THEY CAME to discover there were three venues inside Daryl Roth Theatre. First, there was the main room where the crowd was and where most of the plays at one time took place. Then there was the DR2 theater, a 99-seat room where live productions and musicals were seen.

Except they were seeing it from a unique vantage point — dangling upside down over the stage.

Using the fly system that all theaters employed, sandbags would be attached to ropes to allow stage-hands to change heavy backdrops by raising and lowering them. Only in this case, the rope was wrapped around their ankles and they were hoisted into the air.

"Just when I thought you were redeeming yourself in my eyes," Jade muttered. "Then you pull this little beauty out of your ass. This is just perfect. Absolutely perfect. I couldn't have thought of a better plan myself."

"Hey, do you honestly think they would have bought the idea of joining us to search for your immune mother? They would have headed into Hell's Kitchen without us. The clock was ticking. I made a judgment call. I stand by it."

"Well, you're going to have to now. When they return and drag your ass away to be infected, and you end up showing symptoms, just remember. You brought it on yourself."

"Oh, shut up, Jade. If you're not trying to be a solution you are a part of the problem."

"Am I?" she yelled loudly, her voice echoing off the walls in the room. "If my legs weren't restrained I would..."

"Would what? You're full of hot air. You always have been."

She balled her fists.

"We must be the first people in the history of this theater to see the stage from this angle. Huh. Best seats in the house," Tucker said.

The two of them looked at him like he was equally crazy. "So, you want to tell us who you screwed over, how it happened, and why you left? Because if we're going to die, I would like to get a good reason," Jade asked as she attempted for the fifth time to pull her upper body up so she could untie the rope, but unfortunately, her core wasn't strong enough. Neither was Jonah's.

The rope creaked as Tucker twisted to look at them.

Jonah could feel the blood going to his head. He couldn't imagine they could last very long upside down.

"Her name is Bekah. Dante's sister."

"So, you used to run with them?" Jade asked.

"Used to. Some of them I knew well. Old high school friends. Kai. Nova. When the world went to shit, some of us from the same neighborhood banded together, you know after losing parents and whatever."

"Your parents are dead?"

"Infected. Yeah." He sighed. "Anyway, after some of the others were taken by trappers and scalpers, we wanted to get back at them. That's when we met Dante. He was a beater. Going after those who had taken his family. He had a huge record of capturing these assholes. It's like he can sniff them out. I mean, today they're not hard to find as it seems a lot of folks are doing it but..."

"Did he?"

"Find those who took some of his family?" Tucker asked. "Yep, and he beat them to death with a baseball bat." He paused and let that image sink in. Jonah had to wonder if Dante was willing to do that to trappers, how much more would he do it to those associated with Tucker.

"And Bekah?" Jonah asked.

"He had me watch over her while they journeyed north to seek out the resistance after we heard there was a group forming to go up against GERM and bring about real change. I was told specifically not to leave the warehouse we were staying in at the time."

"So, you weren't here."

"No. This is new. But then again Dante has always been about theatrics. I should have stayed clear."

"That's why you rarely left that recreational center."

"Somewhat," he replied.

"So, what happened?" Jade asked.

"She wanted to see the city. You have to understand, Dante came from a large family. Many died in the Haze, those who didn't were grabbed by scalpers or trappers. When we found those responsible for taking his family, he got them back but it was too late by then. The only one he was able to save was Bekah. He refused to let it happen again. He pretty much locked her up. Gave her no leeway. She couldn't go anywhere that wasn't within the four walls of that warehouse. You can't do that to someone forever. Eventually, they will break out. I told him that."

"So, you took her out?"

"Hell no. But she broke out. I went after her. I found her three blocks away wrestling with someone who was infected. I brought her back and when Dante returned, he went ballistic. Instead of blaming his little sister, he blamed me. Said that I had taken my eyes off her."

"And had you?"

"Was I supposed to take a piss with her standing there?" There was a pause before he continued. "Anyway, Nova gave me the heads-up that he was going to take me out. So, I just left the group. I didn't double-cross them. I had no other choice."

"The highliners? Who are they?"

Tucker groaned. "Just a group that lives over in Hell's Kitchen. I found myself over there living in some shack of an apartment for several months. I would see them, you know, up in the air, navigating through the city on rope. I thought it was kind of unique. Not what you tend to see. Anyway, I ended up breaking into this building to scavenge for supplies. I came across a table with paper all over it and a layout of what looked to be an ambush."

"Someone was going to ambush them?"

"Seems so. They wouldn't have stood a chance. They haven't exactly helped themselves. It was payback for them taking out so many trappers and scalpers. It seems the two groups banded together. So, I gave them the heads-up. They repaid me by asking me to join them. They wanted a scout. Someone who wasn't associated with them, but could dig around and find out intel in exchange for food and supplies."

"That's when you joined them?"

"No. I didn't. But then after a few close calls, I figured it would help to have a few of them watch my back, you know." He glanced off toward the doorway where they could hear voices.

"So what happened? Why did you leave them?"

Tucker got this pained expression. "It was my fault. I should have steered clear of them. It didn't take long for Dante to find out where I was. He realized we were working together to help one another. So..." He got this faraway look in his eyes. "They took one of the highliners. Skitz, the guy who spearheads them had a woman he was seeing. Raven." He shook his head. "They beat her to death then left her body on a roof for the birds to peck at. Skitz found what remained of her and a message blaming me. Dante told them that if they continued to associate with me, more of them would die."

"So you left again?"

He nodded. "This time it was for their sake. Skitz..." He was at a loss for words. "Well, he told me they wouldn't be seen with me again. So I returned to my old stomping grounds. A familiar place. A place from childhood. Avoided people until you two came along."

There was silence for a moment.

Before Jade or Jonah could react, the doors to the venue opened and two of Dante's crew entered, Kai and Orion. "There they are."

"Like we could go anywhere."

They made their way down and lowered Jonah. "Where are you taking him?" Jade asked.

"To prove to us that we should spare all of your pitiful lives."

As soon as Jonah was on the stage, he felt a wave of dizziness.

"Kai. Come on, man. Let us down. We could die."

"Oh, don't be a drama queen. It's a known fact that a person can last at least twenty-eight hours upside down before they die. Of course, that is subjective and varies from person to person," he said, laughing on the way out.

Jonah was led down a corridor and toward the doors of the third venue. There was a thick chain looped through the handles. Orion unlocked it and pulled the doors wide before they thrust him into a darkened room.

"See you in a couple of hours."

The doors slammed shut and Jonah banged on them with his fist. "Hey, c'mon. What the hell is this about?"

From the other side, Kai answered.

"Immunity. Relax. If you're immune you have nothing to worry about."

As he heard them walk away, the footsteps grew distant. Jonah turned and looked back into the pitch-dark room. He couldn't see a damn thing but he heard something, someone, and they were heading for him.

27

Freedom was out of reach.

Jade yelled in frustration after another failed attempt to grasp the rope. She had rocked herself and then swung ever so slightly back and forth, hoping to create enough momentum that it would assist her in pulling herself up and untying her ankles, but it didn't work.

"Give it up. We're not getting out of here. Dante doesn't do things by halves."

She looked back at him in astonishment. "He's going to kill us, isn't he?"

Tucker was hesitant to reply then the words spilled out. "More than likely. He's a man of principle. Even if Jonah's blood could bring his sister out of that coma, he'd still want to punish me just to send a message to the rest of the group."

"Then why let them take Jonah?"

"Because I figured it would buy us some time."

"For what? Blood to rush to our heads?" she screamed, balling both fists. The doors opened and several of Dante's men entered.

"Keep it down!"

"Screw you!" Jade shouted.

"Don't work them up. These folks have a hairline trigger. All they need is a reason and I've already given them one," Tucker added. "Don't give them another."

Jade grumbled.

It was then Dante appeared, striding down the pitched floor toward the stage. "Are you here to gloat?" Tucker asked.

"No. But it is fun to see you on the end of a rope. Though I would enjoy it better if it was around your neck," he replied. "But hey ho! The day's not over yet."

"What do you want?" Jade replied.

"Answers." He stared up at them before taking a seat on the stage and crossing his legs, brushing off lint from his knee with a swipe of the hand. "Your mother. The alleged immune." He chuckled. "Where is she?"

"Why, you've got us?"

"Yes. Leverage. But I like to hedge my bets."

"I don't know. We were searching for her," Jade replied.

"Kai told me you seemed pretty sure of the direction you were heading in. Moving with purpose, I believe his words were."

"As would you if you were outside," Tucker added.

"So she's not at the island?" Dante asked, drumming his fingers against the wooden stage.

"Why don't you go there and find out?"

Dante let out a quiet laugh. "I bet you would like that."

"Hell's Kitchen!" Jade spat out. "She was taken by GERM, I think."

"How can that be when they are the ones in charge of Governors Island?"

Jade frowned. "You must be misinformed. That's the resistance."

"No. Our intel has members of your group conversing with military soldiers in front of a GERM chopper on a roof in Lower Manhattan. It then took off leaving behind others. They went back to the island. Now I ask myself. Why would GERM send in some of their own unless they planned on infiltrating?" He paused for a second. "Or perhaps, they were already running the show and just wanted to replenish those we killed."

"That was you?" she asked.

The corner of his lip tugged up.

Jade considered his words. It wasn't a far stretch of the imagination to think that GERM could take that approach. They'd already shown how underhanded they were. It would have been risky trying to attack, but much easier to infiltrate. She thought Caleb was working for them, used as bait to draw out her mother. But he never said who he was working for.

"So?" Dante asked.

"I told you. Hell's Kitchen."

He smiled and glanced at Tucker. "Did you tell her to say that?"

"No. She has her own mind."

Dante hopped up on the stage and got directly below Tucker. "What did those highliners say to you when we plucked that little bird's feathers in the square?"

"Her name was Raven."

"Irrelevant."

"As are you, asshole." Tucker spat a glob of spit and it landed in Dante's eye.

He smiled as he wiped it slowly from his face with a handkerchief. He tucked it back into his upper pocket before reaching up and grabbing Tucker around the throat. "Keep it up and I will draw out your death for days."

"What is your problem?" Jade asked. "We're here to help and not once since we've arrived have you treated us with even an inkling of decency."

"Decency? Oh, Miss Prissy here wants decency," he said, looking back at Orion and Kai. "You hear that, guys?" He laughed loudly. "Sure, I'll give you decency!" He went over to the rope and lowered her just enough that she was at a level where he could tear her top open. Then, he took a knife from a sheath on his hip and sliced into her jeans, tearing them away until she was only wearing a bra and panties. "There. How's that for decency!"

"Bastard!"

He laughed as he pulled on the rope and she rose back up to the same level as Tucker.

"Some eye candy, Tucker. Don't say I didn't treat you decently."

He smiled as he turned to walk away.

"She's lying to you," Tucker said.

"What?"

"About her mother. She's not in Hell's Kitchen."

"Is that so? Where is she then?"

"North. Hudson Highlands State Park."

"And you would know this because?"

"I heard the resistance chattering over the airwaves."

"They have her?"

"If she's not at the island, who else would?"

Dante stared at him. He glanced away for a second and then shook his head. "You always were a bad liar. Hell's Kitchen it is!"

"Dante."

"Save it."

"Dante."

Tucker's pleas were ignored as Dante went back up the slope toward the exit.

"Keep an eye on them," Jade heard Dante say before he left the room.

As soon he was gone, Jade tore into Tucker. "Why would you say that?

"Because I knew he wouldn't believe me. If anyone can find her, it's him. I can't show my face in Hell's Kitchen but he can and if he does..."

"The highliners will take him out for killing Raven."

"Exactly. Then we don't have to worry."

"Yeah. Well. That only works if he doesn't kill us before he leaves."

She shook her head and thought about her mother and the advice she gave back on the island. Jade wished she'd listened more. Her grief over the loss of her father and brother had gotten the best of her, and seeing her mother close to Jonah only intensified her bitterness. But he wasn't to blame nor was she.

~

IT TOOK a moment for Jonah's eyes to adjust to the darkness and see the individual before him. Instinctively he backed up against the door, swallowing hard. "Stay back."

"Why? Anyone they throw in here is infected," a male voice said.

"How long have you been in here?"

"A week, maybe three, I've lost track of time." He coughed hard.

"But you're speaking? You're moving. You're...."

"Not infected," the guy replied.

"But you said..."

"I told them I was infected. They threw me in here.

I've managed to keep my distance from the others but... are you saying, you're not infected?"

"Yeah."

"What's your name?"

"Jonah. Yours?"

"Tyrone Davis."

There was a short pause.

"You said... Tyrone?"

"Yeah."

There was a pause as Jonah considered something. "Do you have a brother named Malik?"

"You know him?" Tyrone said, stepping closer, his voice raising in pitch. Even though he said he wasn't infected, that didn't stop Jonah from feeling threatened. He'd spent the better part of his time since receiving a transfusion avoiding the outside world, and those infected. "Where is he? Is he out there?"

"I met your brother over in Brooklyn."

"That's where we got separated. I ended up getting grabbed by scalpers, sold, and used to give blood. They kept me for over a year. A blood slave to donate to someone's loved one. Dante's crew raided the house and killed them all. He released those that were still alive, I was one of them. I was going to go back to Brooklyn to find my brother but..." he trailed off. "They told me Brooklyn had fallen. That it was a mess over there. No one had survived. That the military had destroyed it with ballistic weapons."

"So you stayed with them?"

"Yeah. Then once I saw what they were doing. I just couldn't do it. So I told them I was exposed and figured they would just release me, you know. But instead, they tossed me in here with the others." He sighed. "How is Malik?"

Jonah felt a pang of sadness. He didn't want to tell him but in light of all that happened, he thought he deserved to know, especially after two years.

"Well, first off Brooklyn is no different than here. It's not wiped off the map. And as for your brother." He paused. "He's dead."

He reflected little emotion. It wasn't like it was a surprise. To be alive was a gift. Surviving the Haze wasn't a given, it was like delaying the inevitable. "From the infection?"

"No." Jonah struggled with the right way to say it. There was no right way or easy way. Death was death. Pain was pain. "He died trying to protect a young family."

Although Jonah could only make out the silhouette of Tyrone, he heard him sigh. "That sounds like Malik. God. Why?"

"I'm sorry."

Jonah looked around.

Deep within the cavernous room that could accommodate up to 75 people, there was a bar, a sound system, tables, and chairs, and a piano, at least if anything of what Tyrone had told him was accurate. It was hard to tell as he could only see the outline of furniture and...

"Where are the others?" Jonah asked.

"There are only three. I used a mop to keep them back and pushed them into a storage room. It's locked. They can't get out. You're safe here. When I heard the door open, I was going to charge it. You know, try to make a break for it but..." he trailed off.

"There are others out there. Friends of mine. If we can get out of here, you can come with us."

Tyrone slumped down against the wall, wrapping his arms around his knees. He wasn't crying, just deflated by the news of his brother. "And go where? There are no more safe zones."

"Not exactly true. We're from Governors Island. The resistance is there."

"The resistance isn't there," Tyrone said it so matter-of-factly like he knew.

"And you would know because?"

"As I said, I ran with Dante's crew. There are very few things that happen in Lower Manhattan without him knowing. Beaters are the eyes and ears of this city. How do you think they have caught so many trappers and scalpers? They are everywhere. Like a network, Dante continues to recruit. It's easy when so many have lost family." He paused. "No, the resistance is further north."

"In Hudson Highlands State Park?"

"Yeah. How do you know that?"

Jonah exhaled. "A stranger told me. Said there was a group there that could help. What was even stranger was that he knew me."

"Huh. What did this guy look like?"

"I don't know. Short, stocky, he had a full head of hair, was middle-aged."

"Any scars?"

"Yeah. One."

"Was it here?" Tyrone asked, pointing to his neck. "A red X?"

"That's right. How do you know?"

Tyrone got up and walked into the darkness.

"Tyrone?"

A moment later he returned and clicked on a flashlight. "Found it out back." He shone it in Jonah's face to get a better look at him before shining it on himself. "I know because I have one," he said. "Trappers don't care but scalpers mark those they catch. A bit like the way farms brand cattle. Just in case some escape, others know who they belong to. I think you bumped into an old friend of mine who managed to get away. He was branded like me. I'm glad to hear he's still alive."

Jonah didn't want to tell him who his friend was associated with, he'd already heard enough bad news for one day.

Suddenly, from outside the doors, they heard a commotion.

The door opened wide and a figure stepped into view.

Jonah squinted.

Minutes earlier, Dante hurried to collect some of his personal belongings. His mind was awash with thoughts that had consumed him for several years. Now his patience was about to pay off. In an office, he opened a cupboard and collected a large duffel bag that he'd already filled with keepsakes, memories of his life before the event. It was all he had to hold on to. And, despite his outward actions, and those that followed him, his intention was never to lead a group.

As he turned to head out, Nova was standing in the doorway, leaning against it.

"In a rush to go somewhere?"

"It's time."

"To do what? Get your jollies by killing one of our own?"

"Your own is the reason my sister is infected."

"You know that's not true. How many times did you tell her not to go out? Huh? Think about it. You hold a person hostage, you are only increasing their desire to escape. It's your fault she's infected."

Dante scowled at her. He passed her, shaking his head. "I don't have time for your drama right now, Nova. You want to come with me, we leave in ten minutes."

"For where?"

"North. The rumors are true."

"But I was informed we were heading for Hell's Kitchen to find the girl's mother."

"That is a death sentence. Tucker likes to play games. He knows I would do the opposite of what he suggested. We know she was on that island. We also know that people don't venture out into the city without good reason. I believe her daughter."

"Then we should head for Hell's Kitchen."

"If it wasn't for Tucker's influence, maybe. But I'm interested in finding the resistance. They aren't in Hell's Kitchen."

"No one knows where they are and for good reason."

"Exactly. For so long people spread rumors of them being on Governors Island and maybe that was true for a while but announcing it only gave GERM reason to infiltrate it. It's easier that way. No need to take it. Just mingle and pass out information. No. The resistance is smarter than that. They don't just let anyone in like they did on that island. That was all smoke and mirrors like the way the government will create a false narrative to get people looking in a different direction."

"So, are we all going?"

He groaned. "That was never the plan."

Nova thumbed over her shoulder. "So you just used all those people to find out what you wanted to know?" she asked, keeping her eyes fixed on him as he hurried around the room collecting vital paperwork, other items, and ammunition that would aid them in what was to come.

"Used? I gave them a purpose."

"To kill others?"

"That was their choice."

"Oh, c'mon, what did you expect them to do?"

He sighed and stopped what he was doing. "Where is this coming from? You didn't care when I helped you find those who took your father."

"I was in a different head space back then."

"Weren't we all," he said angrily as he continued filling his bag. "That doesn't take away the fact that trappers and scalpers deserve to die."

"Do they?"

He looked at her through narrowed eyes. "Has time dulled your eyes, and deafened you to the cries of those in captivity?" He strode over to her and took her by the arms. "We don't have to do this anymore, Nova. We can go join the resistance. The way it should have been from the start. I was wrong. There, I said it. But like you said. We were in a different head space back then, trying to make sense of this event. The way back is through those who oppose GERM, not by being an outlier and spending our days killing trappers and scalpers."

She folded her arms and looked at him, amused. "And yet that's what we've been doing."

"Yes. Until we could verify the rumors of the resistance's existence and location from multiple sources. It was only a matter of time before their whereabouts would leak."

"If they are so intent on remaining hidden, why now risk being found?"

"Do you really think that the only ones interested in having the cure would be GERM? We've all heard the rumors of this woman who is the cure. Eventually, the resistance would too, and they'd show their faces to collect her. Now we have solid intel, I'm going to follow it."

"No, you have mixed intel." Nova lifted a thumb, then a finger. "You have Hell's Kitchen and Hudson Highlands State Park. She could be in either and with anyone or with no one at all. No, I say we stay put until we make contact with one of them."

"We have the closest thing to it. Her daughter."

Nova shook her head and paced. "You still haven't verified if her daughter or Jonah are immune. It takes time for symptoms to show. No. We need to stay put."

"We'll take them with us and return later for my sister."

"Oh? And how is that going to work? Let's say for a moment that you're right. That the real resistance is in Hudson Highlands State Park and her mother is there. What? You think they're going to open their arms to us when we roll up with her daughter after you've humiliated her, beaten her friend, and killed numerous people?"

He stared back.

"You have no intention of bringing them or returning for your sister. Tell the truth or have you forgotten how to do that?"

Nova was too smart for her good. He'd become so accustomed to bending the truth to get people to do what he wanted that it was out of the norm to do anything but that.

"All right. You're right. But we don't need them."

"I do."

"Geesh. Nova. Tucker walked out on you. Do you honestly think for one second, he won't do it again?"

"You forced him. He had no choice."

"We always have a choice," Dante shot back. "Me? I've always been here. Never once left your side. Made sure you're safe. Helped you find those who killed your father. And yet you want to give this guy another chance?"

"Wouldn't you want that?"

He chuckled and shook his head. "Nova, Nova."

"Don't be condescending."

"I'm not, but as you said, if we roll up with them, we won't get in and I haven't come this far to have anything or anyone stand in the way. Including my sister. She's as good as dead. Now the future is out there and I'm going after it. You want to come, fine, but we go alone."

"Why can't we stay?"

"For the same reason we moved from our last location. It's getting harder to stay ahead of others out there. It's only a matter of time before we're discovered here and maybe next time, we won't get lucky and it will be us hooked up for blood transfusion or worse — dead."

"We've survived this long."

Dante was about to reply when he heard several gunshots in rapid succession.

28

"Max?" Jonah looked on in astonishment. He couldn't believe he was still alive. "I thought you were dead."

"Sorry to disappoint. But, hey, the day's not over. Let's go," he said, holding an M4 low as he eyed the corridor both ways.

"Hold up, I need to get something," Tyrone said, darting back into the darkness.

"It better be worth it. We don't have long."

Tyrone reappeared with a backpack.

Jonah passed the two men who had been posted outside to watch over them. They were lying dead on the ground, their throats slit from ear to ear.

Minutes. That was all they had to get out of there.

Max guided them toward a stairwell that would allow them to get out of the building. "This way."

Jonah shook his head. “Wait! I can’t leave Jade behind.”

Max glanced at his watch. “We don’t have time.”

“Then you go but I’m not leaving her,”

“Damn it! Not again. Where is she?”

“One venue over,” he said. As he turned to head in that direction, Max took hold of his arm.

“Jonah, I’ll get her. This place is rigged to go haywire in less than five minutes.”

“What?”

“C4. You think I was going to walk in here and not rig it before I entered?”

“What the hell?” Tyrone said, waiting by the exit

Max jabbed his gun toward him. “Who’s he?”

“That’s Malik’s brother,” Jonah said.

“His brother?”

Jonah groaned. “Tyrone, this is Max. The father of the family I was talking about.”

Max smiled. “Well now we have introductions out of the way, shall we get the fuck out of here before...”

A slew of gunfire erupted.

At first, Jonah thought it was directed at them. They dropped to a crouch, expecting a group of Dante’s men to emerge. It wasn’t. It was coming from deeper inside the building. The noise was deafening being carried over the ventilation system.

What came next was the sound of a chopper.

Rounds speared windows

And that’s when the real chaos began.

Moving fast, they darted through the slew of corridors toward the second venue. Max had given him a handgun as the last thing he wanted was to have to deal with the expected onslaught alone.

* * *

The noise in the theater had them on high alert. Twisting upside down on the rope, Jade tried to keep her eyes on the left door at the top of the aisle. The two guards posted inside exited at the sound of gunfire.

"What the hell is happening?"

Her body twisted and out of the corner of her eye she caught sight of three people entering, but because of how dim it was, she couldn't tell who they were.

On a second turn of the rope, her eyes widened. "Mom?"

Tucker was quick to point to the area where they were tied off.

Her mother was carrying an MP5. She made it up to the stage and one of her friends detached the rope to free them.

As that was happening, the second door on the right side of the aisle burst open and another three entered.

There was a moment of chaos.

Commands were shouted.

"Let them go!" a familiar voice shouted.

"Jonah. It's us," Alice cried.

"Max. No. No!" he shouted, pushing his rifle down. "We know them."

Once Jade was down, she embraced her mother but Alice pulled back, grimacing.

"What is it?" Jade asked.

"I'll explain later."

Jade looked at those with her mother. They looked unusual. Like hippies from Portland, the kind of folks that hung out at hipster cafes, wore sandals, and burned incense in their homes. "Who are they?"

"Friends," Alice replied, clutching her wrist to lead her away. "We need to get out of here before—"

"This place goes up," Max said, glancing at his watch.

"What did you say?" Alice replied.

"It's rigged."

"I got that. But… why?"

Max sighed. "I'm not having this conversation again. You all want to linger, be my guest but I'm out of here."

Still moving toward the doors, Alice asked how much time they had.

Max glanced at his watch. "Just under two minutes."

Before they made it out, more strangers burst inside.

"Skitz! GERM must have followed us. There are two choppers in the air and even more soldiers on the ground outside. Those inside are holding them at bay but we're going to need another way out," Sky yelled.

Two of them locked the doors by forcing aisle divider bars between the handles.

"This way," Tucker said, guiding all of them down to the stage and over to a door on the left that was hidden in the darkness. There was no exit sign illuminated above and certainly no power to run it even if there was one. He pulled the handle but it was locked. Tucker tried again.

"Shit."

"There must be another way out."

Two of them hurried to the other side but the door on that side was locked as well.

At the top of the slope where the main doors were to the venue, they heard loud banging as if someone was attempting to break in.

"Well great. Now we are truly screwed," Skitz said.

As they prepared for whoever was on the other side to break through, the door they originally attempted to head through was opened. Kai appeared. "Going somewhere?"

As they moved toward him, he lifted a rifle. "Hell no. Stay right there. I don't know how you alerted them but your pals at GERM aren't going to help you out of this."

"What are you talking about, Kai?" Tucker asked, taking a step forward.

"You and I have unfinished business."

"It's over. It's in the past."

"Not to me it isn't."

Max stepped forward. "Look, I hate to break up the reunion but this place is about to..."

Suddenly, an explosion rocked the walls and floor. A second followed in rapid succession. From high above, huge steel light holders crashed to the floor. As panic took over and they went to get out, Kai fired, striking one of the group. An Asian guy fell back, landing hard on the floor.

"Levi!" Skitz said, rushing to his side. He was gripping his stomach, his finger gloved with red as blood bloomed.

"As I said, no one is going..."

Before Kai managed to get the words out, he was shot in the back. When he collapsed, Nova stepped into view. "I never liked him." She tossed some clothes to Jade. "Those should fit. Let's go."

Jade slipped into the clothes, almost losing her footing as they hurried to exit. The floor began to shake violently. The walls trembled and dust rained down from the ceiling, filling their noses and throats with the acrid scent of concrete.

"This way!" Dante beckoned, appearing before them in the dust and grime of the corridor.

"What the hell is he doing here?" Tucker asked.

Nova was quick to reply. "He's helping us."

"Helping? You son-of-a-bitch!" Tucker said, lunging at him.

Nova got between them. "Tucker, please. Not now!"

He didn't have an option; the building was erupting around them.

Skitz and a few others dragged their wounded friend out of the door into the dimly lit corridor that seemed to stretch on forever. The walls were lined with peeling paint and rusty pipes, and the musty air hung heavy with the scent of decay.

Suddenly, another loud explosion shattered the air, sending shockwaves through the tunnel and knocking the group off their feet. They could hear the sound of crumbling bricks and falling debris as the entire building above them shook from the force of the blast. All around, more explosions rocked the walls, sending drywall into the air like a cloud. It was like being inside a machine that was shaking them from side to side. Panic set in at the thought of being trapped. Glass shattered. Cries could be heard deep inside the building through the vents.

They raced ahead, scrambling over fallen concrete and dodging debris, hearts pounding with terror.

Dante leaned into a section of the wall that was a hidden door.

They were hesitant to enter except for Dante. "Follow me or die, simple as that," he said before ducking out of view into a narrow staircase that led into a dark tunnel.

Although the same anger Tucker felt roiled within her, Jade held her tongue because they were minutes away from freedom.

29

Was she dead or alive?

Alice blinked hard. For a brief moment, there was silence and she thought she was the only one that had survived. Although they had made it to the tunnel just in time. As they had hurried down the staircase, she remembered hearing a loud rumble behind them and turning just in time to see concrete crash down, completely blocking the way back.

Instantly the group was shrouded in darkness and dust before being knocked to the ground by even more debris. As she opened her eyes, she heard others coughing hard and choking on the thick air.

"Jade? Jade!?"

"I'm here, Mom," she replied.

A wave of relief flooded her chest.

It was only when one of them fumbled for a flashlight and switched it on that they could finally see their surroundings.

"Where the hell are we?" Jonah asked from somewhere in the darkness.

"In one of the many tunnels built during Prohibition," Nova replied.

It was a fascinating sight — the tunnel was from a different era entirely. It was like they had discovered a piece of history. The walls were rough-hewn stone, and they could see old, rusty pipes running along the ceiling. On the walls were old posters advertising illegal liquor along with gambling dens.

Tempers flared almost immediately. Jade clocked Dante in the chin, knocking him back against the wall. "You piece of shit!" Tucker wasn't far behind, driving a foot into his leg and causing him to buckle.

Not knowing what their issue was, yet clear that this man had helped them escape the hell above, Alice like Nova was quick to intervene. "Jade. Whoa. Back up," Alice said, pulling her back.

"You don't know what he did."

Nova stood between the others and Dante who was down on one knee trying to catch his breath. He wiped his bloody lip with the back of his hand. "If I didn't do what I did, the group above would have killed you," Dante said, trying to justify his actions.

"Do what?" Alice asked. "What did you do?"

"Hung us by our feet, tore away my clothes," Jade said.

"You did what?" Alice balked, the mother in her rising to the surface.

"He's right. He had no choice." Nova kept shifting her body, preventing anyone from getting close to him to continue the assault. "The rest would have seen his actions as a sign of weakness."

"Doesn't make it right," Tucker said. "Piece of crap." He threw out another leg kick, trying to get around Nova, but she pushed him back.

Dante was quick to shift the topic. "Listen, this tunnel will take us out. I have a truck already full of gas and ready to take us north."

"North?" Alice asked.

"To the Phoenix resistance."

"No one knows where they are, let alone if they exist," Max said.

"They were on the island," Alice was quick to correct them.

"Are you sure about that? That ship sailed the moment GERM infiltrated the group." Her thoughts went to what Caleb had said about Sam being dead.

Dante rose to his feet when he saw that everyone was listening.

He brushed the dust from his jacket and in the dim glow of the flashlight, he made his case. "No one has known about the location of the resistance because they have kept it a secret. When we first heard about them, it was just rumors, chatter over the radio. They didn't announce where they were and they certainly didn't invite people to join. Though I bet it was different on the island, right?" he said, looking at Alice. "The real resistance couldn't take the chance of being outed or infiltrated by GERM. No one even knows how they recruit, only that they exist and have wreaked havoc."

"Your point?" Jade asked.

"We kept hearing rumors about a haven. Over the years a few have dropped the location of Hudson Highlands State Park. First, it was from someone we captured, then from Jonah, and then again through radio contact. But they move often. It's my belief that's where they are or at least some of their group is for now."

"A haven?"

"I know. I know what you're thinking because of the island but this is different. We would be safe from GERM, safe from the Haze. Apparently, the Phoenix has been taking in people since the collapse of quarantine zones, just no one has known where or who's in charge."

"And you think it's north?"

"I'm not positive but if I had to place money on it, yeah, I think that's where they are."

"He's telling the truth," a voice said from behind. Alice turned to see a youngster beside Jonah. "I've heard of it too."

"There we go," Dante said. "Now should we all get going?"

Alice backed up, her mind running amok with thoughts about the past, about what Sam had told her.

The interactions with different people like Monroe and others on the island who were tired of the time it was taking to see a permanent cure created.

"Sam didn't want to put me on the operating table but that was because he couldn't be sure that it would work and he didn't want to lose the only thing that has helped to date."

"Your blood?" Dante asked. "So it's true?"

She nodded.

He chuckled and looked at the others. "Holy shit. You know, when I first heard the rumors that there was a woman whose blood was curing people and taking folks out of comas, I couldn't believe it. I thought it was just a ploy by GERM to get people to head to the island."

"How do you know GERM infiltrated them?"

"Because our scouts saw them meet with a group from Governors Island. They sent others back with them."

Alice knew that the only one that ever headed up trips into the city was Monroe. Could he have assisted them and been the one that took out Sam? She dipped her chin. Seven months had given her time to get attached to him, even to believe that the world had a future.

Dante took a step forward, jabbing his finger at the floor. "Listen, I don't think GERM was there from the start but think about it. All those soldiers worked for GERM before they switched sides. How long do you think they would stay loyal to a group that doesn't offer a permanent solution to this?" He paused. "It's said that ignorance is bliss. Not everyone will remain faithful to a cause if they don't see results." He looked behind him down the tunnel. "We don't have far to go. A few more miles and we are home free."

"Pity you won't see it." As Dante turned back to look at the one who said it, Skitz lunged forward, driving a knife into him.

Not even Nova had a chance to stop him. Tabs and Sky held her back. It happened so fast. "Remember Raven? My fiancée. That's for her. You piece of crap!" He twisted the knife causing even more damage before pulling it out and driving it in one more time for good measure. Dante's mouth was agape, shock masking his face.

No words escaped his lips.

He simply collapsed.

Nova dropped to his side. She applied pressure to his stomach but nothing could stem the bleeding, within minutes he took his last breath. "Dante. Dante!" She looked up at Skitz.

Now it was Tucker who intervened, stepping between Skitz and her, his finger jabbing at the ground. "He crossed the line, Nova. You know he had it coming. He had the nerve to think he could get away with that and go with us."

"He helped us."

"He was helping himself. All the time. That's all he ever did and you know it."

She gritted her teeth and looked down at the floor. Somewhere inside her mind, Alice had to believe that she knew that it was true. As they left Dante's bloody body behind to rot in the tunnel, no one looked back, no one mentioned his name again.

As the group ventured further into the tunnel, moving quickly, Alice noticed different items, wooden barrels, empty bottles, discarded playing cards, lost relics of the past, and evidence of the illegal activity that had taken place. The tunnel seemed to stretch on for miles. She could only imagine the secrets and stories that it held.

Their footsteps echoed on the rough stone floor as they pressed on.

After what seemed like an endless walk, they finally reached the end of the tunnel where they found a ladder leading up. "This is it," Nova said, beginning to climb. Alice could see the grief in her expression. As they climbed up the ladder, they emerged into a dusty, dimly lit garage. The air was thick with the scent of motor oil and gasoline, and the floor was coated in a layer of dust. No one had been there in a very long time.

At the center of the garage was a vehicle covered in a cream-colored tarp that had a thin layer of dust and grime.

Tabs, feeling curious, walked over to it and pulled off the tarp to reveal a Ford F-150. It was old, but still in good condition, with leather seats and a sturdy frame, and plenty of room for them all.

A glimmer of hope ignited as they prepared to squeeze into the truck. Skitz opened the garage door, illuminating the dusty interior. Tucker hopped into the driver's seat and pulled down the sun visor. A set of keys dropped on his lap. Skitz got in on the passenger side next to Sky and Tabs while the rest of them filled the extended cab.

Alice buckled up as Tucker turned over the engine a few times before it caught.

"Just as he said. A full tank."

With a roar, they drove out onto a deserted street ready for the hour-and-a-half journey. The truck bounced and rattled over the uneven pavement as they headed north, the sound of the engine drowning out any other noise in the distance. The wind rushed through the open windows, whipping her hair around her face.

As Jade leaned into Alice, placing her head on her shoulder and holding her hand tightly, she apologized quietly, an apology that was overdue but appreciated.

"How are you doing?" Alice asked Jonah.

"Surviving."

"Jade told me you decided to come look for me."

"Well, I didn't get far."

"But you tried, that's what matters. Thank you."

He gave a strained smile and looked out the window.

Abigail's face came to mind and for a second she almost told him, or at least was about to ask him if he could remember her, but something kept her from doing so. A need to protect him from further pain — the pain of what his father had done if Abigail's account was true, and the pain of knowing that his mother had aligned with Robert Weston.

"How did you find us?" Jade asked.

Alice looked at Skitz. "Skitz. He has his finger on the pulse of the city. GERM aren't the only ones who have infiltrated groups."

Skitz glanced back for a second, overhearing his name.

Jade locked onto his gaze. She only now was getting a good look at him in the light of day. He was attractive, someone she could easily have found herself drawn to if there hadn't been a large age gap. As they drove on, the adrenaline of their escape began to wear off, and Alice felt a sense of fear and uncertainty set in. Although they had narrowly escaped a building explosion, they were now driving through a city that looked like a war zone with no idea if where they were heading even existed.

Alice glanced at Max, noting he was looking at her.

"Jonah said you used to be a U.S. Marshal," he said.

"That's right. You?"

"Military."

She smirked. "Well, that would explain the explosions. You boys do love your toys."

That got a smile out of him. The first one she'd seen since meeting him.

"He helped us," Jade said.

"Twice," Jonah was quick to add. "If it wasn't for him, Jade would be..."

"Safe. As you would have gotten her," Max added.

"You give me too much credit," Jonah replied.

"And you don't give yourself enough," he shot back. He glanced out the window. Alice noted the ring on his finger.

"You have a family?" she asked.

"Had," he replied as he noticed her looking at the ring. He twisted it around on his finger, holding it as he looked away.

Alice regarded Max through new eyes.

Despite the uncertainty, at least they had developed a sense of trust with a new group, people who were willing to go out on a limb to save strangers. They weren't resistance, they weren't GERM, they were better than that. They were the last of a dying breed.

"Go that way," Skitz said.

"But this is faster," Tucker replied.

"Yeah, if you want to die. Now take the next right turn."

Tucker grumbled and Alice could tell that there was going to be some fireworks between those two if their egos got the better of them. She leaned over and kissed the top of Jade's head. As a sense of relief came over her, her thoughts turned to what lay ahead and a question that had bugged her since Dante said it.

"Jonah. What was Dante talking about when he said you had heard of the resistance?"

"I encountered a stranger back in Brooklyn." He paused for a second. "He knew me. Like he had seen me before. I just don't understand how."

Right then, Alice knew that she wasn't going to be able to keep the information about Abigail from him. Clearly whoever he'd encountered in Brooklyn had crossed paths with Abigail. Had she told people to be on the lookout for him? Shown a photo to them? It was possible. She was still reeling from her time with her. Abigail didn't strike her as a woman that gave up easily. Her words came back to her. *"From one mother to another, I think more than anyone, you should understand there isn't anything that I wouldn't do to be reunited with my child."*

Even though she was hesitant, she had to tell him. "Jonah."

"Yeah?" he replied, turning his face away from the window.

She was just about to open her mouth when suddenly there was a loud bang, and the truck swerved sharply to one side. The group felt the vehicle shudder as one of the tires was shot out, and they heard the hiss of air escaping from the punctured tire.

The truck fishtailed, the rear end swinging wildly from side to side as Tucker fought to keep control of the vehicle. They felt their hearts race with fear as they realized they were under attack.

The truck came to a shuddering halt, the sound of metal scraping against the pavement echoing through the street. Alice could feel the tension in the air as they looked around, trying to determine where the shot had come from and who had brought them to a grinding stop.

As they peered out, it was impossible to say who had shot at them or why, but the group knew that remaining in the vehicle or leaving could mean a death sentence.

"Do you see anything?" Max asked.

"Nothing," Tucker said, eyeing the terrain.

Skitz went to get out and several more rounds were fired, a couple speared the windows, "Shit." He pulled back. "Now what?"

"We are sitting ducks if we remain here."

They had almost made it to the Palisades Interstate Parkway, close to Bear Mountain Bridge, which would take them on the final leg of the journey. Alice eyed the bridge. It was blocked by a slew of vehicles. Even if no one had shot at them, they would have had to go the rest of the way on foot.

"What do you suggest?" Alice asked.

Max gawked at the tree line. "We create a distraction." He turned back. "You're all armed, yes?" They nodded. "When I say go, we all go toward the tree line, firing in the southern direction."

"How do you know they aren't to the north?"

"Because they would have fired at us from that direction."

"So we're supposed to trust your word?" Tabs asked.

Max glanced at him.

"Hey, I'm just calling a spade a spade. First, you rig a

building to blow it up, now you want us to become human targets. Where the hell did you meet this guy?" Tabs asked the others.

With weapons in hand and adrenaline pumping, they prepared to face whatever lay ahead, determined to protect each other at all costs.

"You want to stay put, be my guest."

"One second," Tucker piped up. "Not to play the devil's advocate, but how can you be sure they aren't just corralling us in that direction?"

"Only one way to find out." Max brought down the window on his side, pulled two smoke grenades off his ballistic vest, activated them and tossed them out, then turned to Jonah. "Go!"

30

It was a ballsy move — dangerous — but it worked.

A thick cloud of bright orange smoke erupted from the canisters, billowing out around the truck, quickly enveloping it and obscuring the view of anyone watching them. They ran in the opposite direction, opening fire as the smoke engulfed everything in its path.

With the smoke providing cover, they were able to reach the tree line.

Alice turned to scan the surrounding area for any sign of danger and to try and get a bead on their attackers, assuming they were still taking potshots.

But all that could be heard was the popping and hissing as the smoke grenades released a colorful plume.

"Can anyone see anything?" Tabs asked.

"Is that meant to be a joke?" Jonah replied.

"I was referring to snipers."

"I'm pretty sure they would see us before we would see them."

"All right, smart ass."

There was a moment of silence as they peered through the fading smoke.

"Maybe they're gone," Jade muttered.

That question was answered instantly at the sound of a whistle. Alice tilted her head up. High above them, camouflaged, wasn't just one, two, or even three people, there had to be more than ten spread out throughout the branches, rifles aimed at them.

"Shit!" Jonah said.

"I was right. Corralled. No one listens to me," Tucker said.

Like a SWAT team or military roping out of a helicopter, one by one rope dropped and the group of heavily armed individuals fast roped down from the branches, landing hard and securing them. They wore tactical gear, their faces masked, their helmets old and scuffed as if they had just stepped out of a war zone.

They quickly established a perimeter around them.

"Drop your weapons."

"All right," Alice said, motioning to the rest of them to do as they said.

"Get on the ground!"

They spoke in terse, clipped tones, barking orders and then communicating with each other over comms. One of the radios crackled static as they updated their base. It was a mixture of men and women from their twenties into their fifties.

"Calm down," Max shouted. "Okay? We just want to get through..."

One of the soldiers tilted his head to the side and then took off his helmet, revealing a full bushy beard. "Max?"

"Nathan?"

Max went to get up and was pushed back down.

"Leave him be. I know him."

Someone replied. "Not until we check." A device was put to his temple.

It let out a beep. "He's clear."

The same was done with each of them.

"Checking for infection," Jonah muttered to Alice. "Same devices used back in Seattle."

Max rose and the stranger hugged him. "Wow, are you a sight for sore eyes," Nathan said.

"Likewise. You scared the shit out of me."

Nathan stood back from him, holding Max's arm and regarding him. "Cut them loose."

"But Isiah said..."

"Cut them loose," Nathan said in a firm tone. One by one their restraints were sliced. Alice rubbed her wrists and watched with a sense of relief and curiosity.

Max smiled. "We served together."

"That we did. A far cry from this though, right?"

"You're right about that."

"Where you coming from?"

"Lower Manhattan."

"And you made it out alive?"

"I always do," he said and the two of them grinned and Max patted him on the shoulder. Right then Nathan got on the comms and gave the all-clear to the rest of them stationed in different areas. "Where's your family?"

Max offered back a grim expression.

"I'm sorry, brother."

He shrugged.

"Where are you heading?"

Max paused almost as if he was embarrassed to say it. "Searching for the Phoenix Resistance. They're supposed to be north of here in Hudson Highlands State Park."

"Huh! You don't say," Nathan replied, shifting from one foot to the next while glancing at the others. "You know they don't exist."

"That's what I've been told."

"Who are your friends?"

One by one they introduced themselves before Max motioned to Alice. "And this is..."

"Alice Walker," she said, holding a hand out.

Nathan regarded her with a smile but then his smile faded as he glanced past her toward Jonah. He backed up, regarding him with a confused expression. He lifted a finger. "One second."

Nathan turned away and spoke with one of the others. A woman. She pulled something out of her pocket, glanced at it then looked around Nathan at Jonah. Nathan cast a glance back.

"Boy. What is your name?"

"Um. Jonah Hayes."

More whispering followed and then Nathan turned. "We can get you where you need to go, follow us," he said, leading the way but without saying any more. They looked at each other, unsure of who these people were or why they had shown interest in Jonah, or why they were willing to help.

They left behind the truck. It would become another barrier for those who thought they could cross the bridge. Bear Mountain Bridge was full of them on either side, a few were even stacked to make it harder to cross on foot. On the other side, they were guided to a group of ten where multiple vehicles were waiting and blocking US-6.

"Are you taking us to meet the resistance?" Sky asked.

Nathan glanced over his shoulder from the passenger seat as one of his crew drove.

"You've already met them," he answered with a smile. "I'm taking you to meet Isiah. He makes the decisions." He looked at Max. "Sorry, brother, but I'm not the one who calls the shots."

"Understood."

Hudson Highlands State Park was a vast undeveloped preserve stretching from Annsville Creek to Dennings Point in Beacon. It would have been a perfect place for the resistance to operate out of with a diverse array of rocky landscapes, rugged terrain, rolling hills, dense forests, and waterways. It was a good fifty miles from the city. As they got closer, they were greeted by the breathtaking sight of the Hudson River and the verdant hills rising behind it.

Just off Stearn Road, they took a right turn.

"I'm afraid there is going to be a considerable amount of walking," he said as he took them deep into the forest. They had to go through several camouflaged checkpoints. "It's to avoid the eyes in the sky," he said, pointing up before they stopped outside a visitor center that was manned by multiple people. Still, there weren't as many people as Alice expected to see. She assumed that they were spread throughout the region.

"So, this is where the base is?"

"One of them. We keep moving. Never put your eggs in one basket, right?"

Max nodded.

"It's getting harder to keep things under wraps. As our numbers increased so did the attention of GERM. We have to be careful."

"Why do they concern themselves with you?" Nova asked.

"Why do you brush away a fly from your plate?

We're annoying. And...we helped bring down the quarantine zones."

"That was you?" Jonah asked.

"Many of us. Our numbers have dwindled since then. We lost a lot of good people when that happened but it was worth it to get back some freedom."

"Is that the goal?" Alice asked.

"Yeah, to stay alive long enough to see this country back on its feet."

"That won't happen without the cure," Max said.

"Well, there are rumors out there that it exists. A woman," he said glancing at Alice as if he already knew it was her. "But from what we hear, GERM has their hands on her." As they were keeping their cards close to their chest, Alice figured it was best she do the same. She'd already had a conversation with the others on the way up that if they were to find them, they were to keep things low-key and not to mention her immunity until they had scoped out the group. The last thing she wanted was to give them a reason to sell her out. Trust was at an all-time low.

"Rumor has it GERM was going to operate and potentially kill her for a permanent cure. Would the resistance do the same?" Alice asked.

"If it meant saving millions?" He paused for a moment. "I would think that would be up to her to decide."

Jonah looked at Alice. Alive, she could help many, but in comparison, it wouldn't even come close to changing the world. If there was a kernel of truth in what had been told to her back in Vancouver, and an operation could turn the tide and save those remaining, she would consider it. This world in its current state was no life for her daughter. It wasn't the one she envisioned. And with each passing day, it was getting worse. But if it could be different. If she could change it. Alice felt it certainly would be a worthy reason to do so even if it meant dying.

After parking the Bronco, they got out and followed a winding trail into the forest and through rocky terrain. The air was crisp and clean, and the only sounds heard were the rustling of leaves and the chirping of birds.

Forty minutes in, they reached a clearing beside a narrow meandering river and rugged, rocky landscape. The sun bore down on them, casting its warm glow across nature and causing the water to glisten.

There before them was a group of people gathered together in a makeshift campsite.

Nathan had already radioed ahead so they were expecting them.

Suspicious faces looked back at them as they entered the campsite, though it was clear from the outset their interest wasn't in Alice but in Jonah. She heard them whispering as they passed by. "He's here. They found him."

"Isiah," Nathan said.

The leader was a commanding figure, a black man with a well-built physique that spoke of his years of labor and outdoor living. He rose from a seated position by the water's edge. He was tall and strong, exuding confidence and authority as he made his way over, protected on either side by loyal followers.

"Have they been checked?"

"They're clear," Nathan said.

He walked straight through the midst of them up to Jonah, walking around him, observing him. Alice noted his sharp and defined jawline, piercing eyes, and thick beard that framed his face. "Astonishing," he said. "It's really you."

"Do you know me?" Jonah asked.

"We've been searching for you for some time."

"Why?"

"All will be explained. Have you eaten?"

When he got no answer, he motioned to Nathan. "Hard to think on an empty stomach. Let's feed our guests. I'm sure they are tired from their journey. Clementine will be with us shortly."

"Clementine?" Alice asked.

"Our leader."

"But I thought you were...?"

He smiled back with a nod. "At times I am." With that said he turned and made his way into a green tent. Nathan told them to relax. He excused himself while he made arrangements for them to have a place to sleep and for food to be prepared.

Alice wandered over to the river and got on her knees, splashing water over her dusty face, and cleaning her hands. "How do you feel about this?" Jonah asked, sidling up beside her.

"It seems they are enamored with you. The question is why."

"I think we should bounce before this... Clementine shows up."

Alice rose and was offered a towel by someone nearby. She took it and dried her face. "You might be right. That's why I've hidden one of the guns," she said, her eyes diverting down to the riverbed where she had set a Glock underneath some rocks. There always has to be a contingency plan. "If push comes to shove, well..." She trailed off, he understood.

"Right. Except I'm hoping we can skip the shoving part."

Alice placed a hand on his shoulder as she turned. "Relax, Jonah."

As she went to walk by him, he continued, "Where did they take you?"

"What?"

"Well, you killed Cabbie. Where did you go after that?"

"Hell's Kitchen. I left a message. Didn't you see it?"

"I get that. But who took you?"

"GERM." She took a deep breath. "Listen. Do you remember that time we were at Ed's house? You know, the place we left the dog."

"How could I forget?"

"You remember I asked about your parents."

"Yeah. Look, if this is about the lies I told. I've already apologized."

"It's not. Jonah. What did your father tell you about your mother?"

"I told you I never knew them. I mean, my biological parents."

"And Eric?"

"He was my foster father."

"Right. That's what he told you."

"What are you getting at?"

She shifted uncomfortably, unable to avoid it any longer. "I met someone in Hell's Kitchen who introduced herself as your mother."

"What?"

"Abigail Hayes. Ring a bell?"

He looked back at her with a confused expression, then looked away. "My mother and father died in a car accident. I was given up as a baby. Placed in the foster system."

"Right. Until Eric adopted you."

"Exactly."

"She said Eric was your real father. That you were placed in the foster system by him to give you a better chance at life. And then later, he came back for you. Abigail said it was to keep you from her."

"No. That can't be. Even if that was true. How could that be?"

"She was institutionalized."

He took a few steps back, grappling with this,

looking unsure as to whether to believe her or not. "You mean, she was placed in a mental hospital?"

Alice nodded. "Except she doesn't think that there was a problem with her. That it was all your father's doing."

Jonah looked at a loss for words. "Where is this woman now?"

Alice swallowed. "I don't know. But..." She was about to say that it was probably best that he didn't meet her when Max called them over.

"Food's ready. Come on. Get it while it's hot."

As Alice turned to leave, Jonah spoke up. "When you met this woman, was she working for GERM?"

Alice had every right to say yes. But in light of the way Robert Weston manipulated people, specifically her sister... Could she have said that Erica worked for him? Instead, she opted to spare Jonah.

"That I don't know," she replied. "I just know she was looking for you."

Jonah dipped his chin and walked past Alice without saying a word.

"Jonah."

"I need time."

He walked off though he was never out of sight of those at the camp, who appeared to keep a close eye on him as he walked along the edge of the river, picking up small stones and tossing them in. A part of her wished she hadn't told him but he deserved to know even if it wasn't the full truth.

Alice joined the others. A feast was laid out on long tables. The spread was impressive with platters of freshly caught fish, ripe fruit, and an array of vegetables.

Isiah sat with the rest of them, engaging in conversation, asking about their journey, and swapping stories of his own experiences in the park and confrontations with GERM. He was charismatic and engaging with a commanding presence that demanded attention and respect.

As they were eating and talking about the resistance, a man approached and whispered in Isiah's ear that Clementine had arrived. He jumped up from his seat and beckoned them to follow him out so they could meet her.

Emerging from the tent, Alice squinted into the sunlight as a knot of people approached.

She froze.

Among them, the one introduced as Clementine, the leader of the resistance, was none other than Abigail. Alice scanned the faces expecting to see Robert Weston but he wasn't there.

Abigail was already speaking with Jonah.

A smile formed on his face. His eyes brightened more than she'd ever seen them before.

Had she told him who she was?

There was a brief hug and she saw it, the same look that every mother had when faced with their child — it was love, a force that would climb mountains, cross rivers, and knock everything to the ground to protect.

"And this is Alice," Isiah said, as Abigail made her way over, a smile forming.

"I don't believe we've met before. Have we?" Abigail asked.

There it was, the question dangling before her.

The chance to throw her under the bus or as a mother let it slide.

Alice recognized intelligence and determination, and Abigail had both. She spoke with a quiet authority, her words carefully chosen and delivered with conviction. Those around her believed she was Clementine, those among Weston's group knew her as Abigail.

Who was she?

The truth was somewhere between the two.

Shaking her hand, Alice glanced at Jonah and then back at her. She could ruin her world but in doing so she would most definitely destroy his. Alice felt her firm grip delivering a message that went beyond words. Was it malicious or from one mother to another, a reminder, a last attempt to give her a chance to explain? That all was not as it seemed. Or perhaps it was. Maybe now they were in the lion's den, in uncharted territory, surrounded by chameleons hellbent on reclaiming power. She wasn't sure what terrified her more, GERM — a group seeking to control the cure — or a mother who would go to no end to find a child.

As it was, Abigail now stood to gain both.

Clever or diabolical, only time would tell.

Without further delay, Alice replied, "I don't believe we have."

~

THANK YOU FOR READING

If you enjoyed that consider reading, When The World Turns Dark, 15 floors, The Aging. Please take a second to leave a review, it's really appreciated. Thanks kindly, Jack.

A PLEA

Thank you for reading The Delay: the sequel to The Haze. If you enjoyed the experience this book gave you, I would really appreciate it if you would consider leaving a review. It's a great way to support the book. Without reviews, an author's books are virtually invisible on the retail sites. It also lets me know what you liked. It also motivates me to write more books. You can leave a review by visiting the book's page. I would greatly appreciate it. It only takes a couple of seconds.

Thank you — **Jack Hunt**

VIP READERS TEAM

Thank you for buying The Haze, published by Direct Response Publishing.

Go to the link below to receive special offers, bonus content, and news about new Jack Hunt's books. Sign up for the newsletter. http://www.jackhuntbooks.com/signup

ABOUT THE AUTHOR

Jack Hunt is the International Bestselling Author of over seventy novels. Jack lives on the East coast of North America. If you haven't joined ***Jack Hunt's Private Facebook Group*** just do a search on facebook to find it. This gives readers a way to chat with Jack, see cover reveals, enter contests and receive giveaways, and stay updated on upcoming releases. There is also his main facebook page below if you want to browse. facebook.com/jackhuntauthor

www.jackhuntbooks.com
jhuntauthor@gmail.com

Made in United States
North Haven, CT
23 May 2023

36898216R00211